My Sweet Curiosity

For Michael —
Very best wishes,
Amanda

My Sweet Curiosity

Amanda Hale

thistledown press

Thistledown Press Ltd.
633 Main Street
Saskatoon, Saskatchewan, S7H 0J8
www.thistledownpress.com

Library and Archives Canada Cataloguing in Publication

Hale, Amanda
My sweet curiosity / Amanda Hale.

ISBN 978-1-897235-61-4

I. Title.

PS8565.A4313M97 2009 C813'.6 C2009-902856-5

Cover illustration: Andreas Vesalius, from *Andreas Vesalius: De corporis humani fabrica libri septem*, page 170 (Basel: Johannes Oporinus, 1543)
Cover and book design: Jackie Forrie
Printed and bound in Canada

10 9 8 7 6 5 4 3 2 1

Thistledown Press gratefully acknowledges the financial assistance of the Canada Council for the Arts, the Saskatchewan Arts Board, and the Government of Canada through the Book Publishing Industry Development Program for its publishing program.

My Sweet Curiosity

THE MEASURED TONES OF THE UNMISTAKABLE Bach suite resounded across Bloor Street to the corner of Sherbourne. A young woman with coppery hair leaned into her cello like a lover, swaying as she bowed the richness from it. She was perched on a stone ledge near the swinging doors of a large grey building from which office workers burst, buttoning their coats, hurrying for the subway. Some stopped, arrested by her music, counterpointed with a steady hum of traffic, the whir of bicycle wheels, the distant scream of planes circling the city overhead, spiralling in to land at Pearson International. The music moaned with that sound that comes when gut is stroked with Siberian horse-hair — taut, strained, exquisitely sweet — this side of agony.

Natalya Kulikovsky stood across the street, eyes cast skyward, listening. She turned, dark hair swinging across her face, looking for the source of the music. She recognized it; the first movement of Bach's unaccompanied *Suite #1 in G Major*. In between cars, buses, bikes, she saw flashes of copper, and hands which seemed small but were not in fact; hands skillfully drawing from their instrument sounds which stirred in Natalya the old childhood grief that came usually at dusk, not in the sun of a brilliant fall day, came creeping to her door in the fading light, begging, *Let me in, hold me, embrace me. I am the pain of un-love, and I will kill you if you refuse me.*

Before the last strains of the prelude had faded, Talya had jumped on her bike and was pedalling east on Bloor, trying to escape the feeling that had crept inside and lodged under her skin. *Keep moving, don't stop,* she chanted under her breath, but she couldn't forget the tantalizing glimpse the music had given her, like a fleeting image through a crack in the door before the light goes off. For a split second she'd almost remembered.

She gripped the handlebars, head down as she sped across the Don Valley Bridge. She imagined the building of it, men hanging from skeletal girders, grappling with metal, lovers flying from the parapet to their deaths, unresolved. She imagined Bloor Street being paved, east to west, across the city, buildings rising like mushrooms in the night, the CN Tower — a grounded missile of eternal aspiration — piercing the Toronto sky. When her front wheel hit a bump she was jolted suddenly, and felt again the deep-throated cello quivering through her body. A different quality of air filtered her darkness and she knew in that moment the paradox of her existence, as a distant memory surfaced in which she merely existed, a pulsing organism with an impulse towards action tempered by the knowledge of futility. Then *phhht,* back to earth, resonating with that split second, every cell in her body wanting to forget, because it was unbearable, while part of her screamed *Catch it! Hold it! Remember! Your life will never be the same now.*

Katya Kulikovsky, after five miscarriages, had been diagnosed at age thirty-five with a hostile womb. Talya had tumbled time and again, into the crumpled sheets of her parents' marriage bed, onto the kitchen floor, down the toilet. She'd even slithered embarrassingly onto a Persian carpet at a Rosedale cocktail party but, being a persistent soul irresistibly drawn to the Kulikovskys, she kept on coming until finally Katya's doctor suggested, as a last resort, ART, assisted reproductive technology. Not *in vitro* fertilization; the Kulikovskys had no fertility problems. (And theirs was a passionate union; after twelve years of marriage they still moved in a haze of eroticism, always hungry for each other. They hoped, by admitting a child into their paradise, to better see each other reflected in her). No, Talya was a subject for lavage, reimplantation and surrogate gestation. She was flushed from Katya's womb three days after fertilization, before she could set up a placental connection or be rejected, and was dropped into a test tube. A whisper of skin brushed against glass. Natalya bounced in rapture, dreaming the future, the past, the living womb she remembered, awash in a sea of cells resonating with memories of her ancestors. Through the darkness she sensed a horizon, a sharp line of vivid orange paling to a yellowish blush flecked with cloud. She was in the hands of the medics, travelling a landscape of towering whiteness, climbing ladders of snowy nothingness, passing through mountain ranges insubstantial as cloud, plumetting into a blistered crater where she rolled over and over, flooded, floating, rising to the surface again, a pinpoint in a bewildered universe. She travelled thus for nine months and burst with an accumulation of energy into a perfect August afternoon. The initial assault was a flash of light, like knives in her eyes, and she screamed, surprising herself with the first unmuted sound in what she had taken to be a permanent sea of tranquility. Katya reached out immediately to receive her daughter in her long arms and as she cradled her, searching her wrinkled face in wonder, Nick Kulikovsky leaned over his wife and touched the tiny head with his finger, stroking her damp hair, already drying in the warm summer air.

"*Moya dochka*," he murmured, "My little girl."

He kissed Katya and stood behind her so that she wouldn't see his tears as he looked down on their perfect child.

They placed her crib in the corner of their bedroom and lay in each other's arms listening to the miracle of her breath. Katya hardly slept. The baby cried for her and was content only in her arms. Nick was overwhelmed by his love for the child, but he felt helpless.

"I'm so tired I could sleep for a million years," Katya murmured.

"This is too much, my darling, after all you've been through. I'll ask Lily to come."

"Not Lily."

"We owe her, Katya. Jack's being transferred to our Vancouver office and he's taking the family. She'll be out of work."

Katya curled into his body and wrapped her arms around his neck, acquiescent.

They moved the crib into the nursery and hired Lily to live in and take care of their daughter. Lily listened from her own room to the child's breath on the Baby Monitor, the soft, even exhalations mixing with her own sobs as she soaked her pillow nightly. Lily had left her own children in Manila with her sister. After Ramón had blackened both her eyes and left her with two kids and no money she'd made a decision to earn her keep in exile. But her heart was filled with longing for her little girl, Carrie, and her baby son, Ramoncíto.

Natalya Tatiana passed her babyhood and early infancy in Riverdale Park with Lily, who wheeled her along endlessly leafy streets, down the sweeping slopes of the park, and past the animal enclosures of Riverdale Farm. The evocative nature of the outdoors made Lily weep, and so, with the smell of lilac, the sound of birdsong, and the whisper of a warm breeze upon her skin, Talya absorbed a line of grief running through her like a fault as she gurgled and cooed with a heavy heart and waved her pudgy hand, the wrist but a wrinkle, at the other babies rolling by. Until one day Lily met a Chinese woman with her young daughter, recently arrived from Beijing and, as she and the smiling woman conversed in faltering English, Talya climbed out of her stroller, took the little girl's hand, and led her to the wading pool.

Dai Ling stood at the corner of Gerrard and Broadview, breathing in the aroma of frosted fruit. Fuji apples bulged from wooden crates; piles of oranges teetered beside persimmon, eggplant, lichens, grapes. An old man nudged the oranges as he entered the store and a handful spilled, rolling onto the sidewalk. People hurried by, avoiding the fallen fruits. Dai Ling stooped to pick them up.

A sudden change of weather had put a stop to her busking. She flexed her fingers inside warm woollen gloves. She'd been in orchestra class all afternoon and her throat and breastbone still vibrated with the power of the cello strings. They'd started with warm-ups, her bow passing back and forth across the steel-wrapped gut of her Helicore strings, creating a vibration that hollowed her from throat to rib cage and on down to the cleft of her; not quite hunger but an emptiness which longed to be filled. She'd felt a great happiness surge in her with the long, slow bowing of her open strings. Sometimes she liked to sing with her cello, harmonizing with it as though it were a human voice of extraordinary range, but today it had become *her* voice. She'd been lost in her own sound, unaware of the other students until she turned suddenly and saw Christie staring at her from the violin section. Dai Ling smiled but Christie had already returned to her tuning and was frowning with studied concentration.

They had been crossing the bridge from the Edward Johnson Building to Philosophers' Walk after class when Christie asked her, "How about coming dancing with us tonight?"

"Where?"

"Isabel's on Church Street. Oh, I know you're not 'one of us,' but I thought you might like to meet some of my friends," Christie had said, swinging her violin case nonchalantly. "They're all in couples and I'm not with anyone right now, so . . . " she'd trailed off. "D'you have a boyfriend?"

"I hang out with Ray Lee sometimes, but he's just a friend." Dai Ling had run at a pile of leaves suddenly and kicked them in the air. "Are you applying to the youth orchestra?"

"You betcha! Wouldn't it be great if we both got in?" Christie's violet-blue eyes had sparkled and her blonde spiky hair bristled. She reminded Dai Ling of Ray, always good-natured and enthusiastic. She wasn't afraid of anything. Last summer she'd hitchhiked all the way to Vancouver to seek out KD Lang. She'd found her too and they'd played punk fiddle together. Christie had even talked her way into a recording session and got to play on KD's new album.

"Deadline for applications is December 15th," Christie had said. "I did mine online. They want a solo and two orchestral excerpts."

"Will you do the Vivaldi?" Dai Ling asked

"The 'Primavera Allegro'?"

"No, I was thinking of the 'Inverno Allegro', third movement. Your technique is brilliant, and that piece allows you to demonstrate your range."

"D'you really think so?"

"Oh yes. Those long mournful melodies, then the sudden crackling of energy as the pace changes. It's your best piece."

"Thanks. I'll try it. Well, what about tonight? Can you come?"

"What's the address?"

"Church and Maitland, just below Wellesley, northeast corner." Her cheeks had dimpled with pleasure. "I'm heading west. See you around 8:30. I'll wait for you in the lobby," she had said.

Absent-mindedly, with the Bach prelude in her ears and her fingers on the phantom cello strings, Dai Ling pocketed an orange while replacing them on the pile. From the heart of Toronto's Chinatown East, she began walking east on Gerrard, toward home. People were muffled against the frosty air, coming so suddenly after Indian summer. Dai Ling's breath vaporized in a long cloud as she exhaled. She delved into her pocket and pulled out the orange, peeled it and slipped the frosty segments into her mouth one by one, juice spurting inside her cheeks as she pierced the membranes and thawed the frozen crystals with her tongue.

She looked down at the sidewalk, stepping deliberately on cracks in the pavement. She'd been told in the schoolyard that if she stepped on a crack the sidewalk would open up and swallow her, and who knew then what might happen to her in the underworld of the city? Over the years this information had been repeatedly disproven, but her ancient ritual of crackwalking persisted, a magical attempt to provoke some change in her life, which was a steady routine of cello practice, chamber music, orchestra and theory, interspersed with a twice-weekly shift at the Riverdale Library where she shelved and re-shelved books with effortless precision. Sometimes a burst of delight shattered the suburban hush of the library. It was Dai Ling letting off steam in the stacks, unaware of her audible joy behind the earplugs of her Ipod, grooving to the strains of Jacqueline du Pré or Yo-Yo Ma.

She wiped her mouth and plunged her hands deep into empty pockets. Her wake was strewn with orange peel. She was a dreamy girl, twenty-one years old, on the verge of something.

She walked up the backsteps of her family home and the screen door slammed behind her as she entered.

"You bought oranges?"

"Oranges?"

"Yes, I smell oranges." Xian Ming turned from the sink, wiping her hands on a towel. "You brought oranges home?"

"No, I ate one on the street."

"That's good, because I bought a big bag of oranges today, nice juicy ones. Mrs. Fox called. She wants you to work at the library tonight. The other girl's sick."

"Oh no! I don't want to, Ma. I'm on all day tomorrow. And Christie invited me to . . . "

"You need the money, Dai Ling, especially when you get into the National Youth Orchestra and go on tour. The scholarship won't cover everything."

"*When* I get in! I wish I was as confident as you, Ma."

Dai Ling was shorter than her mother, with more delicate bones, but they shared the broad capable hands of Dai Ling's French-Canadian grandmother, Geneviève. Xian Ming was, in all but appearance, Chinese. Each time Dai Ling saw her leaning over the wok or crouched in the garden weeding her rose-beds she was surprised by Ma's pale skin, her startling green eyes, her tall, angular body, so different from the other Chinatown women. But Xian Ming was accepted without question on the streets of Chinatown because, though she had not inherited her father's physical traits, she had his fluent tongue and his gestures, and these were enough to assure the Chinese that she was one of them. Dai Ling, entirely Chinese in appearance, except for her coppery hair, demonstrated her Montréal grandmother's ways and spoke Mandarin with a Canadian accent.

"What time do I have to be there?"

"Six-thirty. Your Babá won't be home till late, so we'll go ahead and eat. I made dumplings."

"I'm going to take a shower," she said, already half-way down the hall. She took the stairs two at a time and burst into her bedroom. She stood for a moment, breathing in the silence.

There was her red *shui pao* hanging on the back of the door, sprigs of pale bamboo growing up and down the sleeves and front panels, and on the back a long-legged white crane with folded wings and bowed head. As she took the robe between her fingers and spread it the wings spread too, and she imagined Babá's head appearing round the door, the tenderest of smiles hovering at his mouth, and she, a little girl again, drawing the sheet up under her chin. She smelled the bitter herbs on his skin as he bent to kiss her, felt an alteration in the air as he moved away. Then she heard the door close softly and his bare footfalls continuing down the hallway to Ma's room, the squeak of springs as he climbed into bed, Dai Ling turning to face the thin wall between them papered with creamy-white flowers, like the gardenia in the front room downstairs, its veined leaves shiny with health. Ma had bought it one spring day at the flower shop next door to Cai Yuan Supermarket and had placed it in the front window next to the jade plant. "There," she'd said. "Now it will bloom," and a week later the room had been filled with a heady aroma.

She felt uneasy. *Will I be breaking a date? Maybe it's for the best. Bless you, Mrs. Fox.* Christie was insistent when Dai Ling called. "Oh come on, Dai Ling, you can come after work. You'll be finished by 9:30."

"Too late, Christie. I've got a full day at the library tomorrow."

"Pleeease come. I'll be so disappointed."

"I'm sorry, I can't. I just can't."

"Oh well, another time. Have fun in the stacks," she said, already recovering her cheerfulness.

It was a crisp October Saturday. Talya was perched on a ladder in the Riverdale Library perusing a large book of illustrations from the anatomical works of Andreas Vesalius when Dai Ling, drawn by a tingling sensation in her scalp, rounded the corner and collided with the ladder. It wobbled, Talya tumbled and Dai Ling fell on top of her.

"Sorry. Are you all right?" Dai Ling was the first to recover as they lay in a tangle of limbs.

"I think so. What happened?"

"Shhhhhhh!" A loud disturbance of spittle flew from the Head Librarian's lips. Mrs. Fox kept a close eye on Dai Ling. She liked the girl and took a motherly interest in her. Most of her workers were ordinary girls, plodding through the stacks, dealing with the demands of the reading public efficiently and politely, but Dai Ling was in another world. Mrs. Fox sometimes saw the fingers of her left hand moving with great intention and Dai Ling listening as though some extraordinary music were ringing through the library.

Talya and Dai Ling reached out at the same moment to help each other up and, as their hands touched, *A World Lit Only by Fire: The Medieval Mind and the Renaissance*, displaced in the melée, was kicked open. On the page, Rembrandt's *Le Philosophe* turned his slow head towards the golden window at which he had pondered for centuries.

"I know you! You're the Bloor Street cellist!" Talya exclaimed as Mrs. Fox clicked a rapid path through the stacks and threw up her hands.

"I didn't do anything," Talya said, still clutching her Vesalius. "I was reading quietly and she came out of nowhere and knocked me off the ladder."

"It's okay, Mrs. Fox," Dai Ling said. "I'll deal with it."

"Well!" she sniffed, "You'd better clean up this mess before you go to lunch."

"I'll help," Talya said quickly, catching Dai Ling's eye, "And if you have time on your lunch break I'd like to ask you about your music."

Dai Ling hesitated, then nodded and began collecting the scattered books while Talya looked intently at the Vesalius book of *Illustrations* which, she had already noted, began with a short biography.

1536: Louvain: Capital of the Duchy of Brabant in the Low Countries

ANDREAS VESALIUS WRAPPED A THICK WOOLLEN coat around his muscular body. It was winter in Northern Europe and despite his florid constitution the dampness of the Low Countries entered his bones. After studying medicine in Paris for three years he had recently returned to his homeland, his studies cut short by the outbreak of war and the invasion of Provence by Charles V. Now he was on a night-call, carrying a large sack over his shoulder, flexing his biceps in preparation. There had been a hanging earlier in the day, a middle-aged man, a thief. *Perfect*, thought Vesalius. *Body fully-formed. Fresh.* His boots struck the frosted cobblestones of Louvain, ringing through the sleeping city, twenty miles east of Brussels.

The last one had been a 'Digger,' five days dead and buried. As he'd spaded the earth over his left shoulder, scattering clods of it into the eye of the Devil, Vesalius had stopped to take out a handkerchief and tie it quickly across his nose and mouth. The stench was terrible, but he was not afraid of the Plague. He knew even then that he was born to enter the human body and map it. And he was only just beginning. The 'Digger' had turned out to be an old man, shrivelled and already rotting. Vesalius had doused the body with vinegar and carefully dissected it, moving rapidly to avoid discovery and to beat the maggots. The body had lost its definition even as he worked, cutting and documenting the rotting innards. The dissection had done little more than whet his appetite for a fresher specimen. He had ditched the old man and made a visit to the hangman.

"In four days," he had said. "Come after midnight."

Vesalius found his way to the gallows by starlight. It was the time of the dark moon, but the sky was clear and strewn with stars scattered in clusters like spilled goat's milk. The cloaked hangman greeted him gruffly, emerging from the shadows to grasp Vesalius' arm and pull him through a narrow door. They stooped to enter the stinking hold and the hangman lit a stubby piece of tallow.

"There, he's yours," he said in a gravelly voice, his head jerking towards a slumped body. Then he tugged on Vesalius' sleeve. "First the money."

Vesalius thrust his hand into his pocket and handed him some coins. He bundled the corpse into the sack, hoisted it onto his broad back, grasping the neck over his right shoulder, and shuffled out under the dead weight.

"So it's true," he whispered. "The bowels void as the rope tightens."

The hangman grunted and closed the door silently behind them. "If anyone asks, you got him from the graveyard," he growled.

Talya and Dai Ling walked up Broadview, past the Don Jail and Riverdale Hospital, past the statue of Dr. Sun Yat-Sen and out onto the broad slopes of Riverdale Park, carpetted with flaming leaves.

"That was so strange," Talya said. "I never go to the Riverdale Library. Used to go as a kid, but now I use the university library."

"Me too."

"A student?"

"Cello major."

"So it *was* you! At the corner of Bloor and Sherbourne, couple of weeks ago?"

"I guess so. The Bach suite?"

"Yes! You play like an angel. I've been back so many times . . ."

"It's too cold now for the cello, and for my fingers." Dai Ling, suddenly shy, pulled her black ski jacket tight around her. She wasn't a skier. Xian Ming had bought it for her on sale. "A good price, Dai Ling. It'll keep you warm all winter."

The wind whipped up and scarlet leaves swirled around their ankles. A huge maple leaf blew into Talya's face and she flipped it away with a quick gesture, laughing. Dai Ling laughed too as Talya turned slowly to face her, staring intently.

"I think you're beautiful . . . " Talya said. "Your playing, I mean."

The wind gusted, tugging at Dai Ling's jacket, and white feathers flew from a tiny rip in the elbow of her left sleeve.

Dai Ling clasped her ripped jacket, watching the white down float across the park.

"You're losing your stuffing," Talya laughed as she took hold of Dai Ling's gloved hand and ran with her down the grassy verge, past the skating rink, until they reached the edge of the concrete saucer which transformed into a children's wading pool in summer.

"This is where we came when I was little," Talya said, breathless.

"Me too!" Dai Ling's eyes were shining. "I feel like I've known you forever. Why *did* you come to the library today?"

Talya shrugged. "My parents live in the area. You weren't at the corner so I cycled across the Don Valley bridge and turned down Broadview. Next thing I knew I was in the library and look what I found." She sat on a park bench and looked up at Dai Ling, squinting into the pale sun. "Look, aren't they wonderful?" She held up the Vesalius *Illustrations*.

Dai Ling sat beside her and they flipped through the illustrations of flayed bodies, the muscles and tendons labelled with Greek letters. Each figure was set in a landscape of trees and rocks receding into the distance where buildings with rows of arches nestled amidst rising steeples.

Dai Ling leaned forward. "It looks like a musical instrument," she said, tracing the curved lines of bunched muscle and sinew up the tortured legs of a flayed man — ankle, swirling up calf, wrapping around knee, flaring up thigh to the wing of his pelvis.

"The body *is* an instrument. It plays the sweetest music."

"Are you a music student?"

Talya shook her head. "Med."

"Wasn't it forbidden to dissect the human body back then."

Talya nodded. "Vesalius had to dig for bones and 'rob the gibbet' all over Europe to complete his anatomical work. But after he published his first book he was awarded the chair of Anatomy at the University of Padua under the rule of the Republic of Venice, which gave him free rein to perform public dissections in the cause of scientific inquiry."

"You seem to know a lot about this. Have you studied the Renaissance?"

Talya tapped the book with her long fingers. "Just skimmed through. I'm a quick study," she laughed. "Galileo taught in Padua too, and he was free to lecture on his discoveries. It was only when he went to Florence that he was arrested and charged with heresy."

"Hmmm. What's this?" Dai Ling, flipping through the book, had found a page showing an oval-shaped structure, like a tiered egg with a supine form in the centre.

"The operating theatre in Padua. That's where Vesalius did his dissections."

Dai Ling saw not so much a theatre as a womblike enclosure inside which the body rose and tumbled, its limbs growing within the shrinking space until they could no longer move. The creature was wedged, squeezed inside the last place on earth, its curled spine imprinted with tiered columns.

"And all those balconies? For spectators?"

Talya nodded and smiled. "That's why it's called a theatre. Opening the human body is intensely dramatic, don't you think?"

Dai Ling looked up at Talya, her lips parted. "I don't know. I'm a musician," she said.

~

1538: Padua

Twenty miles west of Venice: A large audience has gathered to hear Andreas Vesalius' lecture on human anatomy. The twenty-four-year-old Doctor of Medicine, knife in hand, is poised to perform a dissection. His dark eyes fix on the cadaver before him, which is held in a standing position with a pulley-rope looped around the back of the head. Vesalius' hand is sure; he has done this many times. He stands on the verge of a great renaissance, backed by Hippocrates, Aristotle, Herophilus, Galen. The young man is afire. Keen and sharp as his scalpel, he reaches forward and makes a swift longitudinal incision from rib cage to pubis, laying open the matrix of the human body, cutting through the veil of time and mystic belief.

Stiff with curiosity, he slits the body, peels back layers of tissue, tendon and muscle to expose the bones. Slowly, meticulously, he examines and documents every vein, muscle, artery and organ. He is on sacred ground, exposing a mystery, revealing a long-held secret. But he does not find the Soul.

Vesalius feels fleetingly within his own muscle, bone and blood a violence simultaneously tempered by another part of him. He does not heed the singing in his blood, the whispering of his heart. He moves like a machine, swift and precise. Rows of dark-headed young men lean forward, straining to see the body laid open, the soft velvet of their voluminous sleeves draping the hard surfaces of wood-grained lecterns as the dissected cadaver dances grotesquely, knees bent, head thrown back, palms dripping gloved skin from the bare bones of its hands. The empty barrel of the rib cage is ringed with yellowing ribs. The Soul has escaped.

Each time Vesalius opened the body, his heart leapt. The first time, trembling with excitement, he had almost swooned with the wonder of it, the clandestine nature of it. "Ah, the true Bible," he had whispered, "The human body." The Church taught that the dead would wreak veangence on those who defiled the body, but when Vesalius saw the helplessness of the flesh, bereft of life, he was moved beyond himself to that other place where gentleness wrestled with cruelty. He felt the suffering of the flesh, the spirit held hostage within. He recalled the screaming of a cat his brothers had tormented in Hell's Lane and how he had watched, helpless, wanting to stop them, wanting to kill the cat to stop its screeching.

With his first cadaver he had delved into the cavity, removing the slippery organs one by one, moving with a speed and urgency that forced his heart into submission. He had laid them on a cloth on the table, beside his instruments. Because the liver was larger and darker than the other organs, he had thought that it might house the Soul. But how could he tell? Would it have a different vibration? Would it answer him when he spoke?

"Immortal Soul, where art thou?" he had asked, his words echoing into the silence of his nocturnal activity. Could it be inside the shrimp-like organ nestling beside the thick, central vein? No, there were two of them. Could there be twin Souls in one body? He'd had a vision of the body as a tree, the extraordinary beauty of its veins and arteries reaching out, roots and tendrils trembling with life, and he had determined to document it. He'd held the curled organs, one in each hand and felt their resonance, their slimy, blood-streaked skin, like sausage casings. He had listened and felt their voices coursing up his arms, thrilling in his veins, but the Soul was elusive. It flitted through his dreams and danced ahead of him, evading him at every turn, as his feet clattered on the cobblestones of Brussels, Louvain, Paris, Padua, Venice . . .

"Dai Ling!" Ray Lee called down from the open window of his bedroom. "You want to go for a walk? I need to be rescued from my studying."

"I was just going home, but . . . sure, okay."

Dai Ling had known Ray forever. Her house was half a block from where he lived with his parents and his brother, Wayne, next door to the Happy Bridal Boutique. They had played in the Lee's backyard as kids, Funeral mostly. Dai Ling remembered the day she had been buried.

"Come on, Dai Ling!" her gang had shouted. "You play the dead girl and we'll bury you."

"How will I get out?"

"We'll dig you up when you tell us."

"What if you don't hear me?"

"No problem," said Ray who had learned the phrase from his father, who completed his every utterance with it. "We'll go into my mom's kitchen for milk and cookies and we'll bring yours outside and dig you up no problem, okay?"

Seven years old and fearless, Dai Ling had climbed into the cardboard box. The children picked her up and lowered her into the trench at the bottom of the garden. They stood around and wept while Ray muttered and crossed himself. He had seen a funeral on his Ma's favourite TV show. They placed the lid on her coffin and she heard the first clod of earth crumbling as it hit the cardboard above her face. She flinched and giggled, then relaxed and listened to the earth scattering and building, housing her securely in her box. At first she'd heard the muffled cries of the children, then they'd grown fainter, until she was in silence except for the sound of her own breathing and the rumbling of her stomach in anticipation of milk and cookies. She had lain silent, no room to move, alert at first, then she'd grown drowsy and drifted into a half-sleep filled with sweet music. When she woke she was cold and cramped. She tried to bend her legs but the box was too narrow. She pushed with her hands against the lid above her face. The earth shifted and fell, buckling the lid. Panic bloomed in her small body. *They've left me,* she thought. *They're in the kitchen eating cookies. They'll all go home and forget me. I'll die here and no one will ever know!* She tried to cry out but the box swallowed her voice and suddenly she couldn't breathe. Her bladder gave way and hot urine trickled through her panties, spreading over her dress, under her legs, soaking into the cardboard.

When they dug her out it was dark. Dai Ling sprang from the box, scattering earth all around her. She ran down Gerrard Street in the darkness, a small child with wet legs and a pulsing red aura, headlong into the arms of her mother. Xian Ming, who had been cooking dinner, had lifted her head from the wok suddenly, exclaimed "Dai Ling is in trouble," and had run out the door without her coat.

Ray Lee had remained her friend and had maintained a taste for the macabre. He was studying film at York University and had just shot his first short movie.

"Let's cut through Riverdale Park to the Necropolis, okay? I'll show you where I shot my movie. There's so much history there, Dai Ling. And everyone's together no problem, okay? Death is a great leveller. It's tragic and full of ritual."

Dai Ling smiled up into Ray's dark eyes. He was tall and very good-looking, like her father. He took her hand and they walked along Gerrard Street swinging their arms.

"*Sansho the Bailiff* is playing at the Bloor Cinema tonight. It's one of Mizoguchi's best."

"I thought *Tokyo Story* was his best."

"That's Ozu. I showed you *Tokyo Story* in the film lab at York, remember?"

"I sure do," she said coquettishly.

Ray blushed and laughed. "Changed your mind, Dai Ling?"

She scuffed her feet in the fallen leaves and shook her head.

"Just asking," he grinned. He always grinned when he was nervous. "You can identify an Ozu movie by his unique style," he continued. "He uses low camera shots with virtually no camera movement, which capture the essence and stillness of the Japanese perspective. And in dialogue scenes Ozu refuses to cut away from a speaking character, as though he insisted that every person has the right to be heard in full."

"You sound like you're reciting from a paper."

"Well I do have an assigment on Japanese film, so that's what I'm thinking about."

They ran down the hill to the ravine that plunges west of Riverdale Park on the southern boundary of the Necropolis. "Ozu is in fact the most brilliant in my opinion," Ray said breathlessly as they reached the bottom of the ravine, "But Mizoguchi is a close second. In *Sansho the Bailiff* a man is sold into slavery and later reunited with his Ma who's been raped and abandoned. She's a cripple. There's a tragic final scene on the beach. It's shot with a crane which rises above the huddled mother and son until all you see is the beach in a long shot with a tiny human figure on the lower left of the frame."

Dai Ling's running shoes were buried to the ankles in red and yellow leaves. She saw their skeletal structure emerging, the silence of winter beginning to take hold. She held up a large maple leaf against Ray's fiery outline. "And who is that tiny human figure?" she asked, looking up beyond the ravine to the top of Riverdale Park, remembering Talya standing there, and the figure in the egg-like enclosure of Vesalius' operating theatre.

"What?" Ray was staring at her, a quizzical expression on his face.

"On the lower left of the frame?"

"Oh." He shrugged and smiled revealing strong white teeth. "I don't know. Mizoguchi uses shots that dwarf his characters to show that tragedy is determined by fate and irredeemable human nature. In the context of this film it's impersonal and unresolvable."

Dai Ling loved his passionate appreciation of the art of film, and she found him so beautiful to look at that it confused her when she invariably became bored and started thinking of other things, like the opening bars of the *Elgar Concerto*, or the pile of books she'd left unshelved in the biography stacks. She had dreamed about Ray kissing her, but when he did, in the York film lab after they'd watched *Tokyo Story*, there had been no spark in it, not like when he talked about the movies. In the embarrassed silence that followed their kiss she had said, "Let's just be friends, okay?"

Ray had stared at her, his brow furrowed, then he'd smiled, his mouth wide and sensual. "Sure, Dai Ling. I understand." He had leaned forward and kissed her cheek, then he'd jumped up and punched the air. "Friends forever!" he'd shouted. And then they had become like siblings again and everything had been easier. But Dai Ling sometimes felt a twinge of regret, which confused her even more and made her wonder if she shouldn't have persisted. *What does love feel like? Is it instant, or does it grow? Perhaps I've known Ray too long to feel romantic about him.*

~

Talya awoke suddenly. She didn't know where she was. Something felt different. The ceiling was sliced with light shooting through the venetian blinds like knives. *My apartment, Brunswick, heart of the Annex.* She looked around at familiar objects; her golden-shaded bedside lamp, the open drawers of her bureau spilling with clothes, running shoes at odd angles like the feet of an accident victim. Then she remembered her dream and her mouth curved into a sleepy smile. Rolling in thick red leaves, tumbling down the gentle slope of a ravine. She stretched her body, feeling each vertebra separating, and lay spreadeagled, recapturing the dream. *Something's going to happen. I know this feeling. Something . . .* She was almost afraid. Stagefright. She remembered, with a thud of excitement, today was her first post-mortem. She jumped out of bed, pulled on jeans and a sweater, brushed her teeth and grabbed an apple on her way out the door. Within ten minutes Talya was cycling down University Avenue, the juice of a golden delicious dripping down her chin.

In the cold basement of the morgue, wearing a thin white hospital coat over her day clothes, Talya tried to focus her attention. She caught Elliott's eye and grinned. A stethoscope dangled uselessly from his neck. The woman on the slab was one of their patients, Mrs. Jacobs, who had died suddenly in the night. The pathologist beckoned them closer and began describing in precise detail how he was to proceed. Talya watched, her eyes rivetted on the naked cadaver, awaiting the first cut. *Oh god, don't let me faint! I've waited so long for this. I didn't expect it to be someone I knew.*

The knife slid into the woman's chest, slicing from the tip of the sternum, through the belly, down to the pubis. Talya leaned in closer and stared at Mrs. Jacobs' tumble of innards. The already shrivelling organs and coagulating blood suggested to her the reverse process — the slow growth of her body, the closing of flesh over vitals, the insistent beating and pumping of a foetal heart that banished the silence and presaged a blinding light. She wanted to take the knife and wield it. She heard the Bach prelude, saw Dai Ling's fingers moving on the stringed neck of her cello, pressing and releasing. The flayed illustrations of Vesalius' *Fabrica* leapt around her as the vital organs were weighed and documented.

"Watch it, do it, teach it," Elliott whispered, watching Talya closely, almost reading her mind. They shared a passionate impatience, a need to break the taboos and take control of the mystery. When she told him afterwards that she had decided to specialize in surgery, he wagged his finger and said, "You'll have to close down, Tal. I know you. You'll have to concentrate on the craft of it, the carpentry and seamstressing of it, or you'll go crazy."

"It was her heart that gave out," Talya said. "Did you see that massive blood clot in her left brachial artery? I wonder what her INR was?"

"Normal yesterday morning. I posted the lab results myself."

"Lab tests don't always tell the story. We should have upped the blood thinners."

"Monday morning quarterback," he quipped. "Come on, we deserve a coffee."

"Let's go by the lockers. I have a marvellous book I want to show you."

"Men in Bondage?"

"Vesalius! Illustrations from the *Fabrica*, the *Epitome* and the *Tabulae Sex.*"

"Oooh! Can't wait."

~

Many attempts have been made to reconstruct the character and personality of Vesalius. He is often portrayed as a fiery, hot-tempered, disputatious extrovert of tremendous energy and ambition, 'the man of wrath.' On the other hand, a recent writer would see in him a shut-in, schizoid, melancholic individual who rapidly passed into depression upon achieving the pinnacle of his success and accomplishment. Such diversity of opinion is no more than a measure of our ignorance of the man and his character, and the extraordinary facility with which writers will lose all sense of objectivity to spin elaborate webs of romantic fantasy from the thinnest of factual threads. Rather, let us confess that the materials with which to reconstruct his personality are of the scantiest and that we are not in a position to view the man except dimly . . . Truly a child of the Renaissance and deeply influenced by humanistic teachings, he sought not refuge in his books but the restoration of the golden age . . .

~

1538: University of Padua

Andreas Vesalius passed under the great stone archway, paused and looked around him, eyes sliding from pillar to pillar of the colonnaded courtyard. The university was quiet and in the silence Vesalius felt the flexing of many minds, heard the tentative footsteps and quicksilver calculations of the young men anxiously awaiting him in the Anatomy Theatre. His footsteps echoed as he crossed the open rectangle of the courtyard and mounted four steps, then silence again as he paused, leaning against a pillar bathed in wintry sunlight. Warm breath condensed on his beard as he savoured the moment, feeling himself at the beginning of something, a sleuth-hound picking up a scent.

As a student in Paris, hungry for knowledge of the inner body, he had spent long hours in the Cemetery of Innocents, digging for bones. He had carried them in a sack, back to his room, where he and his fellow students would sit blindfolded at night, handling the bones, competing for recognition of their shape. Vesalius was tireless. Long after his friends had dispersed, heavy-eyed with sleep, the young man sat, eyes closed, head tilted to the heavens, caressing the smooth bones, imagining the movement and relation of each to the others, the bunching of muscle, taut ligaments binding to bone, the fleshy covering that evoked desire.

One night at the Cemetery he sat on a pile of crumbling earth, his brow running with sweat. Spade at his side, he sorted digit bones and ribs, a humerus brittle with decay, mottled green and yellow, almost ready to snap in his fingers. He sensed the animals before he heard them, a snarling, deep and gutteral, a gathering force. Vesalius leapt from the grave, bundling the bones into his jacket as he tripped over his abandoned sack. The dogs leapt too, almost upon him as he fled. It was a hot pursuit, but an even hotter retreat. Vesalius felt the fangs of the lead dog snag on his breeches and he whirled around, felling the creature with the very bone it sought. Shattered fragments flew around man and dog and Vesalius was left empty-handed. He spun around and hurled himself over the east gate, then dropped to his haunches, panting, and watched the confused pack circle their leader, whining and sniffing. He saw himself, a lone man travelling a darkened path, gathering his own pack around him, drawing them onward.

Vesalius turned on his heel and walked back down the colonnade etched with the names and family crests of the university faculty. He visualized his own name there — Van Wesele of Brussels, his name atop the three-weaseled crest. The name 'Vesalius' conformed to the Latinate convention of the day. He passed the lecture room on the left and glimpsed through the open door a row of shining skulls donated to the university by past professors of Physic eager to serve medical science with this essential part of their cadavers. He did not foresee his own skull in the line-up.

He gathered himself and approached the kitchen where the bodies were washed and prepared for dissection. As he entered he saw the corpse, fresh from the nearby *infermaria*, where the homeless and indigent went to die. He approached and held his hand a hair's breadth from the heart. A whisper of heat crept into his palm. "Bring it in. Now!" he ordered, and entered the theatre, nodding to tiers of students leaning over their railings, circling above him. Vesalius, unlike the other professors, did not seat himself and lecture from the dais, leaving the dissection to his assistants. He stood in the centre of the theatre, scalpel in hand, ready.

He was a handsome man with a stocky frame and a high broad forehead. His head was large, covered with close-cropped dark curls, his face full and open as befitted his questing nature. He led with a thick straight nose, fleshy nostrils resting on a mustache above full lips. His beard reached down, a spade digging into his barrel chest.

When the body was trundled in he instructed his assistants to uncover it, then he waved them aside. He stepped up to the cooling cadaver and raised his arms in a triumphant gesture, causing his shirt sleeves to ride up, freeing his wrists and forearms. Poised, he lowered his scalpel hand slowly, carefully, whispering under his breath. His students leaned over their parapets in the oval theatre, spellbound. Vesalius' ears were red with curiosity and exertion. Shell-like and well-proportioned, they gave him the appearance of a woodland creature caught unaware, alert for a secret signal. He was listening for the breath of the Soul.

The corpse of a man lay before him, a man whose name was long-forgotten, but whose Soul had not yet departed.

Vesalius felt the presence of something lingering and it drove him mad. His eyes gleamed as he sliced and dissected, searching every corner of the body. The Soul hovered, alert like its seeker, waiting for a sign, until suddenly it was pulled, with a silent rush of air, through the roof of the domed building, and into the grey sky over Padua. The Soul had been fused in a fierce relationship with the dying man. It remembered his screams as he'd writhed on his hospital bed, its own staunch alliance to the suffering flesh; all the Souls within all the bodies; the agony and fidelity of the sweet, generous Soul.

Vesalius sensed a subtle alteration in the atmosphere. He paced back and forth, circled the dissected body, searching, until he looked up suddenly, caught unaware by rows of eager faces. Then he cleared his throat, thrust out his chest, and resumed his lecture.

"We are here today, gentlemen, to inquire into the relationship between the vital organs of the human body. Observe," he said with a flourish of his hand as he turned on his heel and strode back and forth across the dais. He approached the diagram of the human organs *in situ* and pointed to the lungs, depicted like bellows in heavy dark charcoal. He knew there was a vital connection between the organs, but he had not quite grasped it, and he rooted, puzzling as he went, like a pig after truffles, following his nose.

As a boy he had hidden in the reeds and watched the swift movement of the river. It had seemed to flow endlessly and he had wondered at its source and destination and at the impetus of its movement. Now he viewed the body's blood in a similar manner, unable to determine the force which drove it through the *corpus.* He by-passed the blood and pointed out the body bellows, the liver, the spleen, the kidneys and bladder, and the great beating heart, vital sign of life, pulsing its rhythm through the body. Thus he created connections between the organs, a human family forced into co-operation by their situation. He guessed at the points he could not prove, inspired in his passion to understand and communicate, but all the time a worm of uncertainty gnawed at his belly and quivered in his gut.

"Oh, help me, Saint Jude!" he implored, appealing to the Patron of Lost Causes and Cases Despaired of. He believed in the impossible; he was determined to put an end to mystery and uncertainty. He twirled like a dancer to face his audience, and once again he was in command, swelling with the authority his students gave him.

"The practice of dissection, gentlemen, is art. And the anatomical discovery of man as the living reflection of God is worthy of the highest personal dedication and risk."

"How can a common indigent or a thief from the gallows be the living reflection of God?" called out a strident voice.

"The form, sir, the form," Vesalius answered. "Anatomical form is everything, and distinct from the behaviour of the vessel. We open the body, remove the organs, laid out thus on the dissecting table," he gestured towards the long trestle, studded with bloody jewels, "And we see it empty, devoid of its animating spirit. And where, you may ask, gentlemen, is the Soul? Where is the Soul?" Vesalius pulled at his beard, brittle black hairs splitting between his fingers.

With a sudden violence he burst forth, "If we cannot find the Soul we must control our lives through the body!"

"But the Church . . . " someone began.

"The Church? The Church?" shouted Vesalius. "Now that we have opened the body nothing will ever be the same."

A flash of lightning erased the stars in the Paduan sky. Vesalius and his students knew nothing of it, entombed in their windowless theatre, until a crash of thunder shook the professor's scalpel hand.

~

Dai Ling gasped as she entered the front room.

"Ma!" she screamed. "It's beautiful!"

She turned to see Xian Ming in the doorway, grinning.

"It'll bring us good luck, Dai Ling. The gardenia is fine for its sweet smell, but an orchid is very important for the house of a doctor and a budding musician. It's a highly cultivated plant."

Dai Ling touched the petals and lifted the head of a bloom with her forefinger. The lip was splotched with burgundy. Above it reared a cobra-shaped petal rippled with red lines running deep into the centre of the flower. Its hooded head concealed a creamy white tip. *Loves me, loves me not, loves me,* her mind chanted, counting the petals. It was automatic as crackwalking. Her finger brushed against a drop of sap oozing from the pale stem.

"It was expensive, but I got a deal. Karen next door has a friend at the garden centre. I know your Babá will be happy," Xian Ming beamed. She had been born Xian Ming Joanne LaCharité in Beijing in 1964. Her mother, Geneviève

LaCharité, had been a student of agriculture in Montréal, and a passionate Maoist. The *Little Red Book* was always on her desk, and when Geneviève wasn't studying she was engaged in passionate cafeteria debates on Maoist doctrine.

"Come to China," she urged her friends, "The country is in a state of dynamic transition, and we can help with our knowledge of agriculture."

"But they're starving since Mao's forced collectivization of farmland," her friend said.

"There's no movement forward without the sacrifice of lives," Geneviève declared, her cheeks flushed.

The name of Xian Ming's father was not registered at the hospital in Beijing and she never met him. Geneviève raised her alone, refusing to return to Canada, and she told the child bedtime stories about her Chinese father. "He's a hero of the Revolution. He was betrayed by a jealous comrade and falsely accused of criticizing Mao Zedong. Now your father is serving a prison sentence," she said. "One day he'll come for us."

But Xian Ming couldn't wait. She fell in love with Jia Song Xiang, a handsome medical student with intense dark eyes and a passion for democratic reform. Jia Song was in the forefront of the student protests at Bejing University. When he realized the danger he was in, and already married with a baby, Xian Ming became their passport to freedom. Five years before the massacre at Tianenmen Square he received a visa for Canada on the basis of his wife's dual nationality. They landed in Toronto in the spring of 1984. Dai Ling was barely two years old.

That Summer Xian Ming headed for the park with Dai Ling in her stroller. A fellow immigrant smiled sadly at Xian Ming; it was Lily, making her daily trip to the wading pool with three-year-old Talya. The little girls immediately found each other in the crowd of toddlers, and splashed ecstatically in the shallow saucer of the wading pool, even though English was not their common language. They met each day and when it was time to go home Dai Ling wept and Talya threw a tantrum, thumping her head into Lily's belly. Though the girls had grown up a half dozen blocks apart they had been channelled away from each other by race and class.

"They don't like direct sunlight," Xian Ming said, moving the orchid onto a side table. "Did you eat lunch?"

Dai Ling nodded. "With Christie and Sylvie in the cafeteria. We had chamber trio practice this afternoon. Our recital is next month. I'm getting complimentary tickets for you and Babá."

The back door slammed. "Hello," a deep male voice called.

"In here Zhuzi," Xian Ming called.

"Why d'you call Babá zhuzi? He's not skinny."

"You should have seen him when he was young — skinny like a bamboo pole."

Jia Song entered, a tall handsome man, padding in his socks. "Starting to snow . . . " he began, then he saw the orchid and his face creased into a big smile. He nodded his head, laughing, and put his arms around Xian Ming. "Good fortune for us all," he said.

"Dinner's almost ready. Five minutes, then we eat," Xian Ming said and hurried to the kitchen.

Jia Song put his arm around Dai Ling and leaned down to kiss the top of her silky red hair. He noticed that she'd had it cut, accentuating her fine bone structure and delicate nose. He recognized in her his own full mouth and dark eyes, and the particular quality of her complexion. When she was little he'd teased her that she had treasure stored under her skin because it was golden and translucent, shining with inner riches.

"Working hard, Dai Ling?"

"Yes, Babá. The audition is in January."

"Don't forget to make time for relaxation. Very important for the body to have balance. Are you going to the movies again with Ray Lee?"

Dai Ling squirmed, "I don't think so, Babá. We're just good friends."

"You got your eye on some other boy?"

"No, Babá," Dai Ling laughed, "I'm in love with you, remember?" She ducked out from under his arm and ran around the room screaming with laughter, making the orchid quiver as she rushed past it. Jia Song lumbered after her, puffing and roaring like a dragon — their old childhood game.

When Dai Ling was a little girl her father's clinic had been in the house, in that very room, filled with the bitter smell of more than two hundred varieties of herbs in large glass jars lined up on the shelves. There had been dried seahorses resting on curled tails, tiny heads bowed over their hollow bellies; long ginseng roots topped with bulbous growths that looked like extraordinary little people; red wolfberries, twisted roots and bark fragments, long centipedes impaled on tiny sticks, dried snake . . .

One time Ray Lee's father had had pains in his chest and Babá let her sit and watch him take the pulses. He had made Mr. Lee lie down and close his eyes while he stuck needles in him. Dai Ling had thought he was dying. She had wanted to run and tell Ray Lee, "Now we can have a real funeral!" But then he'd opened his eyes and smiled at Dai Ling, sitting quietly in the corner. "Your Babá is a very important man, Dai Ling. He knows everything to keep us well in this new country, no problem. In China he would be the most respected man, okay? That is why his true name is Jia Song, a prized name because Song means pine tree and the pine is a clean and honourable tree." Jia Song's concession to his new country had been to modify his name to Jason for his Caucasian clients.

Dai Ling collapsed onto the sofa, breathless from running, and Jia Song, laughing, sat in the armchair opposite.

"Oh, Babá, I don't want to grow up. I want to live with you and Ma forever."

"Marry a Chinese boy, Dai Ling. We Chinese will stay together, one big family."

"I sometimes think how different my life would have been if we'd stayed in China."

"It was lucky for us to leave China, lucky for me to fall in love with your Ma. If I'd stayed I would have been involved in the massacre at Tianamen Square. I was a leader in the protests against Deng's government." Jia Song reached out to touch the orchid, the delicacy of his touch in strange contrast to his studied facial expression as he continued. "There was great hope for a new China when Deng Xiaoping became leader. We were promised revolutionary economic change, but the only changes that came were lower wages, higher prices, and soon a crisis of unemployment. We fought for democratic elections and free speech, then I heard through the student underground that I was going to be arrested. We were lucky to leave."

"I remember when I was little we went to a big demonstration downtown . . . "

"Yes, you were seven years old," Jia Song nodded. "The news came about the massacre, two of my friends died there." He leaned forward, suddenly tense, his words tumbling. "We protested in front of the Chinese consulate, 30,000 people the newspaper said. The massacre was condemned by Canada, the United States, Britain, France, many European countries . . . " He shook his head and smiled bitterly. "Enough of this serious talk." He jumped up and took Dai Ling's hand. "Let's eat or your Ma will scold us."

The next morning Ray Lee looked out his bedroom window and saw Dai Ling hurrying along Gerrard. He tapped on the window, disturbing a tiny pyramid of snow, a remnant clinging to the corner of the pane, but she didn't notice him. He was about to pull the window up and call out to her, but he stopped, hands gripping the sill as she turned suddenly, face lifted to the sky, arms flung out, an expression of bliss on her face. He watched her until she disappeared down the street, then he sat down at his desk. *The directorial expertise of*

Mizoguchi, Ozu, and Kurosawa can be compared and contrasted in terms of . . . he wrote, then gazed at the wall, chewing the plastic cap of his pen.

~

"Talya! What are you doing here?"

"I was on my way home. Thought I'd cut through the campus and see if I could accidently bump into you."

Talya saw the brightness of Dai Ling's tongue as she laughed, blood rising to her face in the chill air. They stood in front of the Edward Johnson Building which housed the Music faculty.

"It's been a while since our walk in Riverdale park," Talya continued with a steady gaze. "How've you been?"

"Oh, working hard. You know . . . classes, rehearsals, the library."

"Me too. We deserve a break. Want to have coffee with me?"

"Oh . . . I have to practise. I have an audition coming up with the National Youth Orchestra. There's a tour . . . if I get in."

"Of course you will. I've heard you play. You're brilliant."

"Thank you." Dai Ling blushed again. "Well I must go . . . "

"Can I come?"

"I'm only practising . . . scales, warm-ups . . . it would be boring for you."

"Oh please! I'd love to hear you play again, even scales."

"Okay," she shrugged, "You win." Then she saw Christie and Sylvie coming down the steps, Sylvie smiling and waving, her body swaying with the movement. Dai Ling was always aware of Sylvie's fluidity when they played together. With her long limbs and the broad span of her fingers she seemed to embrace the piano with a particular kind of elegance, dark hair piled on top of her head, green eyes slit like a sleeping cat.

"Hey, how do you two know each other?" Christie asked.

"You know Talya too?" Dai Ling asked, surprised.

"Do I ever? But we haven't seen you in a long time, have we, Ms. Kulikovsky?"

"I'm really busy with med school," Talya said, bristling.

"Oh yeah? Med school hasn't cramped your style in the past two years." Christie tossed her head and continued, "Your sudden absence has been noticed at Isabella's."

Dai Ling looked from one to the other in confusion. "Talya, this is Sylvie, the pianist in our trio. We're giving a recital in December. Perhaps you'd like to come."

"Sure, I'd love to," Talya said, holding out her hand to Sylvie.

"That was a great session we had yesterday," Sylvie said, "especially the Haydn, but we need to do more work on the *Archduke*."

"Same time tomorrow?" Christie asked.

"Sure," Dai Ling said, waving as she turned and walked up the steps with Talya. She could hardly wait to get to the music room and start playing; to hold her cello and feel the strings pressing into the pads of her fingers.

"Watch out for Talya," Christie called after them. "She's a heartbreaker!"

"What does that mean?" Dai Ling asked.

"Oh nothing. She's probably jealous."

"Of who?"

"Me. It's obvious she has a crush on you."

Dai Ling's mouth was a circle of surprise, but she let it go and concentrated instead on taking her cello out of the locker, carrying it carefully down to the music room. Talya watched as she removed the instrument from its case, holding the neck, extending the endpin, leaning it against a chair.

"Is it yours?" she asked.

"Kind of. Not exactly. It's on permanent loan," she replied enigmatically.

Talya watched her tighten the bow and apply rosin to the fine hairs. She felt a little awkward, even voyeuristic, then Dai Ling looked up and smiled. "You can sit over there," she said. Talya walked across the room and sat on a hard chair. When she looked up it was as though Dai Ling had disappeared and she felt a moment of unaccountable panic. Dai Ling's fingers moved up and down the long neck as her bow slid slowly across the strings, but she was somewhere else, out of Talya's reach.

"I warned you," she said suddenly, like a bird landing. "I'm warming up with open strings and scales. Then I'm going to work on my octaves and spiccato." Her bow bounced off the strings in a controlled rhythm, held so lightly between fingers and thumb. Talya closed her eyes and let the sound enter her. The vibration grew, swirling around her head, setting up a tingling in her scalp. She felt a thrill of anticipation and she remembered that moment in the morgue as the pathologist drew back the sheet. *Is this what Vesalius felt before his dissections? Is this what actors feel as they step on stage; the artist as she lifts her brush, the astronaut as she leaves the earth, the child before she enters the world?*

Dai Ling, twenty feet across the room, was unreachable. She dropped her bow arm and looked at Talya. She was silent, and Talya felt she was staring through her to some other place; she almost turned to look behind her, so strong was the concentration, then slowly Dai Ling raised her bow and the aching strains of the first movement of Elgar's *Concerto* filled the room, in turns pained, pleading, questioning. Talya was shocked. *How could she? How could she look at me so boldly and play like that?* She watched Dai Ling turn inwards with her cello as though Talya, captivated, no longer existed. Her body seemed to travel great distances as she played, her legs thrown apart, thighs squeezing the curves of her instrument. It rested there, the honeyed wood resonating as her head tossed and her hands flew like trysting birds. Her elbows and wrists moved with fluidity, boneless. It was as though she played the instrument with her body, a vibration of wood and gut through flesh, hands and arms flying independently of body and cello, just touching on it. Talya was on Bloor Street once again, watching her through flickering images, glimpsing something strange and intimate — a tease before the door closed — leaving her with a yearning that frightened her.

Dai Ling held her final gesture, head bowed over her cello, as the last note died. Then she looked up at Talya.

"I'm playing the *Elgar* for one of my orchestral excerpts," she said. "They want . . . Are you okay?"

"That was beautiful."

"Are you sure?"

"Yes." Her eyes were fixed on Dai Ling's, insistent, until she broke the silence.

"I'm playing the prelude to the first Bach cello suite for my solo, and I need to do a lot of work on it. D'you want to meet on Sunday, in the afternoon?"

Talya nodded, speechless. She was being dismissed and invited in one fell swoop.

"How about two o'clock by the tennis courts in Withrow Park?"

Talya jumped up to leave, putting on her coat as she walked towards the door.

"I'm glad you came to look for me," Dai Ling called after her, and Talya turned for a moment, raised her hand, then spun around.

What's happening to me? she wondered as she crossed the bridge onto Philosophers' Walk. She walked fast, slipping on the slushy remains of the snow, passing everyone on Bloor Street, and slowed down only when she'd turned onto Brunswick and her house was in sight. Talya had the ground floor apartment; two rooms with kitchen and bath and use of a tiny garden. She closed the blinds and lay down on her bed. The Vesalius book lay open on the floor at Plate 24, The First Plate of the Muscles, with a finely drawn figure, head thrown back in rapture, all the muscles exposed in bunches and weavings, holding the form together. Talya leaned over the bed and began to read . . . *One of the characteristic features of all Vesalian figures is the attempt to represent the dissected body in dynamic fashion with greater emphasis on the living than the dead. In the dissections at a deeper level this has given rise to a rather bizarre and ragged appearance of the figures, but it serves to emphasize the fact that in the sixteenth century there was no separation between morphology and function. On the significance of the background to the figures the reader should consult . . .*

~

1545: Brussels

VESALIUS REACHED ACROSS THE BED AS he woke and found the comforting warmth of Anne's body, the soft downy place in the small of her back. Although his hand wandered, smoothing and cupping the mound of her buttock, his heart raced not with lust but with the immediacy of a dream in which he had eviscerated his own body in an intense desire to know what lay under the skin. *I am a man possessed. I need a fresh corpse, no, a living body on the verge of death and at the very moment of demise I will catch the Soul as it flees.* He dreamed self-destruction in the cause of discovery.

The first time he had lain with Anne van Hamme, on their wedding night, she had run her long fingers through his curls and scraped claw-marks down his back, clasping the buttocks of his vigorous body. As he'd pumped her firm flesh he had held a vision of her inner structure; bones, musculature, venous system. He couldn't help it once he knew. He could not forget what he had discovered and he could not stop seeking that which eluded him, the tripping Soul. Vesalius thought himself the most fortunate of men to have won his heart's desire. Anne was a lusty, full-blooded woman who knew no shame. Their marriage bed was a sea of passion and sensual delight where Vesalius married his knowledge of the flesh with the pleasures partaken of it.

Since the onset of pregnancy Anne had become dreamy and she was most deliciously responsive, even in her half sleep. Lost in dreams, she would murmur and give, pliable as an eel. Many was the night he had taken her like that, and in the morning her secret smile told him she had dreamed an erotic dream. "I know your secret, my lusty wife. It was no dream. I took you and pleasured you in your sleep," he would say.

His hand rounded her swollen belly, but his mind was still on his dream. He felt a pang of frustrated desire as he realized that he had once again been tricked by the scheming Soul who had captured him at his deepest and most private realm, his last sanctuary.

"And where is *your* sanctuary?" he screamed, sitting up in bed suddenly. "Where is *your* hiding place!"

Anne sat up with a start. "What ails you, husband?" she cried, her voice thick with sleep.

But he was already half-way across the room, hopping on one foot as he stumbled into his breeches, his foot slapping the cold tiles. "Go back to sleep," he barked, "It's early," and he thrust his arms into the voluminous sleeves of a rough cotton shirt.

"Where are you going at this hour? You'll catch your death of cold, Andreas." She nestled into the bedcovers, a smile tugging the corners of her mouth. He hesitated a moment then leaned down and kissed her brow. "I'm going to greet the dawn" he said. "I'll be home before you wake," and he strode towards the arched doorway.

"Put on your woollen cloak," she called after him, but he was gone, leaving Anne wakeful and lusty. A sensual, earthy woman of generous proportion and voluptuous form, she was never happier than when her sturdy legs were wrapped around her husband's hips, the bed creaking, rolling with him as one body. But nowadays, when she woke and reached for Andreas, she often encountered the still-warm imprint of his body, and then she felt the nagging frustration of being outrivalled by something she did not understand. This strange man to whom she had given over her life had places in him that were unintelligible to her. Even in the throes of their mutual passion she sensed a cool place in her Andreas, a pulsating red place veined with cool blue, that would never come to terms with its own paradox. "Hot and cold you are," she murmured, "all at once, like a fever. I'll never fathom you Andreas Van Wesele," and she rolled over, a restless hand nestled between her thighs.

Vesalius crossed the courtyard as dawn broke with a blush of frozen light across the Flemish sky. Back home in Brussels after his long sojourn abroad, he relived his childhood every day, a childhood dominated by the absence of his father who had travelled with Charles V, Emperor of the Holy Roman Empire and King of Spain, as his pharmacist, leaving Andreas in Hell's Lane with his mother, Isabel Crabbe, his brothers, Nicolas and Franciscus, and little sister, Anne. The house on Helle Straetken had been a dark hole, gloomy as a cave, given by Jacob Crabbe as dowry for his daughter. It was near the Bovendael, a desolate area of Brussels, near the southern gate of the city, inhabited by prostitutes and indigents. Between Hell's Lane and the Bovendael lay an area called Galgenberg.

It was a partly wooded field, mounded into a hill, at the top of which hung the remains of condemned criminals along with the instruments used to torture them. It was here that young Andreas had been drawn daily, to the Montagne de la Potence, to mark the transformation of flesh into bone.

Andreas had been a lonely child who missed his father and longed to travel with him. "But who will look after Mother and Little Sister?" the elder Andreas had asked in his booming voice. "I'm relying on you, my son, you and your brothers." But young Andreas fought with his brothers, then he would run to the Montagne and there hold his nose and gaze upward, fingering the instruments until a raven's cawing or a gust of wind sent him tumbling down the hill and through the woods, racing for home. There was a lake, hidden by trees, and sometimes the boy would lurk there, dipping his hands in the water, watching the other boys swimming. He was afraid of the water. He'd had a dream one night that the Souls of the hanged men had entered the lake with the dipping of his hands, and that they waited there to drag him down. But he couldn't keep away.

It had been the magnetism of that grisly hill, seen from the distance of his childhood home, that drew his life before him like a roadmap; and the Van Wesele coat of arms with three weasels riding one atop the other, contained in arms flaring outward, that had imbued Vesalius with his questing spirit. When he had frequented graveyards in the darkness of his studious nights, digging, digging with his bearded spade, he had imitated the family totem. Andreas Vesalius was that anomaly of the Renaissance — a man who embodied the curious conflict between fidelity to the past and the vision of a new future. While he adhered to tradition, walking in the footprints of his male ancestors who had for generations served as imperial physicians to the House of Hapsburg, Vesalius had a new way of perceiving the world around him. He had gained a reputation with his rebellious insistence on hands-on dissection of the human *corpus*, and his vigorous challenging of Galen the Greek's 500-year-old structural analysis of the human body, on the grounds that it was based upon the body of the ape.

When Van Wesele the elder had died in the winter of 1543, he had left Andreas a handsome inheritance, which enabled him to marry Anne van Hamme in the golden September of the following year. In the year of his father's death he had published, to great acclaim and controversy, *De Humani Corporis Fabrica*, (structure of the human body), with the accompanying *Epitome.* The *Fabrica* was a revolutionary remapping of the human body, documenting his discoveries of its inner workings; the scaffolding upon which the flesh hung, its arterial roadways and muscular bunchings. With this publication he had gained a reputation sufficient to earn him an invitation to join the court of Charles V, as physician to the imperial household. His first task had been as field surgeon in the Holy Roman Empire's war against France, which ended with the Peace of Créspy in September 1544, the same month he had married.

Vesalius had built a house in Brussels. He had planted an orchard. He had built stables. He had laid the courtyard stones himself, digging into the soft earth, flattening it, laying broad pink stones one by one. When he'd finished he had stood in the centre of the courtyard and taken stock.

He had become a man of means with a wife, a house, a private practice in Brussels, but it all left him peculiarly dissatisfied. His reputation was made, but still he was a man held hostage by an insatiable passion for discovery, drawn away from his dreamy Anne as the baby tugged her inward, away from him.

Vesalius was oblivious to the coldness of the dawn. Stiff with passion and curiosity, his tightly-curled head tilted in an ancient and ecstatic gesture towards the heavens, as Don Quixote, fifty-two years hence, would tilt at the windmills of Cervantes' imprisoned imagination, tilted like a dervish, eyes wide to receive the early morning light. He was a good Catholic and felt himself illuminated by God. "Oh Lord," he prayed, "share with me the secret of the elusive Soul. It is all I have ever wanted. All I ask is to be privy to this knowledge." He humbled himself, proud and puff-chested, his mercurial mind already slipping down another avenue, remembering the fervour and dirt of Hell's Lane, his knobby-kneed tumbling through puddles harbouring sharp-angled stones which bled the boy, doctored in his own laneway.

It was a strange day from the beginning, unseasonably warm for November, with a tight oppressive feeling in the sky. The early snowfall of the previous week had melted overnight. People spoke of global warming and climatic change, presagers of disasters to come, but Dai Ling had woken with sunlight on her face and a tingling anticipation. After practising all morning, her breastbone still vibrating, she walked up Logan Avenue to Withrow Park. The tennis courts were empty, the tarmac pooled with rainwater from yesterday's downpour. There was electricity in the air, Dai Ling felt it. She heard a dog bark and as she turned it came running towards her, chasing a stick that was flying through the air.

"Talya! I didn't know you had a dog."

"Her name's Ruby. She's a rescue dog."

Ruby dropped the stick and sniffed Dai Ling's legs, exploring every inch of her jeans for information. She scratched the dog's ears absent-mindedly, but her eyes were on Talya. "Looks like she's part red setter. And maybe some terrier or shepherd?"

"She's like the Greek Chimera. She has the tail of a fox, the body of a silky red goat and the head of a dog. She belongs to my parents, but they left for Europe yesterday, so I'm dog-sitting at their house. D'you want to come visit? It's only a couple of blocks away."

"Sure."

They walked briskly across the park, Dai Ling's mind racing. *What am I doing here? Did I set myself up with a date? Oh my god, maybe she thinks I'm a lesbian. What are we going to talk about?*

The Kulikovsky house was surrounded by a secret garden, protected by a high stone wall with a wrought iron gate giving onto a pebbled driveway. The virginia creeper which had flamed up the west wall of the house in October was ashen now. The winter garden lay curled and pale, shocked by sudden changes; the heat of late fall had lured many of the shrubs and rose bushes into a second blooming, only to be stunted by plummeting temperatures and a snowfall. The November return of the heat mocked nature, unable now to respond anew. While some plants were made stronger by these extremities, others died. But each corner of the garden was alive with the memory of lilac scenting the spring air, mock orange at the open summer windows, honeysuckle cascading over the front door, roses and peonies filling the beds around the house. A giant maple towered over the driveway like a brooding ancestor, and rose hips swelled with promise.

The garden was Katya's domain. This was where she wandered, pushing a green wheelbarrow, stooping to pull weeds, deadheading roses to make way for new blooms. As she tended the borders, clearing around the Jacob's ladder and her sage-leafed rock rose, she thought of Nick and the pleasure she felt made her laugh out loud. She'd never recovered from the wonder of him, or from the miracle of their daughter. If she'd not been able to give him a child to continue the bloodline her life would have been a failure. Of course she'd felt a twinge of disappointment when they'd told her the gender — she'd been hoping for a boy — but once the doctor placed the baby on her breast, still joined to her by the umbilicus, she'd been unable to imagine anything emerging from her body other than her beautiful daughter. But Natalya had grown into an impossible child, sullen and rebellious, and by the time she was a teenager she'd had Katya in tears almost every day. She'd tried to hide their conflict from Nick, but the hostility between mother and daughter filled the house. And the girl tried to come between them, demanding her father's attention.

"This is what adolescent girls do. Sexuality is their only power. She's competing with you," her analyst friend had told her over coffee on the terrace. It was impossible to discipline Talya; she had a will of her own and she was herself punitive, lashing out and then retreating into vengeful silence for days on end. Katya had long since admitted defeat and given in to her daughter's demands. "Of course, darling, of course you can have your own horse, of course you can go to Europe, of course you need your own apartment."

It had been a mixed blessing when she'd moved out, because Katya missed her terribly and craved intimacy with her daughter. "Why does she separate herself from us, Nick? She's part of us. Why doesn't she want to share in our life?"

But in reality it was a relief to have Nick to herself. It was like beginning all over again. *Love is lovelier the second time around,* she would hum to herself, *even lovelier with both feet on the ground* . . . She loved the old romantic songs. Ironic that her illness had been diagnosed exactly then, as though bliss could not exist without the threat of death. That day, before she'd phoned for the result of her biopsy she had clipped a perfect red rose for the dinner table. A thorn had pierced her wrist and a drop of blood had fallen into the centre of the rose, disappearing into its redness.

"You're going to get better, Katyushenka. Nothing can happen to you, my darling, because I love you too much." Nick was confident. She believed him and rested in him, drawing the strength she needed to refuse conventional treatment.

Dai Ling stood in the entry hall. The air was cool and empty. *This house feels like a showplace,* she thought. *All the life is in the garden.*

"I'll fix something for us. Would you like a drink, something to eat?"

"Sure, I'm always hungry," Dai Ling said, following Talya into the kitchen. She had noticed Ruby nosing a line of light under a closed door leading off the hall, watched her whiskers quivering, sensed the keeness of her cold nose, soft and black with a blush of pink circling each nostril. There were seeds in Ruby's fur where she'd been rolling in the garden. Dai Ling watched Talya moving around the kitchen, the sweep of her long arms, the curve of her mouth as she looked up, smiling, a bottle of white wine in her hand. She scattered olives, grapes and soft cheese onto a plate and began to uncork the wine.

"Did you step on cracks in the sidewalk when you were little," Dai Ling asked.

"All the time. And I made myself invisible." Talya shut her eyes tight and made a face.

"Me too," Dai Ling laughed.

"I hid in the garden under the giant rhododendron and I travelled to Russia, Italy, Cuba, Guatemala . . . playing doctor, like my uncle Vassily. I never met him until I was seven, but Dad used to talk about him, and I'd lie awake at night imagining the day he'd come back – a dashing Cossack on a white horse. He was my hero."

"Are you Russian?"

"I'm a Romanov. But actually our family's more Germanic than Russian. We're part of the Hapsburg dynasty. And of course we're all in exile. None of the Romanovs have set foot in Russia since the Revolution."

"Where does your uncle live?"

"In Montréal. But he used to travel as a Doctor without Borders. He worked in Guatemala, El Salvador, Columbia . . . that's why I didn't meet him till I was seven. He was just back from Ecuador."

She popped a grape into her mouth and offered one to Dai Ling, watching her as she ate it. "Help yourself to cheese. You're the hungry one."

Dai Ling cut into the Brie and began eating, standing close to Talya, as though they were at a cocktail party, as she continued her story.

"I woke up so excited! I dressed in my red velvet frock and new patent leather shoes, and I brushed my hair one hundred times. I heard the knocker at the front door and I ran downstairs and opened it, but when I saw him I thought it was a mistake. He said, 'You must be Natalya Tatiana. I'm your uncle Vassily,' and he swept me up in his arms and gave me a big kiss and I burst into tears." She poured the wine into tall blue glasses. "He was so ordinary; no sword, no red coat, no Cossack boots or fur hat. I ran down the front steps and hid behind the rhododendron. I still hoped there might be a white horse, but when I came out of the bushes and walked up the driveway, I saw it."

"What?"

"A rusted out, dirty-white Toyota van. Worst of all, my new shoes were pinching me like crabs!"

Dai Ling laughed as Talya handed her a glass. "Here's to travel," she said, holding Dai Ling captive with her eyes. They clinked glasses and sipped the dry wine, pursing their mouths around the coolness of it, savouring the taste. Dai

Ling felt the effect immediately, a lightness in her head. She wasn't used to drinking.

"If I get into the youth orchestra we'll be touring. It could be my first time away from home."

"Really? You've never lived away from your parents?"

"Chinese families are very close. Lots of people live with their parents till they get married. Anyway I couldn't afford my own place." She leaned down and stroked Ruby's silky fur. The dog was panting. "I think she wants a drink."

"Oh sure, I'll get it." Talya was already at the sink, running water into a mixing bowl. She plunked it on the tiled floor and they watched Ruby's pink tongue lapping.

Dai Ling took a slice of cheddar and a handful of Italian olives. When she was nervous she ate. It filled up the emptiness and dulled the vibration inside her.

"How does a Chinese girl get red hair?"

"From my French-Canadian grandmother. She had a cloud of curly red hair. And she smoked cigarettes. I used to sit in her lap and stare up at her blowing smoke through her nostrils, like a red dragon. But I don't remember her very well. We came to Canada when I was two. My father is a doctor of traditional Chinese medicine. He studied at the university in Beijing."

"Does he practice here?"

"He has a clinic on the Danforth, but he used to work in the front room of our house, and I liked hanging out there, opening the big jars of herbs and smelling them. My favourite was the hawthorn berry wafers, for the heart. I used to fill my pockets and suck on them like candies until my dad found out. He was so mad at me!"

"You must have a very strong heart. Let me listen." Talya pressed her ear to Dai Ling's breast and felt the steady beat quickening. "Perfect," she murmured, and smiled up at her.

"It's my metronome," Dai Ling said, blushing. "I listen to my heartbeat and the music follows." With the wine and the closeness of Talya she was beginning to feel rather strange. "What about your family?" she asked quickly. "Are you related to the Tsar? I was looking at a book about the Romanovs in the stacks yesterday. Is that why you're called Natalya? Is it a Russian name?"

"Not really. It's a name for children born at Christmas, which I'm not. But my second name is Tatiana . . . for one of the Tsar's daughters. Dad said it would be bad luck, but Mom insisted, so they put it in the middle. What did the book say?"

"That the Tsar's family were shot. There's a photograph of the skulls, seven of them. But someone claimed that Tsar Nicholas and his hemophiliac son were executed and that his wife and daughters were spared. They said the four girls were kept in a cellar after the murder and that Anastasia, the youngest, escaped from there."

"Uncle Vassily says they were all shot. He says the Romanovs are a close family and if anyone had survived they'd have been in contact through the Family Association in Paris. The Romanovs who laid claim to the inheritance said the whole family was executed in that room in the house in Ekaterinburg in 1918."

"Sounds like quite a mystery. What do *you* think?"

"I don't know. I've talked about it so much that sometimes it seems unreal. No one knows the truth. D'you have a boyfriend?"

"What a switch of subject," Dai Ling said, taken aback.

"Well, do you?"

"Not really."

"Sort of? Maybe?"

"You're teasing me."

"Come on, I'll show you the stables," Talya said, scooping up a handful of olives. "There used to be a farm on this land back in the thirties before Riverdale was developed. My grandpa left a lot of money so my parents were able to buy this place when they married. I was born here. My whole life is here, in the garden, at the stables, in the parks."

"Your Romanov grandpa?" Dai Ling asked, following Talya into the hall.

"No, on my mother's side. The Romanov fortune was taken by the Bolsheviks. They took everything, including Alexandra's famous collection of Fabergé eggs. She had fabulous diamond tiaras and ropes of pearls. The fortune was apparently worth a billion dollars, but the Romanov descendants haven't seen a cent of it. They say the nuns hid a suitcase of jewels for the royals, but Stalin had them tortured until . . . " Talya stopped suddenly in the centre of the hall as the phone started ringing. "Not now," she said impatiently as the message machine kicked in and a woman's voice, deep and sensual, said, "We've arrived safely, darling. It's so beautiful here. I wish you were with us. Daddy sends love. We're going to bed now, but . . . "

"Why don't you answer?" Dai Ling asked as Talya turned down the volume. "It's your mom."

Talya gave a gesture of annoyance. "The phone is so invasive, don't you think?"

"Not when it's your mom."

Ruby was ahead of them, jumping at the door, whining. As Talya opened it the dog went bounding down the stone steps.

Dai Ling saw that line of brightness again, flooding under the closed door. "What is that?" she asked. "What's in that room?"

"I'll show you later. Come on!"

They ran, Ruby at their heels, through the rose garden and across the grass, past a clay tennis court, overgrown with weeds and skeletal lupins rattling their seed-pods.

"There are the stables," Talya said, pointing. "Empty now, but we used to have three horses, Dublin, Limerick and my horse, Corky, a dapple grey. Come on, I'll show you the tackle room."

She had lost her virginity with Corky, galloping breakneck for a jump at the Newmarket Gymkhana. As Corky sprang into the air Talya flew with him, imagining golden wings spread wide above them, girl and horse carried as one body, then Corky's hooves bit the earth and something released in her, freeing her body forever into the ability to fly. Talya and Corky had trotted to the judges' podium to receive their red ribbon, bloody but victorious. The ribbon hung still in Talya's bedroom in her father's house, a tattered red memory of girl-power.

"Where are your parents anyway?" Dai Ling asked.

"In Geneva. My mom was diagnosed with uterine cancer. They've gone to a clinic Uncle Vassily recommended. He's an oncologist, but he knows about alternative therapies. She refused to have surgery or any of the conventional treatments so . . ."

"Oh Talya, I'm so sorry," Dai Ling broke in, reaching out to touch Talya's shoulder, but Talya stiffened and shrugged her off.

"It's all right," she said, "She's going to get better."

Light filtered through the thickly cobwebbed windows of the tackle room. There was a smell of old leather; two saddles hung on the far wall. Dai Ling walked over and touched the leather. It was dry and dusty. Her shoulder nudged a hanging bridle and the bit jangled, startling her. She grasped the reins. They were dry and cracked and one of the straps on the headpiece was flowered with a fine powder of mould. A fragment of dry grass clung to the bit.

"This tackle hasn't been used in years," said Talya. "Dad got rid of the horses when I left."

"Where did you go?"

"To Europe, for six months, after I graduated from high school. I travelled all over—Italy, Spain, Greece, France, Germany . . . I liked Italy best. That's where I first heard about Vesalius. I went to Padua and saw the operating theatre."

Dai Ling felt a presence passing through the dappled light. Tall, quick, shadow-people passing to and fro, weaving in and out of each other. She turned and saw Talya standing in the doorway. "Come on," Talya said, "I want to show you the orchard." By the time Dai Ling had caught up with her

Talya was weaving through the apple trees, ducking her head under low-hanging branches. The orchard looked neglected, the trees full of suckers in need of pruning, and the ground beneath them soft with rotted windfalls, frozen then thawed, some with dead wasps embedded, their bodies frozen as they fed.

"This was my favourite place to hide out," Talya said. "Mom never knew. She'd be shouting for me all over the garden, but she never went further than the tennis court. Mr. Brewster knew where I was but he never ratted on me."

"Who was Mr. Brewster?"

"My grave digger." Talya laughed, throwing her head back. "Actually he was the gardener, but he dug the grave when Felix was run over . . . my cat. Here, I'll show you." She took Dai Ling's hand and led her through the trees. They stooped under lichen-covered branches and hunkered beside a little cross, barely visible now that the wood was rotting and only a few chips of white paint remained.

"We had a proper funeral with an oration and a blessing, then he let me shovel the first clod of earth. And when I cried he gave me one of his sticky old woolly toffees; he kept a stock of them in the pocket of his overalls. I couldn't believe Felix was really dead. What does that mean to a kid . . . death? I lay in bed every night thinking about him all alone in the dark under the earth and I knew I had to save him. So I took the shovel and dug up the box we'd buried him in. I was sure he'd jump out meaowing and rub himself against me."

"What happened?"

"I knelt here, right here and lifted the box out. It was too light. I placed it on the ground and leaned over it. When I lifted the lid the smell made me jump back, but I could see something moving and I thought it was Felix coming to life. Then I saw that he was alive with maggots squirming around his eyes and nose, his belly, his anus. His eyes were gone, fallen back into his head and he was all shrivelled up, a tiny thing transformed into a nest of maggots."

Dai Ling was silent, thinking of her own small body lying under the earth, but she wasn't ready to tell Talya about that. She stood and leaned against the old tree, feeling the gnarled bumps pressing into her spine, remembering Ray Lee's garden; Sam Ngan, Dee Dee Chong and Celia Quan standing above her as she lay in the ground.

Talya jumped up. "I'll show you the stables," she said, and strode ahead through the open gate. Dai Ling caught up with her at the double door of the centre stable.

"This was Limerick's stable," Talya said. "Dad's horse. A thoroughbred from Ireland and very high-spirited. Once, when I was about two, they lost me. They looked everywhere and finally Dad found me in this stable. I was crawling around under Limerick's belly, patting his legs and singing. I had no fear. When you're afraid, animals sense it and they get spooked. They're like people. They either attack or back off."

"Which kind are you?" Dai Ling's voice was almost a whisper. Talya smelled the sweetness of her breath.

"I don't waste my time backing off. We only live once."

"Do we?"

Talya stared at her, taken aback. Dai Ling was intensely aware of their closeness. She kept very, very still.

"Oh well — figure of speech," Talya said dismissively, and she turned quickly, her dark hair swinging, and began pacing the perimeters of the stall. Dai Ling watched her with a disturbing mixture of relief and disappointment as Talya continued talking, talking, always talking.

"I'm quite determined," she said. "When I want something I go for it. How d'you think I got into Med school? There were 1700 applicants in my year and only 190 of us were accepted."

"Music school is competitive too. That anatomy book you showed me . . . is it one of your texts?"

"No, we use *Gray's Anatomy*. It's more pedestrian. The Vesalius illustrations from *De Humani Corporis Fabrica* are works of art. They were made as woodcuts by students of Titian, the great master, under his supervision in his *atelier.*"

She was leaning against the far wall now. They watched each other silently in the growing dusk, taking the sensory measure of each other; a curve of shoulder, jut of cheekbone, rise of lip; small essays in visual intimacy.

"What happens when someone loses a library book?" Talya asked.

"A fine, up to fifty dollars."

"Maybe I'll keep the Vesalius. It's out of print. Don't tell Mrs. Fox. I can't give it up."

"You're making me your accomplice," Dai Ling teased. "You could try renewing it."

"Too risky. There might be a waiting list. I feel it belongs to me. I had my first post-mortem the other day, and when the pathologist opened up the cadaver I felt I was looking at an old map I'd studied long ago. I thought of the Spaniards mapping the Americas, Vesalius mapping the interior of the human body, Galileo mapping the skies . . . "

"Was it a man or a woman?"

"What?"

"Your post-mortem person."

"It was one of our patients. Her heart had failed, but I didn't think of her in a personal way once the body was open. It takes you beyond the personal, Dai Ling, beyond gender even. The history of the universe is encoded in our cells and when you cut into the human body it's all there, a microcosm. I felt like a traveler on a journey to an old, old familiar place." Talya walked across the stable and stood very close to Dai Ling. "I can barely see you from over there," she whispered. "Have you had a lover, Dai Ling?"

"Not yet." She could barely breathe. It was all too weird. She wished she was home in the kitchen with Ma, that she had never invited this crazy woman for a Sunday afternoon walk.

"Your cello is your lover, isn't it?"

Dai Ling laughed, too loud. "I guess so."

"I had my first lover in Italy, in Padua as a matter of fact. I was sitting in a coffee house, Caffé Pedrocchi. A man walked over to my table. He'd been standing at the counter drinking an espresso. He wasn't particularly handsome, medium height, curly brown hair, green eyes – pleasant but unremarkable. I thought he was going to ask me something and of course I couldn't speak Italian, my head was still full of the words I'd learned in Greece."

Even though she stood so close to Dai Ling, her body insistent, Talya's eyes had a faraway look.

"But he didn't speak. He just smiled at me and lifted his hand, and with the tips of his fingers he touched the nape of my neck gently and began tracing little circles there. My whole body started humming like a crystal wine glass when you run a wet finger around its rim. His eyes were on me and he said something in Italian. I stood up and followed him down the street and through an archway into a courtyard. It was filled with plants, and a fountain playing in the centre. There was a high stone wall on the far side, in the shadow of the courtyard. He pushed me up against that wall and very gently began to touch my face, tracing his fingers over my mouth, my eyelids, the bones of my face, then down my neck feeling the pulse of my throat, over my breasts and belly, my hips and thighs. His journey was so slow. It was as though time had stopped and all I could hear was my breath coming faster and the trickle of the fountain. Then he kissed me, slowly and sensuously, the kind of kiss you dream about, not rough and aggressive like the high school boys I was used to, but like a prince disguised as an ordinary man. And as he kissed me he began to move his body against me slowly until I was gasping with the pleasure of it. I wanted him so bad. I was wearing a full skirt and he let me lift the skirt and invite him in. He gave me all the power. I took his hand and made him touch me there. When I came he released himself and entered me. There was no blood, he slid into me so easily as though I'd been waiting all my life for him."

"I thought you were a lesbian." Dai Ling's lips were parted. "Christie said . . . "

"I am. I never saw him again." She laughed. "Perhaps he was a dream. Men aren't *really* like that, are they?"

Dai Ling thought of Ray Lee and his abrupt kiss, of how much she liked him even though she didn't want to kiss him. She couldn't imagine kissing a complete stranger. Over Talya's shoulder she saw a patch of sky, an ominous grey-blue, heavy with pigment in the gathering darkness. She could hardly see Talya's face. As she'd spoken her features had slowly disappeared until she was a disembodied voice. The air was weighted by a growing silence, broken by Ruby's insistent whining as she cowered by the door, tail between her legs. Dai Ling felt a brush of skin as Talya touched her lower lip with her finger. A flash of light revealed Talya's face for a split second, then a clap of thunder cracked directly overhead, shattering the stillness.

"Let's make a dash for it before the rain starts," Dai Ling said, and she was already half way across the stable yard when Talya started after her, Ruby at her heels, a warm, almost tropical rain falling, as though the heavens were unaware of the season. Talya caught Dai Ling's hand, spun her around and kissed her, rain streaming over their eyelids, down their faces, drenching their bodies. Dai Ling felt the flash of light through her skin. She opened her eyes, saw the forked sky and ran for the house, pulling Talya with her.

As they ran up the back steps and opened the door the kitchen was illuminated by another flash of lightning. Then came a frightening crack of thunder followed by a crash.

"What was that?" Dai Ling gasped. "It was in the house, wasn't it?"

The girls froze, staring at each other as Ruby slunk past and slid on her belly under the kitchen table. Talya ran through the kitchen into the hall and stopped suddenly, teeth tight against her bottom lip. The first thing Dai Ling noticed when she reached the hall was that the line of light under the door had vanished.

"What's in there?" she asked. "Show me."

Talya shook her head and tried to block the door, but Dai Ling grasped the handle and opened it, pushing against Talya as she grabbed her arm. Thousands of fragments of glass crunched under her feet as she entered the room, pale green shards.

"Now you'll never see it."

"What?"

"My mom's prized possession. It's broken."

Dai Ling stared at Talya, remembering Ma's face when the news had come of Geneviéve's death. "It's all right," she said, holding out her arms to Talya. "I'm here, we're all right."

Talya screamed and spun around, her long arm sweeping in a circle, striking Dai Ling's breast bone.

~

1545: Brussels

"BOOKWORM! BOOKWORM! WIGGLY LITTLE WEASELWORM!" THE children chanted, pressing in on him, deafening him. Andreas jumped up and ran through the library, down a long corridor of books, his twelve-year-old legs short and stumpy, flying over the flagstones. He heard the crowd behind him getting closer, felt the big boys breathing down his neck. Faster and faster he ran, turning corners, knocking books off shelves with his pumping elbows until suddenly a tall stack quivered and shook and he was knocked to the ground by a heavy, black book to the back of his neck. Books cascaded slowly from shelves, falling, falling, burying him. He tried to scream but there was no sound. He struggled to rise to the surface and finally a strangulated sound escaped his mouth as he woke, heart pounding, breath vaporizing in the cold night air. He heard Anne's moaning, a sultry, disgruntled sound, a slight grinding of her teeth as she settled into a steady rhythmic breathing, the six month foetus pulsing in her belly.

Vesalius rolled onto his side, his forehead beaded with sweat. "Genius lives on, all else is mortal," he whispered. How the boys had taunted him, but he had shown them.

He had made a name for himself, greater than any of his ancestors, greater than anyone from Brussels. When the boys had tumbled into the lake he'd hugged the shore, hiding in the reeds, shamed by his inability to swim. Little Andreas hadn't known what he would grow into. But his curiosity had inflamed him and led him on the path to great renown. With the publication of *De Humani Corporis Fabrica* he had changed the face of science. *Bookworm indeed! I have published my own book. I have mapped every inch of the human body. I am the first. I am the definitive man!*

He closed his eyes and saw before him a row of worm-infested corpses. He was transported by his vision to Montfaucon, a grim mound by the north wall of Paris, where sixteen stone pillars, each thirty foot high, formed a colonnade connected by strong wooden beams. From these the corpses were suspended, fifteen circles darkening the ground beneath the dangling feet, causing his stomach to clench as he remembered the foul air of the place. But the twelfth century structure remained the finest gallows and charnel house in France. *What I have done for my genius*, he thought. *I burned with so great a desire that I was not afeared of snatching in the night what I longed for.* He saw himself wearing the raven's beak filled with winter thyme and rosemary, his hands encased in thick leather gloves, handing down the best preserved to Gemma Frisius, a fellow physician. Frisius had wrapped the grisly specimen against disintegration, and together they had skulked south, back to their shared quarters.

He opened his eyes on the cold darkness and lay, wide awake, listening to Anne's gentle snoring. She lay with her back to him, her generous buttocks pressed into his lap. "What have I missed?" he whispered. "What more can I do?" His mind delved inward through the labyrinth of its mysteries. *Ashes to ashes, dust to dust, all is food for worms. But the Soul! Where is the elusive Soul? This is my genius, to discover the eternal.*

Slowly he shifted and, without waking her, Vesalius penetrated his sleeping wife. He probed her gently with the prehensile, cyclopic being who rose to attention, sharing his quest, slowly, slowly drawing his mind from its torment, until at the last moment it claimed governance.

"There must be *something* inside the body to prove that we are immortal!" he gasped as he wasted his seed inside the fecund body of his dreaming Anne.

"I'm sorry, I'm sorry, I didn't mean to strike out, but I hate to be . . ."

"It was an accident." Dai Ling's voice was soft, her lips close to Talya's ear as she held her. She'd been shocked when Talya hit her, but she had been kissed by her, touched by her and with that touch invisible threads had been woven. Dai Ling was a girl with a vision of a crane hanging in its red caul, a girl with a handsome father who watched her sleeping. Dai Ling had been buried alive and survived under the earth. She had resources.

"Help me sweep it up," Talya begged, "I can't do this alone."

"You're not alone."

"But I've always . . . I always *feel* alone, ever since . . . My mom will kill me."

"It wasn't your fault. Must've been the vibration of that thunderclap." Dai Ling went into the kitchen and tried various cupboard doors until she found a broom.

"Something terrible's going to happen. I know it is," Talya said, following her.

"Nothing's going to happen. The storm's over."

Dai Ling picked up a dustpan. "We'll need a box for the glass," she said.

Talya disappeared onto the back porch and returned with a cardboard box. "Here," she said. "Will this do?" She'd surrendered all authority and Dai Ling stepped into the empty place. She led her out of the kitchen, across the hall where Ruby skulked, hesitantly wagging her tail as they passed through into the shattered living room.

"I'm going to open a window," Dai Ling said. "There's no air in here."

"French doors," Talya whispered. "Windows don't open."

Dai Ling turned the key and threw open the doors onto a flagged terrace shining wetly in the darkness. As she stepped outside something caught her eye; a white rose blooming, impossibly late. She stooped to smell its strong scent then snapped the green stem sharply between thumb and forefinger. She entered the room holding the rose at her aching breast bone and walked towards Talya, tracking damp steps across the floor. Talya took the rose with a curious smile.

"A rose? At this time of year?"

"This is a strange day," Dai Ling laughed. She could still feel light flashing on the wet skin of her eyelids, the slippery sensation of Talya's tongue against hers, but she couldn't believe they had actually kissed, like that, like lovers.

"What will I tell my mom?" Talya asked.

Oh my god, what will I tell my *mom?* Dai Ling wondered.

"Here, sit in the armchair while I sweep up." She pushed gently at Talya's shoulders, making her fall into the chair. Dai Ling started sweeping the shattered glass into a pile. The larger pieces she picked up carefully and placed in the box.

"Don't cut yourself."

"Stop worrying." There were wet swirls where the brush swept over Dai Ling's footprints. Then there was a flash.

"Dai Ling! Look!" Talya's face was aghast. Dai Ling followed her gaze onto the terrace where lightning zig-zagged across the wet stones, clustering by the door like a knot of vipers. Then, as a thunderclap burst directly overhead, an electric current flashed across the floor, swirling in the pattern of her brush strokes. She leapt in the air as the lightning shot beneath her.

"Lift your feet!" she screamed and Talya balled her body into the armchair. Then it was over and the rain streamed down again.

"Oh my god, what was that thing anyway, some kind of huge vase?" Dai Ling dropped the broom and threw herself onto the sofa.

Talya closed the french doors and sat down next to Dai Ling. She took a deep breath. "It was . . . a glass uterus. I was gestated in it."

"You're kidding!" Dai Ling laughed.

"No, I'm not. My parents really wanted me. They wanted me more than anything, but my mom kept miscarrying . . . " Talya hesitated a moment, her eyes guarded, "So her doctor suggested ART — assisted reproductive technology. The doctors plucked me out as soon as I was fertilized and transferred me to a test tube. They monitored my progress and transferred me from tube to larger tube until I was perfectly formed, then they decanted me into the ARTwomb."

"That's not possible."

"Yes, it is. I have memories of it," she said, her hand gripping Dai Ling's arm, urgent.

"But never to have been inside your mother's body, never to have been . . . borne?"

"I've been inside her body many times. She had five miscarriages."

"But that wasn't you."

"It was," she insisted. "I told you, I'm a very determined person. I remember. I remember everything in a . . . a feeling kind of way. When I heard you playing on Bloor Street I remembered . . . the sounds as I floated in the ARTwomb . . . not exactly sound, but a vibration all through my body."

"I feel that when I play cello. From here," she put her hand to her throat and let it sweep down her body.

"So you know what I'm talking about." Talya's voice trembled and for a moment Dai Ling thought she was going to cry, but she continued. "Medical scientists had been working on the artificial womb for years. The difficulty was the placenta. It took decades of intensive research to discover the physiological process involved in the diffusion of oxygen and carbon dioxide across the placental barrier in order to create an artificial placenta." She laughed and angled herself to face Dai Ling more directly, leaning forward, intent on her topic. "The placenta is a miracle and it cannot actually be simulated. It's a biochemical dialogue between mother and foetus. The embryo sets up a placental connection between itself and the host body, mixing its embryonic cells with the endometrial cells in the lining of the uterus to form the placenta. That's why babies can't distinguish between their own bodies and the bodies of their mothers during the first months of life." She watched Dai Ling, anxious for her reaction. "I was the only success, which makes me a miracle of ectogenesis, because I developed entirely outside the human body. My survival was against all scientific odds."

"You already talk like a doctor."

"They train us to talk like this. It doesn't come naturally."

Dai Ling noticed how pale she was, the faint blue shadows under her eyes.

"My parents never tried to hide it from me. How could they with the media on the case? I was big news on the medical beat. *Healthy girl born after reimplantation—a medical miracle!*"

"D'you think it was a true memory or your imagination?"

"What?"

"The memory of being in your mother's body."

"You don't believe me, do you? You're so cynical."

"No, I'm not! But it's really weird. I've never met anyone like you."

"What is the truth anyway?" Talya asked softly. "I brought myself into this world with the power of my imagination."

"If it was so difficult to create an artificial placenta, how did you survive?"

They were sitting so close that they felt the heat of each other's bodies. Dai Ling found it difficult to concentrate. She'd lost all sense of time. Something in the back of her mind was tugging at her, but she was rivetted by Talya's story.

"I don't know for sure, Dai Ling, but this is what I think. That I remembered all the times I'd been in Katya's body, remembered the sound of her heart beating, the rush of water through her kidneys, the slow river of her blood flowing into my veins. I felt the vibration of her voice and the bouncing of my fluid sac as she moved, and the silence as she slept. I actually believed I was in her body again."

Ruby whined from the hallway and Dai Ling started to get up, but Talya grabbed her arm and continued, "I wasn't alone there. I created my own environment with memory and maybe it acted like a placebo. Because I *believed* I was in Katya's body and she was finally embracing me to term, I was nourished and I grew." She leaned back a moment, taking stock, realizing she held Dai Ling captive, so when she spoke again it was at a more leisurely pace. "Of course the medics did their thing. They probably pumped culture fluid into me to simulate the natural hormone release of an actual pregnancy. They'd stimulate me with gentle agitation of my container during daylight hours, just as though I were in a live, moving body. They had total control of me, but it was all virtual and I don't believe it would have been enough without my participation. I take credit for my existence."

There was a sudden yelp as Ruby padded across the threshold. She circled, whimpering, and ran out to the hall leaving bloody pawprints in her wake.

"Oh Ruby, what happened?" Talya exclaimed.

They both ran after her and Dai Ling brought a wet cloth from the kitchen sink and dabbed at Ruby's paw.

"She's all right, it's only a nick," Talya said, "But look at the blood on Mom's carpet."

"Oh my god, I have to go," Dai Ling said, suddenly realizing the time. "I've been here for hours. I'll just finish sweeping the glass, it's so dangerous."

"No, no, I can do it," Talya said. "You go."

"Really? I'm so sorry, but my parents . . . they'll be wondering where I am. We always eat dinner together on Sunday."

"It's okay, I understand."

Talya bandaged Ruby's paw and sent her to her basket in the corner of the kitchen. After she'd scrubbed the hall carpet and swept up the rest of the glass, she stood in the hallway staring at the blinking red light of Katya's message, listening to the silence of the empty house, the beating of her heart. She climbed the stairs and heard the clink of the brass rods holding the dull gold carpet as her feet tugged the pile. At the top she paused, listening. Ahead of her the door of her parents' room was open and she walked in hesitantly, almost expecting them to be there. She crossed the room and sat in the bay window facing west towards the stables.

Everything was dark. Katya's perfume filled the room. Talya imagined her mother's body being scrutinized and tended, her immune system being boosted so that her body could heal itself, her whole being transformed and renewed, like a garden in spring. She was glad Katya had refused surgery; she would have hated that, would have felt it in her own body, the sharp entry of the scalpel, the dull ache of the aftermath.

Talya stood and walked across the room, touching the quilted bedspread and the glass-topped dressing table where Katya's silver-backed mirror and hairbrush lay. She pulled at one of the long hairs trapped there and wound it around her finger, then glancing up she caught herself in the mirror. So many times she had stood behind her mother, watching her in that mirror, wondering if she could ever grow up to be as beautiful. Katya was like someone from a fairy-tale and Talya had wished passionately to enter her magic world.

Outside on the landing the curve of the bannister was smooth under her hand. She remembered sliding down, screaming with joy, Lily catching her at the bottom of the stairs. She remembered how Lily and Mr. Brewster had become friends, Lily calling him 'Mr. B,' because she couldn't say Brewster . . . it came out like 'rooster,' and he'd always tease her, crowing and slapping his knees. Lily used to make him a big cup of strong tea at noon and he would drink it sitting on the back steps in the sunshine, eating his sandwich, sharing it with Talya. Then her mom had been mad when she couldn't eat her lunch.

She walked down the long corridor, the bathroom branching off on the right with its cool blue tiles, the open door of her room at the front of the house, the bed a twist of sheets, and next door the old nursery converted into a guest room. She turned the handle and entered the cold room, the quilted counterpanes of the twin beds smooth as glass. Towels hung rigid on the metal rail by the corner sink. She remembered Lily's sad song in a strange tongue, lulling her to sleep, Lily's eyes glistening in the half light, the sweet smell of mock orange. A sudden longing pierced her; Katya was always somewhere else, in the next room, in another country, another house, otherwise occupied. She wouldn't phone her, not yet. She crossed to the window and looked out on the garden – lilac bushes, the giant rhododendron, maples with scraps of sputtering flame clinging – everything was dripping wet, drinking in the storm, roots clenching around rainwater trickling through the earth. She felt the quenching, battering, drowning in her body like the satisfaction of a summer thirst. But it was winter and she was an invalid thrown into confusion by her own condition. The outside light went off and the garden disappeared, revealing her own face mirrored at the window. Night of the dark moon. She tried to remember Dai Ling's face, but she couldn't conjure it. There was nothing but a white oval, her own face wiped clean.

Talya went back to her parents' bedroom, sat on Katya's side of the bed and picked up the telephone. She dialed the Montréal code and a number. It rang four times before the message machine came on. *You've reached the Kulikovsky home. We're sorry we're not home to talk to you right now but leave a message for Vassily, Riva, Nathan or Sandra and one of us will get back to you as soon as possible.* Aunt Riva's bright voice. The beeps.

"Uncle Vassily, it's me, Talya. I need to talk with you. Has there been any news? Are you coming to Toronto soon? It's Sunday night. Please call me. I love you."

~

Dai Ling was re-organizing the magazine section at the Riverdale Library when the cover of an art magazine, showing a glass sculpture, reminded her of Talya. She had been trying not to think of her since the bizarre events of almost a week ago. It seemed like a dream, or perhaps something she'd imagined. It occurred to her now to look up 'ARTwomb' online, and sure enough there it was on the cover of the spring 1980 edition of *Art in America*, with an article entitled, "The ARTwomb by Belle Cloutier at Galerie DesJardins." *So it* is *real,* she thought, her heart beating faster, *at least as a sculpture. And the kiss was real, and the way I felt was real.*

There were more images of the ARTwomb and a description: *A sculpture of pale aqua glass the color of a sun-soaked ocean, with sides blown out in sweeping curves — molten liquid shaped by breath — nestled amidst a crafty arrangement of mirrors, producing multiple images of itself.*

The article described it as . . . *feminist sculpture at its best, addressing the problem of the Assisted Reproductive Technologies of the future. With this dramatic piece Cloutier warns of a future in which the human body may be bypassed in the regeneration of the species. 'Imagine woman-as-creator usurped by the womb-envious, science-obsessed patriarchy,' she invites, 'ART could result in a story more horrific than Mary Shelley's Frankenstein. Men have always been jealous of women's ability to create life inside their bodies,' Cloutier opines. 'Rendering the role of woman-as-childbearer redundant with the invention of a functional glass uterus would elevate the role of the patriarch to mythological levels, like Zeus giving birth to Pallas Athena through his head.'*

Dai Ling glanced up and saw Mrs. Fox bearing down on her from the check-out desk. She quickly closed the site and hurried back to the magazine stacks to resume her tidying. *Maybe Talya's mom saw the exhibit in Montréal and got the idea from Belle Cloutier,* she thought. *Or maybe she bought the sculpture and that's what I was sweeping up the other night. It's such an incredible story, I don't know what to think. Talya's a mystery to me, but behind all the weirdness she's so warm and full of desire.*

During her break Dai Ling checked the online library catalogue and punched in, *Vesalius: The Illustrations From His Works.* There was only one copy and it was registered as 'Lost.'

~

1545: Brussels

"WHAT ARE YOU GROWING IN THERE, wife?"

Andreas' hands rested on the dome of Anne's belly, swollen now beyond the cupping of a single hand. Her smile was enigmatic, like the maddening smile in the Italian, da Vinci's, portrait of Lisa Gherardini, wife of Francesco del Giocondo. "What are you growing in there?" Under his teasing tone was a great impatience. He was a father, waiting and longing to see his child. So great was his desire to claim possession of the infant that he sometimes wished to crawl inside Anne and curl there, observing the source of life, and in those moments of absurd passion his throat seized up and he sobbed his impotent love into the hollow of her shoulder. Then he slept, nuzzling her, and *dreamed* himself inside her.

With his wife's pregnancy Vesalius had turned his attention to the study of the foetus, a topic which would occupy him for the next ten years. For some months already he had been studying the development of the human foetus and now his own child, flesh of his flesh, was about to enter the world. His eyes were ravenous for sight of its emergence. Boy or girl, whole or deformed, breach or headfirst, he awaited it, curious as the cat who drowned in the well pursuing its own image.

His colleagues gazed at the stars and invoked demons, their lively discussion splashing the night sky, creating new galaxies, but Vesalius was entrenched in the human body, all his desire for the discovery of its mysteries. He longed to draw his fellow-explorers from their cosmic visions and into his own microcosm, to see their wonder at a new world revealed through his eyes.

"Wait and see," Anne said finally, as though she had been in a trance, drawn inward for an answer. "Boy or girl, Andreas, wait and see," and her hands cupped his bearded face with a gentleness and generosity reaching beyond all his inquiry. He leaned on her belly, his heart pounding against the foetal heartbeat which, as he felt it, shocked him and opened his heart to its own beating.

"Thanks for coming, Uncle Vassily."

"Natalya, you're family! When I got your message I called the hospital right away and arranged for someone to fill in for me, called Air Canada, booked the next available flight." Vassily ran a hand through his thinning hair. His appearance was unremarkable — medium build, brown hair, a neat beard, well-manicured nails — except for luminous eyes which gave him the look of a Biblical character who'd seen a vision and accepted responsibility for it. "Riva sends her love, Nathan and Sandra too. They said you should come down and visit us. Will you? You could travel back with me tomorrow."

Talya shook her head. "Third year med, Uncle Vassily. You remember what it's like."

"Crazy, eh? Clinical clerkship rotation?"

"You got it. Here, let me take your coat."

"Where are you assigned?"

"General mostly. Sometimes Mount Sinai."

"I did my internship at the General. Must've been running on three or four hours sleep a day. It's a form of torture you know, sleep deprivation."

"It hasn't happened to us yet." She took his hand and led him into the living room.

"It will. You'll have to make sure you get enough rest, otherwise you'll lose your connection with your patients. It can become like automobile maintenance." They both burst out laughing. "I'm proud of you," Vassily said. "Maybe we're starting a family tradition here, a line of doctors. My kids show no interest in anything remotely scientific. Sandra wants to be a night-club singer and Nathan wants to go to film school."

"Is she going to be cured?" The question hanging over them.

"I don't know, Talya." Vassily sat down heavily and sighed. "The Geneva clinic has had some remarkable successes, but you know as well as I do, my dear, the human body is a mystery." He patted the sofa next to him and Talya sat, leaning forward, her body tense.

"What exactly are the immunotherapy treatments she's having?"

"A couple of hours a day on an IV nutritional detoxifying cocktail. High doses of vitamin C — 62.5 grams at a time — alternating with hydrogen peroxide. Huge quantities of daily supplements, coffee enemas to cleanse the liver and blood, and to decrease pain." Counting them off on his fingers he continued, "A diet of organic whole grains, legumes, vegetables and fish. No sugar. Cancer, as you know, feeds off sugar. No dairy, flour, soy, no fruits except berries. An hour a day in a hyperbaric oxyen chamber zipped into a cocoon-like pod while the pressure is raised and pure oxygen is piped in." He turned to Talya and smiled. "The oxygenation is apparently very relaxing." His eyes narrowed as he leaned back and looked up at the ceiling, thoughtful. "An hour a day in the infrared sauna — cancer doesn't like heat, in fact it doesn't survive above 105 degrees. Acupuncture twice a week, lymphatic massage, counselling and guided meditation. Homeopathics and light therapy, electrodermal screening and autohemotherapy."

"What's that — autohemotherapy?"

"Removing blood, mixing it with saline and reinjecting it intramuscularly. It strengthens the immune system because the body must mount a fresh immune response to the disease-causing substances inside the red blood cells, sort of like rebooting the computer."

"Do you think she should have had surgery?"

Vassily spread his hands in a shrug. "Your mother refused categorically, so I found her the best alternative available."

"But can they cure her?"

"We can only hope. I'm part of the system that's given her a terminal prognosis, but it's the exceptions that make fools of us every time."

"If anyone would be an exception it would be Mom."

"She's one of the most determined women I've ever met."

"What d'you mean?"

"Your birth for a start."

Talya stood and walked over to the empty sideboard. She saw her face mirrored there. "Did you notice?"

"What?"

"It's gone."

Vassily leaned forward, elbows on his knees, puzzled.

"The ARTwomb."

"Oh, that ugly thing. I never liked it."

"Uncle Vassily, she'll be heartbroken. It was her pride and joy."

"*You're* her pride and joy."

"But I came out of it."

Vassily laughed. "*Diévochka!* That's what you told me when you were a kid. You marched me in here and stood there in your little red velvet dress, hands on hips. 'That's where I came out,' you said. 'I'm a medical miracle.' Precocious little brat you were! I went along with it, because I wasn't up to telling you the facts of life at that point."

"What are you talking about?" Talya's face was white and pinched.

"That monstrosity Nick bought for Katya when she was carrying you."

Talya froze. "Wait a minute. I was nurtured in that 'monstrosity' as you call it."

"Surely you don't believe that?"

"It's true!" she said vehemently.

A softness spread slowly across Vassily's face as he reached out his hand to Talya. When he spoke his words were measured. "Look, Talya, you're an adult now. We don't need to play these games."

"It isn't a game. That's where I came out. The *Globe & Mail* was here, the *Toronto Star*. I was big news."

"It was an unusual case. Flushed out of the uterus and reimplanted."

"In the ARTwomb."

"No, Talya. In your mom."

Talya pulled back her hand and kneaded her upper arms with scissorlike fingers.

"I was working in Guatemala," Vassily said gently. "But this is what Nick told me. Because of all the miscarriages they decided to go with a surrogate, a Philippina woman who later became your nanny. But when it came time to reimplant, Katya wanted you back. She was so desperate to bear her own child that she was willing to take the risk. She spent close to nine months on her back in order to give birth to you. Of course the media were onto it. 'The twice-born,' they called you, 'The one-bodied twins.' Nick hated the publicity. They were so thrilled with you they just wanted to be left alone."

Talya was shivering so hard that her teeth were chattering. Vassily gathered her in his arms.

"I feel so stupid," she said, speaking into the tweediness of his shoulder. "Here I am studying medicine . . . I should have known better. But I've always believed in magic . . . "

"Send some of that magic to your mom, Talya. She's getting the best care possible, and Nick will do everything to keep her alive, that I know. But she could use some magic."

Talya nodded, nestling into him, unwilling to let go. "I remember when you came back to Canada. You were my hero. What took you so long? I was waiting for you."

"Didn't want to live in North America again after what I'd seen in the Guatemalan villages. It was a grim time in the early eighties, Talya, hundreds of Mayan villages destroyed in a US-backed genocidal campaign. Widespread terror. Impossible to do anything to help. So I kept on going – El Salvador, Colombia, then Ecuador. I only came back to see you. I thought it was about time. My trip was supposed to be a vacation. Then I got work at the Royal Vic and I met Riva. Amazing how quickly you can be seduced by your old life, fall into the familiar and forget what moved you beyond yourself."

"You moved a long way from your Romanov background, Uncle Vassily."

"Tell you the truth I don't know a lot about the family history. Nick's the one. He kept all the family photos. I turned my back on it all when I went to work in Latin America."

"Sometimes I wonder if it's real. Dad never talks about the past, only about him and Mom, as though nothing was real until he met her. I don't even remember my grandparents."

Vassily shook his head. "They died relatively young. I missed our dad's passing. I was somewhere in the Highlands of Guatemala and by the time I got the news it was too late." He shrugged. "But you do understand about your birth now, don't you?"

"Yes." Talya's voice caught as she spoke, "I wish you lived in Toronto."

"There's a bat mitzvah tomorrow night — Sandra's friend Naomi. I have to be back, I'm speaking for the family, but how about I take you out for dinner tonight?"

"Yes, I'd like that," she nodded. "Uncle Vassily, I'm so scared."

"Talya, if this treatment fails . . . "

"Please! Don't talk about it." Her voice had become a whisper.

"All I'm saying is . . . "

"No, you'll make something bad happen. Let's drop it."

"But will you call her? Promise?"

Talya nodded. "Promise."

"I feel much better about the Beethoven," Sylvie said, turning from the piano to face Dai Ling and Christie. "But could we go over the Mendelssohn once more?"

"I was going to ask the same thing myself," Christie said, "There's a couple of places where I'm not clear on my entry. How about you, Dai Ling? Dai-Liiing . . . dreaming?"

"Oh . . . I was just marking my pages."

"Come on, you never look at the music anyway. Doesn't she have the most brilliant memory?"

Sylvie nodded, twirling a stray lock of hair around her finger. "She spends all her time practising, that's why. Dai Ling, you should live a little."

"I love to practise. It's my idea of fun."

"Really?" Christie said archly. "I thought you were getting some new ideas, running around with Talya Kulikovsky?"

"Oh, she's just a friend. The Mendelssohn you said?"

Christie and Sylvie laughed. "Is she coming to our recital?" Christie asked.

"I don't know. Maybe."

"You're so secretive."

"Oh come on, let's play," Dai Ling said impatiently and she put her head down and began re-tuning her cello.

Christie and Sylvie exchanged a look and Sylvie, sitting at the grand piano slightly behind Dai Ling, brushed her cheeks with her long fingers to indicate that Dai Ling was blushing. Christie, trying not to laugh, picked up her violin in readiness for the *D Minor Trio*.

Dai Ling found freedom in the music. It was her refuge and her joy. As a little girl in grade one she had learned that she was different from most of the other kids, with her slanted eyes and her Mandarin words. Nobody could pronounce her name and they laughed at her when she told them. "No, no, Dai Ling! Dai Ling!"

"Let's call you . . . Daisy," Mrs. Westerly had said. "That will make it easier for all of us." So that's who she had been, Daisy Xiang, until they had moved to Chinatown East. Many Chinese lived there and she had found her gang at the new school — Ray, Dee-Dee, Celia and Sam, and she had become Dai Ling again.

When she'd first picked up the bow with the tight hair and rosin dust her teacher had fixed for her, as she had touched it to the strings of her little cello, Dai Ling had begun to travel. The sounds she made lifted her into another world where time stopped and she encountered many spirits, many shapes and forms dancing in the universe. As she played now, finding harmony again with Christie and Sylvie, her grandmother Geneviève came, her hair a cloud of soft redness, curling like smoke from the cigarette in her hand. She seemed to float above Dai Ling and her cello, emitting her own strange sound, sad and piercing. Dai Ling sensed a figure which formed and dissolved before she could properly distinguish it — a man with dark eyes, broad cheekbones, a half-open mouth, Geneviève lying in his arms. There were no words, only strains of sound wrapping them around like a new language, their flesh joined, singing.

There was dirt under Geneviève's nails and her muscles ached from digging. She worked alongside her Chinese lover. As soon as she had seen him she'd known it was for him that she had come to China. It was in the first days, before she had learned more than a few words of Mandarin. In Montréal she had studied Cantonese, thinking she would be sent to South China, but when she arrived everything was different from how she'd imagined and she knew she would never leave China. Liu Zhen, her lover, was a *pipa* player. The four-stringed lute was like a honey-colored teardrop, the strings callousing his fingers long before the sharp-stoned earth marked him. Liu had a family, a wife and two children, but like many families in Maoist China, they were separated, the children with their grandparents, he and his wife sent to separate provinces to work on the land. He fell in love with the tall, red-haired foreigner and love made him careless. He dropped his guard and spoke his heart. Geneviève was not sure of their child until a week after they had taken him.

"Where is he? Where is Liu?" she asked in her fractured Mandarin. A young woman, proud of her English, said, "Liu is taken for special training in correct political thinking."

She had not known how to ask for a pregnancy test, and she had not known how to tell him of her suspicion. After they took Liu, Geneviève had no one. She kept on working in the dirt, digging and planting, imagining him at her side. In the night she called his name, *Liu, Liu,* her throat aching with desire. They all watched her belly grow and no one said anything. The big-boned stranger with a wide-brimmed hat shading her freckled face kept on working, bending and straightening, turning the earth, digging and shovelling until one day she cried out and fell to the earth, her legs buckling under her. When they picked her up to carry her to the hospital the earth beneath her was muddy with the waters of her child and a thread of blood clung to the newly turned furrow.

Geneviève never gave up hope of Liu's return. She learned to speak Mandarin fluently because she believed that one day he would come and they could speak for the first time. Her child could not wait. Xian Ming had her own love, Jia Song Xiang, a student dissident protesting the undemocratic process by which rapid economic change was sweeping across China, flooding it with western ideas. Moments after Dai Ling's birth, Geneviève held the baby on her arm, the dark wet head cradled in her palm, and she saw herself there and heard Liu's lute strings. Two years later Xian Ming and Jia Song begged her to go with them to Canada, but she said, "I must wait here. This is my country now."

When the trio was over and Dai Ling dropped her bow to the ground she was unable to speak. Her ears were ringing with a 2,000-year-old song.

~

Talya picked up the phone from its charger, dialled and paced the hall waiting for Dai Ling to answer. Ruby sat in the kitchen doorway watching her, ears pricked, ready for a walk.

"Hello, Doctor Xiang's household," a voice said.

"Can I speak to Dai Ling?"

"Dai Ling's not here. Who is this?"

"Talya. I'm a friend of hers from the university."

"Ah, you're a musician too," the voice stated. "Dai Ling is practising for her recital. You playing too?"

"No, I'm a medical student."

"Oh, I see. You want me to give her a message? I'm her Ma."

"Could you ask her to call me when she gets home."

"Sure. She has your number?"

"Yes, yes, I believe she does."

"Maybe I'll see you at the recital."

The phone clicked and Talya replaced the receiver. She stood a moment, indecisive, then picked it up and held it against her shoulder while she searched through the papers on the desk. She found the number and dialled. An excruciating silence then it began to ring finally, that familiar far-off sound.

"Hello?"

"Dad."

"Talya, finally! We've been waiting for your call, *moya dochenka*."

"Sorry, Dad. I couldn't call earlier."

"Wait a moment. Your mother's here. Hold on."

"Darling! Is it really you?"

"Hi, Mom. How are you?"

"I'm fine darling, fine."

"I'm so worried."

"We've been worried about *you*, haven't we Nicky?"

"It's not too late? I know there's a six hour difference, but . . . "

"You know us, we're night owls, tucked up in bed, reading. Daddy and I have our own room in the clinic with a gorgeous view of Lake Geneva."

Talya imagined her, leaning back against a pile of pillows, reaching for his hand. They were always touching. She'd be in her silk nightgown, her hair loose around her pale face, skimming her shoulders as her head moved, turning to smile at him.

"Any news, Mom?"

"Nothing yet. They're keeping me busy with treatments. It takes time, darling. I miss you so much. How's Ruby?"

"Oh, she's fine. She cut her paw, but it's getting better."

"Ouch! Poor Ruby. Did you break something?"

"No, no, just a bit of glass in the garden." The line began to crackle. "Mom? Mom, are you there?" Her voice came in fragments, words cut in two with a staccato rhythm, like a slow rain of bullets. "The line's very bad, Mom. I'll call again. Give my love to Daddy." She put the receiver down, trying to swallow the pain that bloomed in her throat; the old childhood grief that came creeping in the fading light, begging. *I lied, she knows, I lied, I'm bad.* It was gloomy in the dimly-lit hall with the silence of the big house surrounding her. She felt Ruby's damp nose pushing at her leg and she crouched down and hugged the big red dog, burying her face in her fur. Ruby always knew. *I'm not going to phone again*, she thought, *it hurts too much. It's worse than missing her.*

She walked into the living room, Ruby padding after her, nails clicking on the hardwood floor, and lit a small fire, scrunching newspapers, laying kindling, striking a match. When the sticks were burning well she added a few small logs from the alder Nick had taken down in the spring and flopped onto the sofa to watch the flames. But she was restless, even after an eight hour shift in Emergency. She picked up the Vesalius book from the coffee table, rested it on her stomach and flipped the pages until she came to the illustrations of the female reproductive organs. Strangely there were no illustrations of the foetus, except for a peculiar little man with crossed legs, sucking his thumb, floating by a cord attached to a nutshell. *Plate 62*, she read, *In his figures of the foetus and its coverings which appeared in the first edition of the* Fabrica, *Vesalius committed the unpardonable error of illustrating the annular placenta of the dog as part of the human investments. Writing some three years later, he excuses himself on the grounds that he had had no opportunity of examining the human foetus and that Jacobus Sylvius had informed him that the arrangement in the dog also held for man. This and other errors he corrected in the second edition. His three membranes are the placenta, the chorion and the amnion. But he confused the placenta, his outermost investment, with the chorion, as described by Galen. His second investment, the true chorion, he mistakenly described as though the allantois of the dog. His third investment, the amnion, he believed . . .*

The book slipped out of Talya's hands and slid onto the carpet. Ruby whimpered and her paws twitched as she dreamed of running, running . . . On the horizon a thin line of orange light bleeds as a roll of thunder shakes the sky. The corners of Talya's mouth tremble. A curled foetus looms, its ancient eye rolling as it floats by, pulled like a toy by its umbilical cord. A flood of light sweeps across the map, up through northern Italy, igniting beacons all over Germany and the Low Countries, southwest into Spain, pocking the red earth with light. Like flags mapping a war zone, men born of brilliant women cover the earth with extraordinary visions, men with free minds, drunk on the light ingested with their wet nurses' milk, fill the air with thoughts that have never been thought before, imprinting space with new patterns. Alchemical codes are captured with the screams of the tortured, resounding through the universe, down the centuries; music is composed and notated on fine paper which crumbles away leaving harmonic overtones echoing in the sky; brightly coloured oils are dabbed on canvasses with fine brushes, a breathless will to beauty shining through layers of glazes; codes for the restructuring of the entire planetary field are embedded in paintings filled with light and darkness. Talya hears a whisper. A thrill of fear passes through her body, then the sky turns red and she sees faggots being piled, fires being lit, racks assembled, gibbets built. The sky darkens and the lights are extinguished one by one, swallowed by the sheltering earth as flesh tears and burns, bones crack, and screams die. The earth spins faster and faster until the light cannot be contained, but seeps out bit by bit, slow and stealthy as a thief stealing the darkness. It is 1600, the beginning of a new century and Giordano Bruno cannot contain his knowledge of multiple dimensions and extraterrestrial civilizations. With ink squeezed from the octopus he scratches his knowledge onto paper. The pope declares his writings heretical and decrees his execution; the sky blazes anew as Bruno burns at the stake. Souls fill the sky, lost, confused, fugitives seeking safety from proof of their existence. Everything which defies verification becomes the domain of the 'weak-minded.' Bleating flocks are shepherded across the earth by men who preach Belief, powerful men who hide beneath feminine robes, ritualized, fetishized, men with licence.

When Talya woke she didn't know where she was. All around her was darkness except for a pile of glowing ashes. Slowly she came to, rolled off the sofa and crawled across the floor towards the light. Ruby nuzzled her as she threw some sticks into the fireplace and lay there in the sudden warmth, watching the flames.

Vesalius was hurrying from the hospital, anxious to get home to Anne, when the gimpy-legged watchman tugged at his sleeve.

"Doctor Vesalius, sir, something of interest to you, sir."

Vesalius shook himself free. "What is it, man? Don't waste my time."

"Follow me, sir, if you please."

"I am in haste, I tell you. What is it you want?"

"Please, sir, I think you'll find it worth your while, sir," the man wheedled.

He followed the hobbling fellow down the stone steps to the basement of the hospital and into the morgue.

"There she is," the man whispered hoarsely as he whipped the sheet off the mounded belly of the corpse. "An indigent with child. One of those from the Bovendael."

"Ah," said Vesalius, stroking his beard.

"I heard you saying, only yesterday, sir, that . . . "

"Yes. Very good." Vesalius pressed a guilder into his open palm. "Leave me now."

The watchman limped across the flagstones and up the steps, massaging his guilder between finger and thumb, thinking of the nice piece of pork he would purchase with it, the surprise on his wife's tired face. Vesalius listened to his crippled footsteps ringing into the distance and raised his face to the heavens. "Saint Jude Thaddeus!" he exulted, "I did not know you would come to me in the form of a humble hospital watchman and with such goods. Thank you, thank you for providing the impossible! And blessings upon your holy remains in the basilica of St. Peter at Rome." He kissed the air and, pulling up his sleeves, began to lay out his instruments.

"After all my efforts, to publish in error . . . but I'd had no opportunity of examining a human foetus. Until now! Thanks be to Saint Jude!" He rubbed his hands together, surveying the cadaver before him. "My error in illustrating the annular placenta of the dog was a minor detail in the context of my opus. Surely it is my genius that will be remembered?" he questioned his absent audience. "No matter. Now I will rectify my errors," he declared, aflame with the fervour of anticipation.

The woman was indeed an indigent, dirty and emaciated but for her mounded belly which shone in the half-light.

"No one to claim her body, no one to miss her. I am merely robbing the pauper's grave before it is filled," Vesalius said, reassuring himself. A thin red line snaked up her thigh, running from a festering wound at her ankle.

"Ascending lymphangitis," Talya murmured into the flames, as she watched him with her mind's eye.

"Poison of the blood," Vesalius said. "The blood travels, how does it travel? The river runs, from whence to the ocean?"

He made his incision carefully. It was the foetus he was after. His previous illustrations had been made from supposition, based on the the foetal sacs of animals, and his text had carried the same thread of error. Now the secret would be revealed. Talya leaned over his shoulder as he sliced cleanly through the surface of the uterus. It fell open like an egg, revealing two foetal membranes in one sac — the chorionic, fused with the placenta at this advanced stage of pregnancy, and the amnionic.

Vesalius took up pen and paper and sketched rapidly, cutting and delving as he went, exploring every detail of the foetal sac. He noted with delight a cluster of coalescence he had not guessed at. The allantois formed part of the umbilical cord which was fused with the chorion to form the placenta. As he probed and punctured the final layer of the amnion, a trickle of water leaked into the cavity of the woman's body, leaving her baby stranded and shrunken inside the collapsed amniotic membrane, a dead wet thing, dark with the mystery of its source, like a fish thrown up from the deep. Vesalius caught himself, his heart swelling, moved by the perfect premature form. Tears started in his eyes and as he turned to wipe them with his sleeve, which still bore the imprints of the watchman's greasy fingers, his form merged with the body of Talya, standing behind him.

"What is this that occurs each time I cut into the body?" he whispered. "Perhaps it is, as the Church says, sacred ground not to be trodden on." He resumed his work, refusing to be distracted from the scientific nature of his activity. He did not pursue the *source* of his feelings, his own quivering abstraction. He did not pursue the *source* of the rhythmically spurting blood of his living patients. Andreas Vesalius quested outward in the spirit of his time, searching for evidence of an abstraction. And Talya, invisible in her reverie, followed him.

The hall grew humid as people removed their snow-encrusted coats, shook them and hung them on the backs of chairs where they started dripping onto the grey carpet. The recital was the first of the *Young Artist* series held in Walter Hall. It was mid-December and truly cold finally, as winter should be, with a big snowfall. Dai Ling had given Talya one of her three complimentary tickets. She peeked through the curtain in the wings and saw her, third row centre, staring up at the organ pipes rising above the circular stage. A grand piano stood waiting; in front of it two chairs with music stands, and her cello leaning against the chair. Talya must have come early to get such a good seat. Dai Ling saw her parents in the front row and next to them Ray Lee and his Ma. She felt a quivering in her belly and she didn't know if it was nerves about playing for them or fear of introducing Talya to her family afterwards.

There was a murmur throughout the auditorium as the musicians entered. Dai Ling held her bow, freshly rosined, dangling from her right hand. Already she had removed herself, in preparation for entering the world of her music. Sylvie sat at the grand piano and shuffled on the bench until she was comfortable, then flexed her fingers over the keys as though she were warming them at a fire, while Christie and Dai Ling tuned their instruments, Christie with a pad on her shoulder, chin gripping her ruddy violin. Dai Ling flourished her bow and drew it across the strings. The brief call and response of their tuning was followed by a hushed silence. The musicians nodded to each other, then there was a slight intake of breath from Christie into which floated the first notes of Haydn's *Trio #1 in G*. As she played, Dai Ling was aware of Talya leaning forward, watching intently and she remembered that day in the music room when Talya had come looking for her. Did she know Talya any better now than she had then, despite all their talking? Her heart was sure of one thing; she had been kissed.

They were well into the third movement, the cheerful "Gypsy Rondo", when Dai Ling looked out to the audience and caught Talya's eye. She let her in then, let her spiral with her, travelling a pathway of sound in which they formed a heavenly ladder, connected at intervals.

A sudden burst of applause and Talya was on her feet, along with Ray Lee, Jia Song and Xian Ming, shouting, "Bravo!"

The rest of the program flowed smoothly—the Mendelssohn *Trio in D Minor*, and Beethoven's *Archduke*, the music travelling down two centuries, each rendition an attempt to recapture the spirit of that original moment of inspiration, each time different from the last, from the first, each an attempt to return to the source. Then it was over and the audience applauded and cheered, calling for an encore. The musicians consulted briefly then Christie nodded and they launched into the first movement of Mozart's *Trio in B Flat*.

People were putting on their coats and gloves, crowding into the lobby, as Dai Ling pushed her way to the back and found Talya.

"You were wonderful!" Talya threw her arms around her. "I should have brought flowers!"

"Oh, thank you. Come and meet my parents."

"Ah, here's Talya. We hear so much about you from Dai Ling," Xian Ming said. Talya smiled and looked up at Jia Song as he gripped her hand and shook it firmly. She immediately detected Dai Ling's resemblance to her father in the warmth of his eyes, in his sensual mouth, the slight angle at which he held his head.

"You have the most extraordinary daughter," Talya said, "I'm in love with her music!"

"Thank you, yes, we are proud," Jia Song bowed slightly. "We must go out and celebrate. Will you join us, Talya?"

"Thank you. I'd love to," she beamed.

Dai Ling introduced her to Ray Lee and his mother, then Christie and Sylvie joined them and finally everyone was ready to leave.

"Dai Ling, you're the best cellist in Toronto!" Ray Lee shouted across the table once they were seated at the Szechwan Gardens restaurant. "One day I'm going to make a movie about you, okay?"

Dai Ling laughed. "Sure, Ray. We'll both be famous."

Talya sat between Jia Song and Dai Ling. Everyone talked about the concert, what a great success it had been, and Xian Ming, seated next to her husband, leaned across and said to Talya, "I remember when Dai Ling was a baby, so tiny in her crib, her fingers were always moving in the air, as though she was playing invisible music. She's been playing the cello since she was four years old. She's going to have a big career," she finished proudly, and Jia Song nodded and smiled. Then Xian Ming turned to Mrs. Lee and began talking in Mandarin.

Dai Ling's hand crept into Talya's as the food began to arrive—big dishes of steamed dumplings with fat pink prawns and green vegetable shoots atop a tangle of ginger and garlic-flavored noodles.

"You were brilliant tonight," Talya whispered. "All I want is to be alone with you right now."

Dai Ling blushed and bowed her head as she picked up her chopsticks and balanced them between her fingers.

"We talked on the phone," Xian Ming said, leaning across to Talya. "You're the doctor."

"Not yet. Still studying."

"My husband is a doctor."

"East meets west," Jia Song said, laughing.

"Dai Ling told us your mom is sick," Xian Ming said. "Maybe my husband can help her."

"Dad took her to a clinic in Europe. They've been gone more than two weeks now. Maybe when she comes back . . . " There'd been more phone messages, and enigmatic e-mails — *Geneva's so clean and orderly . . . The lake is beautiful . . . No news yet . . . It's early days.*

As Talya told Jia Song about her medical studies he nodded silently, filling his mouth with loaded chopsticks, chewing hungrily. She hadn't much appetite herself and finally she said, "I'm afraid I must go. We have clinical evaluations early tomorrow and I have to prepare." She bid her farewells to Jia Song and Xian Ming, then she leaned into Dai Ling and whispered, "Call me later, will you? I'll be up."

Dai Ling squeezed her hand before she let go. Talya waved to the blur of faces around the table and hurried out.

When she got home she sat at her father's desk upstairs and turned on the laptop computer. A message came in, from Geneva. Her heart rose. She clicked on it.

The news is not good, Natáshenka. Your mom is very sick. I think you should come. All our love, Daddy.

His study was stale with cigar smoke; it clung to the curtains. The shelves were thick with books, the desk covered with toppling piles of papers. Talya's stomach clenched into a fist, bending her double. When she recovered she sank into Nick's black leather chair and swung in a double circle, until the chair came to a standstill and she found herself looking out onto the moonlit rose garden, filled with thorns and a memory of soft voices.

What does he mean? What in hell does he mean? She jumped up and paced the room, her heart insistent. She started for the door, but turned back, her movements sharp and jerky. She sat in front of the screen, hands poised over the keyboard, then she jumped up again and ran to the window. *What will I do? Oh god, what can I do!* She turned and walked briskly onto the landing. She paused, her hand on the doorknob of her parents' bedroom, then she opened the door and stared at the huge bed, wide as it was long. There she was, distorted in the mirrored headboard. Talya flung herself and landed in the centre of her parents' bed, the mattress soft and giving, and she lay silent, her face buried in the quilt, barely breathing, until the phone rang. She reached out, her hand brushing the lip of the bedside table, where her father's hand touched every morning, reaching to switch off his alarm.

"Talya? It's me, Dai Ling."

"Dai Ling. Oh, my god . . . "

"What is it? Are you okay?"

"Yes, yes, I'm fine. Where are you?"

"We just got home. I'm upstairs in my room. Are you in bed?"

"I wish you were here."

"I'm not so far away."

"Can you come?"

"Now?"

"I think I'm falling in love with you." There was silence on the other end of the phone. "Dai Ling? Are you there?"

"Yes." Her voice a whisper. "I . . . I don't know what to say."

"Am I alone in this?"

"Oh no . . . no, but . . . I can't come now. My parents, they would think it strange for me to be going out so late . . . "

"It's all right, I understand. So long as you . . . "

"Yes, yes, I think so, I mean . . . "

"Don't say any more. When can I see you?"

"Friday evening?"

"I'm on late shift at Mount Sinai. Saturday?"

"After the library. We could go to Riverdale Park like when we first met."

"It'll be dark."

"Full moon."

"Perfect. Five?"

"Five-thirty. Bring back the Vesalius."

"No way. It's mine now."

"You're bad."

"Yes, I am. Sweet dreams."

"Good night."

Talya got up from her parents' bed and went next door to her father's study. She sat in his chair and stared at the screen for a moment, then she clicked on 'Reply' and wrote, *Bring her home. I'm waiting. All my love,* and sent her message flying out of its little folder on a curved arrow into the trusting void of cyberspace.

She had been standing in her white coat, scalpel in hand, surrounded by an audience of music lovers. They had each held a program with a diagram of the heart floating on a white background — showing the spacious chambers contained within the pericardium, the ventricles and atria, the aorta, the pulmonary artery, the vena cava — like pipes breathing sweet music, blood flowing through the heart, oxygenating, pumping, splashing. "Play! Play!" they'd shouted and she had raised the scalpel like a baton and brought it down slowly, oh so slowly, entering the body, draped in a sheet. Blood had spread, a dark blot, but she couldn't see the body, so she had asked the audience to remove the sheet. A little girl in a red dress had tugged smartly at the corner of the sheet and raced across the room with it. When Talya looked down there was the heart revealed inside the gaping chest, but it was black with tentacles like an octopus, spurting ink. She had looked in horror at the child who was racing around the recital room, in a black dress now, and when she looked at the face of the corpse she saw herself and heard weeping all around her. Then the face had disintegrated into a mass of writhing maggots. She had watched, horrified, as the face of the corpse reformed into her mother's face, and she had woken sobbing.

Elliott nudged her and Talya snapped to, her nostrils filling with the antiseptic smell of the men's ward.

"I'm nauseous, doctor. My stomach's bloated and I feel tired all the time."

Talya nodded, looking straight through the patient.

"Abdominal examination?" Elliott suggested, his thin face bright with irony.

"Of course," Talya said. "Lie down, please, Mr. uh . . . " She fumbled with the clipboard.

"Fraticelli," the old man said.

Classic symptoms of parasites, she thought, grasping at the obvious. "Have you been out of the country?"

Down the hallway the elevator doors opened and a group of carol singers launched into a thin rendition of *Jingle Bells*, their voices swelling as they gained confidence.

"Anywhere tropical?"

"Not for many years, doctor. Stopped going back to the old country when my wife died. 'Course there was the Korean war, I was there . . . "

Talya palpated the stomach and Mr. Fraticelli cried out suddenly.

"I'm sorry. Did that hurt?"

"Took my breath away," he gasped.

The singers had entered the ward now. They were bright-faced, dressed in festive red and green. "*O come all ye faithful*," they sang.

Talya whispered to Elliott, "Is this one for real or is he a patient simulator?" The hospital hired out-of-work actors to study up on specific diseases and simulate the symptoms for the students as part of their diagnostic training.

"He's for real. And it's ten in the morning and we're at the Toronto General on clinical rounds. Is that enough of a reality check?"

The old man watched them, straining to catch their words.

"I can't do this, Elliott. There's a massive growth on the lower end of the liver. Will you cover for me?"

"Sure. Just try to look less like a zombie or you'll have Dr. Mukherjee on your case." He stepped forward and began palpating gently, his cheerful face suddenly serious.

Talya was so relieved she felt like crying. She fell back into a blur, losing herself in the crush of students around Mr. Fraticelli's bed. The hospital corners on the bedsheets made her think of Lily. She had made Talya's bed like that, with a neat overlap of cloth, always lined up equally on each side. When she'd been sick, lying hot with fever, Lily had sponged her down and made the bed around her with fresh cool linen. Her bed had been smooth as the surface of water and she had imagined herself lying in it, a tragic heroine, floating away, her hands trailing among water-lilies, fingers clinging to their rubbery stems . . . She was cold, so cold suddenly, mist all around her . . .

When Dr. Mukherjee, leading rounds that morning, had finished his assessment and released the students, Talya hurried down the ward, her white coat flapping, the sound of Christmas music and the murmuring of hospital staff muffled around her. She couldn't feel anything. She was numb. And in her mind was an insistent image of her heart frozen in a small glass coffin. Someone touched her arm and she spun around, pulling her arms in close to her body. Elliott stood there, holding out a tangle of rubber tubing. "Your stethoscope. You forgot it," he said. Talya stared at it for a second, uncomprehending, then the stethoscope took form and she laughed. "Are you all right, Tal?"

"Yes, I'm fine," she said, laughing harder as the carol singers swept down the ward towards the elevator.

"No you're not."

"Oh Elliott, fuck off!"

He grabbed her arm. "I'm not letting you off so easy, sweetheart. Tell me what's happening."

"I'm waiting to hear from my father. It's touch-and-go with Mom and I don't have time to get to Europe." Elliott stared at her with raised eyebrows, holding his silence until Talya burst out, "I really don't, Elliott, I don't want to go!"

"We need to talk. When are you free?"

Talya shook her head impatiently. "I can't think, Elliott."

"Wednesday, after your day shift on Emerg? Oh yes, I have a photographic mind. Looked at the schedules this morning. Is it a date?"

"Okay. Five-thirty in the solarium at Allen Gardens."

"Are they serving cocktails in there now?" He raised his left eyebrow which usually made Talya laugh, but she was unresponsive.

"Oh Elliott, it's warm in there," she replied, shivering.

"Whatever. We can always sip nectar from the passion flowers. Go home and get some rest now, okay?"

Talya fled, her jaw aching with false laughter, running down seven flights to avoid crushing into the elevator with the cheery-faced carollers. They terrified her. And she couldn't stand Elliott's concern. She grabbed the Vesalius book from her locker and raced for home. Ruby had to be walked.

Ray Lee and Dai Ling trudged through the snow down Broadview Avenue. They had met at the university bookstore where Ray worked part-time, and had taken the subway together.

"Come on, Dai Ling, let's walk instead of waiting for the streetcar connection. I have to get home and finish that paper on Ozu, Kurosawa, and Mizoguchi. It's only a compare and contrast, but it's taking me forever."

"That's because you're a perfectionist," said Dai Ling, pulling up the hood of her ski jacket.

"What about you? I never see you because you're always practising," he teased. "Your concert was impressive, Dai Ling."

"Thanks."

"Who's that girl that came to the Szechwan Gardens with us?"

"Talya. She's a friend from U of T, a med student."

"She looks at you kind of funny for a girl."

"What d'you mean, Ray?"

"Well, you know, like a guy might look."

"Really? Does she really look at me like that?"

"Yeah," Ray grinned, nodding his head. "I don't mean to pry, Dai Ling, but we've been friends all our lives, okay?"

"Don't ask me, Ray. I don't know. I'm so confused."

"How d'you know what I was going to ask you?"

"I just know. I know you too well, Ray. You're my best buddy and . . . well . . . promise me you won't tell anyone?"

"How can I promise when I don't know what you're going to tell me?"

"Oh Ray, just promise, okay?"

"I promise, Dai Ling, on the memory of Ozu. He died very young, you know, cancer of the throat."

"Ray, I think I'm falling in love . . . There, I've said it! But I'm not sure because it's never happened before. I keep thinking, 'Oh my god, what's happening to me' . . . all these feelings . . . "

"Like delicious melting chocolate ice cream feelings? Like a hot day on the tennis court, Dai Ling? Like last summer?"

"Well, not exactly, more like floating in the sky. She kissed me, Ray!"

"Oh my god!"

"Exactly. How could I ever tell my parents?"

"Don't tell them, Dai Ling. Look what happened to Mei Li when she married a white guy. My mom disowned her. She still won't speak to her and it's been two years. Talya's not only a rice ball, she's a girl!"

"D'you think I'm weird?"

"No way. Friends forever, Dai Ling, okay?" He punched the air and almost lost his balance in the snow.

"The thing is it's not just her. It's me. I called her, and I invited her to the concert, then I called her again . . . I'm not sure . . . but maybe she thinks I'm coming on to her."

"Dai Ling, you have to be honest with yourself. Forget about your parents. We're the next generation, so it's different for us. I might marry a white girl, and you might be . . . a lesbian."

"Oh, don't say it. I can't imagine telling my parents. They'll throw me out."

"They might. Don't tell them till you're sure. They'll get over it, and I promise to always be your friend, Dai Ling. You can share my room, no problem, okay?"

Dai Ling scooped up a handful of snow and threw it at him. The snowball caught him on the neck and Ray squealed as it melted under his collar. He chased after her as she turned the corner onto Gerrard and began running towards home. He took a flying tackle and brought her down with him into a snowbank. They lay there laughing and when Dai Ling recovered her breath she turned to Ray and said, "I love you like a brother, Ray. You can't imagine how good it is to be able to talk about this. I've been going crazy."

"You are kind of crazy, but I love you too. Your secret is safe with me."

~

Talya was waiting outside the Riverdale Library, perched at the top of the steps, when Dai Ling came out. "I thought you'd never come." She touched Dai Ling's shoulders, smiling, trying to contain the joy bubbling up in her.

"You look as though you have a bird in your mouth trying to escape," Dai Ling said and Talya laughed, revealing her mouth, pink and moist behind the whiteness of her teeth.

They linked arms and walked up Broadview like two old friends, familiar enough to be quiet with each other, savoring the weight of words hanging in the silence.

People waited for the streetcar. Others hurried by with bags of groceries, eager to get home for dinner. As the moon appeared behind the clouds, slowly flooding the slopes of the park, Dai Ling turned her face to the sky, caught by the moonlight. Talya watched the slight parting of her lips, the curve of her eyes. "I want to know you forever," she breathed, so quietly that she wasn't sure if Dai Ling had heard.

"Make a wish on the moon," Dai Ling said.

"I already did."

Dai Ling reached out and touched Talya's dark hair. She imagined the weight of it, let it drop in her mind. *Oh my god, what's happening to me?* Ray Lee's kisses had bothered her, making her feel like a cat, wanting to be stroked, bristling with annoyance at the same time. But Talya had ignited her.

It was a mystery. In the darkening silence she felt the lid closing. She heard the whispering of children above her. She waited for the first clod of earth. She knew there would be fear and then there would be music. She shivered suddenly and Talya gathered her in her arms and hugged her for what seemed like a long time, until they began to stamp their feet and jumped up and down, grounding the delight they stirred in each other.

"Let's go up to the Danforth," Talya said.

They walked slowly despite the cold night air, each intensely aware of the other's body, not wanting to break contact. When finally they sat facing each other across a small table in the window of the Second Cup, Dai Ling stirred way too much sugar into her hot chocolate, aware only of her foot touching Talya's. As her hands wrapped around her cup Talya's finger brushed against Dai Ling's right thumb. Their eyes met.

"The callous is from my bow, holding it for six hours a day."

Talya took her left hand and flattened it out in the palm of her own hand. She traced the lines there. "You have a long life line and a very strong heart line."

"Must be all those hawthorn-berry wafers I stole," Dai Ling laughed, trying to ignore the fire shooting through her body.

Talya touched the tips of her fingers, one by one, tracing tiny circles with her middle finger. Dai Ling's were calloused, patterned like contour maps of the earth.

"It's the pressure of my cello strings," Dai Ling said, barely breathing. Then, as Talya's finger spiralled into the palm of her hand, sending a thrill of arousal up her arm and shooting into her body, she pulled her hand away and took a gulp of hot chocolate. "When I first started playing my fingers were so sore. The callouses protect me."

"Your fingers are miraculous. They remember the notes of cello music written by all the great composers. Each fingertip is densely encoded with information. Imagine, your skin rising up in response to the music like a kind of genetic Braille, meeting the strings, allowing themselves to be read. I can almost hear the music as I touch your fingers."

"I never thought of it like that," Dai Ling said. "Sometimes I dream the most exquisite music. Well, it's not exactly music, it's more like a silent harmony, but I can feel it in my body — it's like all the sounds of the world — bird song, the wind, the oceans and rivers, everything together in a crazy harmony. In my dream I think, I must remember this and play it when I'm awake, but when I wake up everything's different, then I feel so disappointed and for a while I think that all our playing is just a shallow echo of that . . . heavenly music."

"That's what happens," Talya said, something dawning on her, "when you meet someone and they make you see things differently. They illuminate a part of you that's been in darkness. When I was in Padua . . . "

"With your Italian lover?"

"No," Talya laughed. "I was alone in the Caffé Pedrocchi . . . "

"Waiting for him?"

"No, not exactly, but waiting for something. Pedrocchi is a tourist trap, but I liked it. There was something about . . . the placement. I could see the big picture, with me like a dot on the map of Europe, moving from place to place, and there was a red flag in Padua, right by this coffee house. I crossed the street, diagonally, towards the right . . . "

"What was there?"

"Palazzo Del Bo. The faculty of Medicine at the university where Vesalius lectured. I didn't know anything about him at the time. I was just out of high school, didn't know what I was going to do with my life. I felt paralyzed by the array of choices. Then I walked into that big grey building with the stone-pillared courtyard. It didn't happen consciously, not like an idea resulting from a thought process, but when I walked out of there I knew I was going into medicine, not like something new, but like old knowledge that had suddenly been uncovered. I forgot about Vesalius. It was only when I found that book of illustrations and saw the picture of the operating theatre that I remembered."

"I've been remembering things too." Dai Ling wished Talya would touch her hand again. "Memories popping and crackling inside me, usually when I'm playing. The other day I saw my grandma and heard some strange music — it must have been from China — sounded like a lute. When we left, Ma wanted her to come with us, but she stayed in China waiting for my grandpa. I haven't seen her since I was two. Now it's too late."

"She died?" Dai Ling nodded. "Do you remember her?"

"I remember how big she was, like the whole world. I'd sit on her knee looking up and her face was like the moon inside a red cloud. But the clouds didn't move. They stayed around her always. I remember feeling so happy in her arms. She had soft round arms and when she laughed her whole body shook and the sound came out rich and throaty."

"What about your dad's parents?"

"He was separated from them when he was little. In Maoist China many families were separated when the parents were sent to work in the countryside. My dad went to live with his aunt in Beijing."

"Are you the only child?"

"Mm hmm."

"Me too."

"It's a big responsibility — they expect so much of us."

"Look, it's snowing again," said Talya.

Dai Ling stared out at the snow falling so softly. She felt as if she were inside one of those glass domes where everything is silent and watery, as though some great hand had shaken up her world and the snowflakes were settling around her now in all her newness.

"When's your audition?"

"In two weeks, just after New Year." Dai Ling took a deep breath. "I want more than anything to get into the youth orchestra."

"More than anything?"

"I want everything, Talya, but most I want . . . "

"What?"

"To really hear the music."

"But you're the one who plays the music."

"Something I haven't heard yet."

~

Brussels: July 1545

Anne van Hamme laboured in the dead of night, bringing the candlelit darkness to life with her noisy complaint while the midwife ministered to her, massaging the dome of her belly, mopping her brow. "Bear down, my love," she urged, her own brow shining with the sweat of her exertions. It had been a long labour and her brawny arms were streaked with blood and excrement. Anne seemed deaf to her entreaties, oblivious to all but the tearing within her body, and she screamed again.

Vesalius sat hunched in a corner. Despite his years of medical research, he felt unsure of his place in that room. *Whelping is women's domain. But this could be the answer to all my inquiry,* he thought. *Here, tonight, with the birth of my own child.* He sprang to his feet as Anne let out a curdling scream, and drew near to the bed in time to see blood spurting onto the sheet from her torn perineum. As ever he wondered at the force behind it, the force that expelled the red river from the body in pulsing jets. Her scream was followed by a long moan as the child crowned. The midwife scooped her hand under the wrinkled little face and pulled gently. Vesalius crouched, looking up through the crook of her elbow, his eyes sharp. A sudden gush of oily water splashed in his face, slithering into his eyes as he blinked. He saw a red bundle of limbs slide out of his wife's body, still sheathed in the membrane of its sac. *It's dead*, he thought and in the same instant the midwife yanked the creature, holding it by the ankles, and slapped its shrivelled buttocks. Then came the cry and his wife's answering cry as she lifted her arms.

"A girl! A lusty little girl!" exclaimed the midwife and she plopped the baby down on Anne's breast where it nosed for her nipple.

If she was dead when the midwife pulled her out and the Soul entered her or awoke within her when the midwife slapped her flesh, then ... He could not think. He felt a stirring within, drawing his mind away from its wondering. He shook his head and resumed ... *then the Soul is part of the body, but animated, unlike the other organs, with the ability to be outside and enter, or to leave when the body is dead like the Souls of my cadavers when I feel them hovering, uncertain where to go. Or perhaps the Soul lies dormant in the unborn, playing dead, waiting for the slap as a signal to inhabit the flesh, or ...* All of a sudden he was overcome with a fury and frustration which caused him to beat his bulging forehead on the bedpost.

"Oh, husband!" exclaimed Anne, looking up in adoration, seeing her Andreas in the ecstasy of fatherhood, "Our little girl!"

Vesalius, his brow throbbing, surrendered to the insistence within as he gazed in wonder upon his wife and child.

"My beloved," he said, "Oh, my beloved!"

They celebrated baby Anne's birth with the remains of the winter wine during a rare storm in the dogstar days of July. Rain cascaded into the dry earth. The baby lay cooing in her cradle as Vesalius and his wife recalled the harsh winter of her confinement spent huddled by a spitting fire of frosty wood, or shivering in the kitchen as she instructed the new cook and tended Griet, the parlour maid whose chilblained feet turned blue as wine froze in the barrels and was chipped off by the flagon with an axe.

"You have worked a miracle, my love," beamed Vesalius, glowing with fatherly pride. "Drink, my beloved, never-to-be-sufficiently-praised wife," he tipped the warm cup to her lips, "to replenish your blood."

Red wine drizzled down Anne's chin as she basked in her husband's effusiveness, listening to her baby gurgling contentedly. She seemed to be exactly where she wished to be with no nostalgia for the Heavens, an odd child, singularly pleased with her condition. Vesalius brought his wife invigorating conserves, flagons of barley water mixed with syrup of citron, for she had a voracious thirst. He made bugloss water, drawn from the red roots of the oxtongue, and fed it to her for her blood. He dandled the baby, already a week old, and gazed on the tiny mystery of her. He waxed amorous with Anne, but she laughed a deep throaty laugh, held the baby to her breast and pushed him away.

"Not with my parts in their ragged condition, Andreas. You must wait for their healing. Go on now, go on," and she shooed him away and snuggled into the bed covers with her new baby.

~

Nicholas Kulikovsky sat at his wife's bedside, his face drawn with sleeplessness, afraid that if he slept she would slip away from him. Katya was peaceful, her hands curled around the edge of the white sheet, gripping it loosely. He leaned towards her, listening for her breath, which rattled suddenly through her exhausted body, sour and pungent. Her chest heaved, then subsided, and Nick sighed, relieved. He leaned down and kissed her cheek, filmed with a salty dampness which clung to his lips. He imagined himself licking her all over, like an animal grooming its mate, absorbing and defusing her sickness. He took her hand in his and kissed each finger tip, then rubbed the bristle of his chin into her palm. Their charmed life had come to this, a bedside vigil in a white room in a foreign country. They had always been together since that first moment when he had walked across the room and whispered in her ear. It had been a risk and for a moment his heart had stopped as she'd stared into his eyes, then she'd thrown back her head and laughed, her white throat trembling. "No one's ever thrown me that line before," she'd said, and he'd known he was home. A smile stretched his mouth painfully as he remembered, but without her seeing it what use was a smile? What use was anything? A determination rose in him to keep her alive, to believe in a future. Nothing else was conceivable. He stroked Katya's sleeping face and reached for the phone.

She answered on the first ring. "Dai Ling?"

"Talya, is that you?"

"Oh, Dad, I'm sorry, I thought . . . "

"Oh Natáshenka, will you come?"

"I can't. I'm on a six week rotation at the General."

"Don't you have time off for Christmas?"

"No, Dad. I can't come, really. There's a huge snowstorm and all the planes are grounded."

"We're in the depths of winter here too. Only a few days till Christmas. Darkness falls so early . . . "

"You said there was bad news. Can you bring her home? There's a Chinese doctor I've met who might be able to help."

Nick stared down at Katya's pale face. He felt her listening, her eyes moving back and forth under thin, blue-veined lids.

"Dad, can I talk to her?"

"She's sleeping."

"Shall I call again later?"

"No, no, you'll disturb her."

"What do the doctors say?"

Nick turned away from the bed and whispered into the receiver. "They're not hopeful, Natáshenka, but if we can keep her alive until spring I know she'll get better. I'll bring her home and she'll sit out in the garden when it's warm. You know how she loves her garden."

"The white patio rose bloomed until the snow came."

"I'll tell her. She'll like that. Take care of yourself, darling. I'll give her your love when she wakes."

Nick put the phone down, then reached towards a vase of red roses on the bedside table and caressed the softness of a drooping petal with the tip of his finger. He ran his thumb and index finger down the long pale stem, manoeuvering around thorns which seemed to pulse with all the life and beauty of the flower, protecting it. He pressed his thumb into a large thorn, held it there, watched his blood well around it, trickling down the sappy stem. "Your life is there, Katya. I should never have brought you here. Forgive me, my darling. Don't leave me, Katya, Katya, Katyushenka, don't leave me . . . "

When Talya left the hospital that night she felt so exhausted she almost hailed a cab, then she remembered that she was supposed to meet Elliott. She glanced at her watch and started walking, heading east on Carlton, past Maple Leaf Gardens and across Jarvis, trudging through deep snow. The snowfall that had begun so gently as she and Dai Ling sat together on the Danforth had continued for three days, silencing the city and cloaking it in a thick blanket of whiteness. She walked through Allen Gardens to the botanical solarium, a Victorian glasshouse surrounded by overhanging trees, their branches weighted down with snow. She stamped her feet, watching a couple of drunks passed out on a park bench, one of them still clinging to his bottle. It was Christmas Eve and all Talya wanted was to get some sleep. She was on duty again the next day.

As she entered the vaulting glass structure a rich mushroomy smell rose from the debris-covered earth and her body began to relax, lulled by the humid warmth. Mulched pathways snaked through the solarium, flanked by banana palms. There were benches at intervals, and when Talya sat under a cloud of flowering jasmine to wait for Elliott a tiger swallowtail butterfly landed on her hand and caressed her with its furred yellow wing as she watched, her mouth curving into a smile, almost languid in the depth of winter. She closed her eyes and saw her mother's face, always that face, waiting for her to surrender to sleep, then haunting her dreams. *It's your body, you must know. Send me a sign, say something!* Her eyelids fluttered, teased by light reflecting off the snow.

She remembered walking with her mother on Bloor Street, a sharp autumn day, shopping for clothes for her trip to Europe. *Why doesn't she just give me the money?* she'd thought. *But no, she insists we go shopping to fulfil her fantasy of the kinds of things mothers and daughters do together.* The wind had blown in her face. She'd felt crabby, irritated, something cramping her spirit. And when Katya had taken her arm and steered her into Holt Renfrew she'd wanted to shake her off and run. Admittedly Katya had exquisite taste. It was she who had found the magenta silk blouse, the one that had become significant to Talya, the one she had worn in Padua. She remembered the hot lights in the changing room, the sickly blend of perfume and sweat. "How's it going in there, darling? Come out and let me see you." Pulling back the curtain — the gushing shop assistant, Katya's shining eyes — she'd felt twelve years old again, holding her breath, waiting for it to be over, waiting to grow up. She had never been able to yield to her mother despite her best intentions. Always, at the last minute, she drew up short, gagging, like

Corky at a fence that was just too high, then standing there, chewing on the bit, filled with regret.

There was Elliott, waving through the misted glass. He burst through the door with that energy that never seemed to desert him.

"Is this the Hawaiian Lounge? May I join you? Oh thank you, I'll have a Missionary's Downfall with triple rum," he said, waltzing towards her, twirling an imaginary cane. "And for the lady, a Zombie," he said, addressing an invisible waiter. Talya smiled weakly as he leaned down to kiss her cheek. "Come on, sweetie, let's get you out of here. You look exhausted."

"You should have seen me when I came off duty. I'm about fifty percent recovered already."

"Well thank the Goddess I didn't arrive early. Only She knows what kind of wreck I would have found. Come on, Tal, we need a drinkie-poo. After all, 'tis the season to be merry!" Elliott strong-armed her out of the solarium and across Allen Gardens to Carlton Street. "How about a taste of the grape?"

"I need a scotch."

They walked west on Carlton to where it turns into College and went into the Bunch of Grapes, a pub which Elliott frequented. He ushered Talya into a corner booth with red velvet banquettes and ordered. Despite their mutually exclusive sexual orientation, he always played the gentleman with her, as though they were out on a sixties retro date. It satisfied his theatrical leanings.

"God, I don't think I can handle another day of Emerg."

"You're on tomorrow, eh?"

"*And* Boxing Day."

Elliott turned to her with raised eyebrows. "Why don't you take Christmas off like everybody else?"

"'Cause I'm doing an elective, like *you* did last year," Talya said pointedly. "Keeps us busy, doesn't it?"

"But not this year. I've got plans," he said smugly.

"Going home for Christmas?"

"Are you kidding? Stuffed turkey with mashed guilt smothered in goopy gravy love? No thanks, sweetheart. I'm shacking up for a couple days R and R."

"With whom?"

"Lawrence, with a 'w', my dear."

"Is he cute?"

"A Greek god no less, with a truly immortal hard-on!"

"I'm jealous."

Elliott threw his hands up in mock surprise. "You're not going straight, darling?"

Talya laughed and leaned across the table. "I could never take a man seriously," she said and kissed Elliott on the mouth.

"Neither can I. That's my problem. Now how about some serious drinking?"

A couple of times when he'd been drunk Elliott had talked with Talya about his sado-masochistic sex play — "It's like wrestling, darling, looks dangerous, but it's so theatrical, and we do have rules." Talya never raised the topic; she left that to him.

"Cheers, Elliott. Happy Christmas."

"Oxymoron." They clinked glasses and drank, then he pulled out his *kama sutra* enamelled cigarette case and flipped it at her.

"You know I don't."

"Oh, but I love to offer," he said, taking a cigarette and lighting it with a flourish. "And who knows, you might change your mind one day and give me an embolism. Don't you love that word? Emmm-boooh-lismm."

"I don't know how you can smoke, Elliott, after the lungs we've seen."

"But I'm immortal, don't you know?"

"You're impossible," Talya laughed.

"That's what they all tell me, but honestly, Tal, I just have to live in the moment. What's the point of being a good boy and denying myself a few little pleasures when we really don't know what's going to happen. Maybe there is no future. Let's face it, the planet's a mess. I buy ciggies with the money I save on life insurance. How is she?" he asked without skipping a beat.

"No news."

"Is good news, right?"

"Right." Talya gulped her scotch.

"Another?"

"You don't miss a trick, do you?" Elliott signalled to the waiter. "No, Ellie, I must go home," Talya said abruptly, fumbling for her coat.

"Expecting a call from your dad?" he asked, frowning.

"The time difference is impossible. I won't be able to talk to him again until my day off."

"So you did talk?" His hand was on Talya's arm, restraining her. She nodded. "And? Come on, tell me, what's going on? You were such a zombie on rounds the other day. I've been worrying about you, Tal."

"Oh Elliott," she exclaimed, trying to pull away, "this is like an episode from a hospital soap opera . . . "

"Don't run away," he said, gripping her arm harder.

"Dad wants me to go to Geneva."

"Are you going?"

"You know I can't! Don't look at me like that, I hate you. Look at the weather, it's dreadful, the airport's closed down."

"Have you talked to her?"

"What's the point? She'd be incoherent. The drugs . . . Anyway, he won't let me."

"Did you hear about the woman with acute angina?"

"No, what about her?"

"Nice little titties too."

"Oh Ellie, get your Lawrence with a 'w' to teach you some new tricks."

"Tricks I got. Jokes I'm short on, given our long association. How about the new girlfriend? Do we have a ray of sunshine there?"

"She's doing Christmas with her parents and their neighbours. Don't know why. They're all Chinese."

"You know the immigrants, got to fit in, more Canadian than the beaver. But you didn't tell me how it's going."

"It's going . . . good. She's the only spark in my life right now . . . apart from you."

"Why, thank you."

"Even though your jokes are corny as hell."

"You know I'm always here for you, Tal. If there's anything . . . *anything* . . . all you have to do is call. You have my pager number, right?"

"Of course," she laughed.

"I'm on duty New Year's Eve *and* New Year's Day, can you imagine? Hangover City!"

"People don't come to Emerg with hangovers, Elliott."

"But I might. Not to mention all the alcohol-related violence. Split noses, blackened eyes, women dragged screaming from their kitchens . . . "

"Home is where the heart is."

"Multiple bruisings and shattered femurs, drivers hauled unconscious from the mangled wreckage of their vehicles. Oh, the holidays are such fun."

"You old cynic." She gave him a high five and he grasped her hand and kissed it. "Dai Ling's a lucky girl. But wait till she tells her parents, then the chopsticks will fly."

"I've already met them. They're wonderful people. I'm sure we'll work it out."

"Gay rights are not part of Chinese culture, my dear. Can you imagine, Gay Pride in Tiananmen Square? Gay life was completely underground in China until a few years ago."

"Hey, Elliott, reality check. This is Canada. Since when were you so political, anyway?"

"Well, maybe I'm a closet activist. People do change you know. Especially when you've been through what I've been through."

"What d'you mean?"

"Oh sweetheart, you don't have time," he said, rolling his eyes dramatically.

"Elliott, I always have time for you," Talya stared him down, "Tell me what you've been through."

He opened his mouth and took a deep breath, then he took a gulp of his drink and rattled on, "I've been through *all* the boys at Woody's, and at the Lub Lounge. I really have to find a new bar to frequent. This town is just too small for me, Tal. Did I ever tell you about . . . ?"

"Look, I really have to go, Elliott. I'm exhausted. And Ruby's alone in the house. She'll be starving."

"Omigod, poor little pooch, I see a front page sob story . . . 'Young medical student devoured by starving chihuahua on Christmas Eve!'"

"She's not a chihuahua, you idiot!" Talya laughed heartily, relaxed finally by the whisky and the festive atmosphere of the pub.

"No, no, the drinks are on me," Elliott said, pushing back the ten dollar bill she'd laid on the table. "I'm feeling expansive tonight. Did I say expensive? Oh, I hope the Ontario minister of health is listening. Take it easy, sweetheart, only two more days then you can crash."

~

The thrummed strings of a perfectly pitched instrument vibrated through the deserted basement of the Johnson Building; Dai Ling, practising for her audition. The strains of the *Elgar Concerto* echoed in the silence and entered the circles of sound that kept the planets spinning. The deep tone of her open C string vibrated through the silenced world of the immortal Beethoven, whose genius circled the universe, setting the spheres spinning in the cosmos, each sphere a circle of fifths, crossed by a ladder of seven — the octave, forever climbing, repeating itself, circled by its own twelve tones.

As Dai Ling played she imagined fissioning circles dissected by ladders climbing to the Heavens where a belt of twelve zodiac signs mapped the path of seven classical spheres . . . Moon, Mercury, Venus, Sun, Mars, Jupiter, Saturn . . . each sphere turning to its own rhythm, planets creating the harmony and dissonance of the Heavens, resonating in each creature, a microcosmic part of the whole, like DNA, perfect, ordered, a great puzzle holding the sentient world together, struggling for freedom in an indestructible web.

When she left the building, darkness had fallen and the streetlights cast their peculiar glow on the whitened world. But the music was everywhere, a suffusion of color in the sky, the trees, on the tall buildings, the memory of it in her body, a muscle that moved her fingers obsessively — the music would not be stopped.

Dai Ling dodged her way through crowds of Christmas shoppers, half expecting to bump into Talya. Even in the rare moments when she wasn't thinking of her consciously, Talya was there, hovering, entering unbidden into her music. They talked on the phone and their voices wove a cocoon that held them in torturous restraint.

"I can't meet you. I'm waiting for my dad to call."

"I can't come. I have to practise."

"I can't, I'm on late shift at the hospital."

When they did meet Dai Ling's skin tingled, prescient. Was it nerves about her audition or anticipation of something more? She was beginning to feel uncomfortable in her own house, as though she were leading a double life. And yet nothing had happened, only a kiss. *It probably meant nothing to Talya. Is that what girls do, kiss each other casually?* The thought of kissing Celia Quan or Dee Dee Chong like that made her giggle. Christie had warned her about Talya, said she was a flirt, but Dai Ling didn't quite trust Christie. She wished she could talk to Ray again, but lately he never seemed to be home. She grew tired of her uncertainty and played the *Elgar* in her head as the subway screamed eastwards.

Toronto, gripped by winter, slept through a silent Christmas and into the new year. The mouths of angels in cemeteries all over the city froze in silent circles, their wings stiff with ice, eyes glazed, ears deaf to all but the memory of vibration.

Katya's garden was obliterated by the snow. Humped bushes loomed around the house, turning blue in the afternoon shadows; every branch of every tree was weighted with hardening snow, encased with ice as night closed in.

Talya had thought she would escape Christmas by working through it, but when she returned from the hospital on Christmas night the weight of it descended on her. Not even Ruby's disproportionate welcome, her crazed dash through the snow, biting and barking at it, could lift Talya's spirit. She lit a small fire in the living room and sat before it, hostage to her memories of all the lonely Christmases. *It's something in me,* she thought. *Something wrong with me.*

She'd bought herself a gift — a *Classic CD Cello Special*, which included a track of the *Elgar Concerto* played by Jaqueline du Pré. As she listened she closed her eyes and saw Dai Ling playing; how could she not? The music perfectly expressed her feeling of passionate desolation. Talya had confidence in her own staying power despite the depth of her discontent, because it was a dynamic discontent that she suffered, and she was caught in it, a fly in a web of curiosity, struggling until the end. She read in the CD notes that Elgar had composed the *Cello Concerto* in 1919 while in the throes of despair following the first world war. He'd been hospitalized for a tonsillectomy and as he came around from the anesthetic after the operation he wrote down the melody that would become the first theme of the concerto. Talya wondered where the music came from and why it was that she heard it during the post-mortem. Was it something to do with the opening of the body, the heart's reaction to assault?

1547: Brussels

IT WAS NOT AS ANNE HAD imagined it would be, their life together. Aside from a sometimes intrusive passion for his work, Andreas had been wholly hers, but since the baby came something had changed. It was as though they had stepped apart even though in reality Andreas was frequently at her side, his hands upon her. He held her close through the sleepy nights and honoured her with his body as a husband should. And yet she felt a sense of loss, yes, that was it, she felt that she had lost Andreas. Not that he had changed, but perhaps *she* had, with the birth of her child. She blamed herself but failed to understand of what she was guilty. *Doesn't a woman alter with the birth of a child? Do all men stay the same?* Sometimes she felt that their life together existed only in the darkness of their bodies, moles tunnelling and rooting in the night. It was difficult to reconcile night with day, her puzzled husband with the man who entered her body and completed her then fled, a fugitive, while his body remained.

One evening in the parlour she looked up from her embroidery and caught him staring at her with a puzzled expression.

"What is it, Andreas?"

"Nothing, my love."

She rose and crossed the parlour, her full skirt swaying. She sat next to him on their tapestried loveseat and lifted her hand to his furrowed brow. He grasped her wrist and held her.

"Now I have you. Mine."

She laughed and nestled into him like a bird puffing its feathers out for the night, luxuriating in the closeness of him, the manly smell of him mixed with the pungent herbs and spirits he used in his Physic. "I've been too caught up with my baby," she said.

"No longer a baby. Annie is walking now. And she is weaned." His hands cupped her breasts, lifting the weight of them, kneading. "I will not miss the soured milk of our bedsheets. How you sprayed in the height of your pleasure, my wife."

Anne blushed, but her throaty laugh revealed her.

"Perhaps you will conceive again now that your milk has dried."

"Do you want another child, Andreas?"

"But of course. I want a son."

"Isn't our daughter sufficient?" She feared another child might increase their distance.

"A man must have a son to carry on his work. I walk in the footsteps of my father and he in the footsteps of his."

"But yours are larger." The blood had subsided, leaving her pale as Andreas continued, seemingly oblivious.

"Yes, and our son will walk larger and taller. We live in an age of expansion. *Plus ultra*, yet further. There are no limits, Anne, to what a man can do."

His spark had returned, but she felt strangely empty. *I must try harder*, she thought. *As Andreas flares I fade, yet in our bed we flame together.* Her spirit rebelled against the separation.

Xian Ming was bent over the kitchen table chopping vegetables when Dai Ling arrived home. She wiped her hands nervously on her apron, picked up a long white envelope and handed it to Dai Ling.

"It came already?"

Xian Ming nodded, her eyes fixed on Dai Ling's face. She'd been restraining herself all day from peeking at the letter.

"Oh no, I've been dreading this. Are you sure it's from them? It's only a week since the audition."

"Come on, be brave, Dai Ling. I know it'll be good news."

They hovered over the envelope as though it were a bomb, then Dai Ling tore at it and pulled out the letter. She opened it, holding her breath, then a sudden inhalation and tears in her eyes. "They accepted me! Oh Ma, they accepted me!" She threw her arms around her tall mother and they danced around the kitchen.

"I knew it!" Xian Ming shouted, "My clever daughter is a member of the National Youth Orchestra of Canada! How proud your grandma would be. Her own country."

"I can't believe it, Ma. I've wanted this for such a long time."

"It's just the beginning of a big career, Dai Ling. I'm so proud of you. Wait till your father gets home. His face will crack with smiling."

"The adjudicators looked so stern after I finished playing, especially on the Boccherini. I thought they didn't like my interpretation."

"I guess they were impressed. Remember how we started with the Suzuki when you were four years old? We went every week for your lesson and the teacher showed me how to help you at home, learning repetition, rhythm and phrasing. And it's all lead to this!"

Dai Ling hugged her tight. "Thank you, Ma, for giving me my music and helping me to play."

"Only until you were seven, then you left me behind. I couldn't help you any more."

"Ma," Dai Ling said, sitting at the kitchen table, pouring herself a cup of tea. "I know the reason you didn't go to visit Grandma was because you had to pay for my lessons."

"No, no!" Xian Ming leaned on the table, supporting herself with her hands. "Your Babá was still training to be a doctor and money was tight. Once he was established we had to save our money for this house. So many times I asked your grandma to come to Canada, but she wrote to me and said, 'I'm waiting here for your father. I cannot leave my country.' I always intended to go back and see her."

"Never mind, Ma. Maybe one day we'll all go back to China together—you and me and Babá."

"Come on, you can drink tea later. I have something for you."

Xian Ming took Dai Ling's hand and led her down the corridor to the front room where the orchid bloomed in the window with the gardenia and the jade plant. She picked up a small box from the table and gave it to her. Dai Ling opened the box and stared at the jade bracelet inside.

"Oh Ma!" she breathed, "It was Grandma's."

"And your great grandma's. Now it's yours. It's time."

"Tell me the story again."

As she spoke, Xian Ming lifted the thin bracelet and slipped it over Dai Ling's left wrist. "In China the funerary jade is very important. This bracelet was worn by many generations of your female ancestors and it contains their essence. When your great grandma died she was wearing this jade and it was buried with her. After seven years they dug up her bones and reclaimed the jade. After many generations we believe that if you put it under the light you will see the blood of your ancestors."

Dai Ling held her wrist under the lamplight. The translucent jade seemed to glow with a dull red hue.

"There must always be someone to burn incense for the ancestors or they will be lost and will wander the underworld without a home."

"But Grandma Geneviève was Canadian."

"It doesn't matter. She came to China and mixed her blood with a Chinese man — my father. He gave her this bracelet which had belonged to his mother and to her mother and grandmother. I remember my Ma wearing this bracelet all those years, waiting for my father to come home. It is the wearing of it that gives the essence. And the mixing of blood. Blood is life, Dai Ling. When we left China she gave me this bracelet and she told me to give it to you one day. Maybe she knew that she wouldn't see us again."

"Did you tell Babá you were going to give it to me today?"

"I didn't know until that envelope came. Besides, this is women's business."

"But your dad gave it to Grandma."

"That's true. Lucky for us, Dai Ling, that he was crazy enough to break the rules," she laughed. "I made a special dinner, a Szechwan dish — pork with sesame paste and flower pepper, spicy-hot, the way you like."

"Mmm, delicious. I must phone Talya and tell her the good news. And Christie, I wonder if she got in, and Sylvie . . . "

"Don't talk for hours. Your Babá will be home soon and we'll eat."

The answering machine blinked at her as she opened her bedroom door. She knew it was Talya and a tremor of anticipation rippled through her. She pressed her finger into the red eye and the tape rewound briefly. *Please come. Something terrible has happened.* She dialled Talya's number. The phone rang four times then the message came. *Kulikovsky residence. You know what to do.* She played the message again . . . *something terrible . . . please come.*

"Oh no, what can I do? I'm so scared."

When Dai Ling arrived she found the front door unlocked. She walked in and immediately Ruby bounded into the hall, barking and wagging her tail, jumping at her.

"Talya! Talya, where are you?" Dai Ling called as she hunkered down, hugging Ruby, burying her face in warm red fur. The house was still and silent. Everything was dark, only a pool of light on the telephone table. She ran upstairs and searched the rooms, a sense of foreboding rising in her as she raced downstairs to the kitchen. A steady hum of electricity filled the air; the overhead stove light was on, shedding a half light on the gleaming white refrigerator. Dai Ling opened it and stood in the cold light staring at saran-wrapped packages lying on metal rungs, vegetables and fruits blurred by the glass cover of the crisper, bottles of colored liquids. A faint haze of frost floated like mist, causing her to shiver and slam the door. Suddenly she knew. She headed for the back door and bolted across the grass, Ruby at her heels, past the tennis courts and the orchard, towards the stables, pulling at the door of Limerick's stall, breathing fast, heart racing. Talya was huddled in the corner of the stable.

"What happened?" Her arms around her gently. "Tell me what happened."

Talya looked at Dai Ling as though she were a stranger. "It's too late," she said.

"Too late for what?"

"It's too late for me to go to Geneva." Her voice was flat. "My father's on his way back with her body."

"Oh Talya, I'm so sorry."

For a moment it seemed as though Talya might weep. Then she pulled back suddenly.

"She's dead!" she shouted, "She's dead, she's dead!" and she laughed, an ugly desperate sound, bouncing off the closed walls of the stable.

Dai Ling grasped her shoulders. "Stop, Talya, stop!" Without thinking, she slapped her face. After a moment of shocked silence Talya started shaking. Dai Ling held her shivering body and pulled her up.

"Come on. I'm taking you to the house. You can't stay here. It's too cold."

Ruby was shut in the stable. She jumped at the door and the top part swung open as her paws hit. She jumped again and again, but it was too high for her to clear. She lay down in the musty old straw, head on paws, then raised her muzzle and sniffed the air, searching for Talya's scent. Ruby carried the history of the earth in her unassuming nose. She lived through it; she relied on it. She could scent a charged cluster of emotion fifty feet away and a cat from half a furlong; she could sense the earliest tremor of a minor quake or a fit of existential angst; she could detect the aroma of barbecued chicken three blocks away. The whiskers on her muzzle quivered now and her body tensed as though held for the chase. She leapt up and rose on her hind legs, nosing the top of the lower door, then she threw her body at it, over and over, rattling the bolt until, with a mighty leap she rose in the air, her claws scrabbling at the edge of the locked door, and she was over, her belly grazed and splintered, flying across the grass towards the house. She was a red streak of rippling silk, a memory of wings fluttering at her legs as they scissored towards the Kulikovsky house. Nose to the ground, she rounded the corner and sniffed in circles till she arrived at the back door. It was closed. She snuffled along the edge of it, whining and whimpering. She jumped back impatiently, her snout quivering in the frost-bitten air, and barked, a short, sharp bark. She barked again, she craved and crept, belly to the ground, then she sat back on her haunches and howled.

In her dream Talya sat in a pool of sunlight after a long, long journey. She was in her mother's house and Katya sat on the other side of the room. Talya laid her arms on the table in front of her and cradled her head. Katya crossed the room and stood behind her, and Talya lifted her head and lay back in her arms, pulled back, overcome by a weight that threatened to suffocate her. She couldn't breathe; she was dragged backwards by a deep undertow until she had no breath left to exhale and still it held her, blind, deaf, unable to speak. She was dying in her mother's arms, and then she woke to a howling and found herself in Dai Ling's arms.

"It's Ruby. I have to go let her in."

"I'll go." Dai Ling was already up, shrugging Talya's robe over her nakedness.

Talya watched her cross the room, her small bare feet padding down the corridor. The miracle of Dai Ling was still tingling through her body as the terrible knowledge of Katya's death began seeping into her mind, unacceptable, unbelievable, mixed with the remnants of her dream. A shadow had escaped her drowning body, and it floated in her mind now, on a long cord into the sky. And then, oh yes, it had dropped to the ground, she'd heard it in the corridor outside, crawling with an ancient crablike motion, a newborn creature like an old man, desiring its passionate life. It had passed through the closed door of her room, risen above the bed, hovering there, then she'd been part of it, watching herself cradled in Dai Ling's arms, an extraordinary light emanating from their separate skins, forming a caul surrounding them like a third skin.

Ruby leapt onto the bed and licked Talya's face, her feathery tail brushing Dai Ling's leg. Talya ruffled the thick fur of her neck and the dog growled with pleasure, her growl becoming a whine of surrender as she rolled on her back between the two women.

"Her fur's so cold. How long did we sleep?"

"Not long," Dai Ling replied. "It's 9:30. I just called Ma and told her I'm staying over, okay?"

"How could I possibly let you go now?"

"I've never done this before," Dai Ling said shyly, still unable to believe what had happened.

"You're a natural," Talya laughed, then Ruby lunged at her, big pink tongue lolling from her mouth, and began licking Talya's swollen eyes. "Come on, Ruby, get down," she said with an edge of impatience, pushing her off the bed as she reached with her other arm for Dai Ling.

Talya's mouth found Dai Ling's, the fleshy beak of her lip swelling as she kissed her. Through half-closed eyes she saw the blur of Dai Ling's face, felt the soft yielding of her flesh, like a flower opening, and a confusion of pain and desire welled in her. A shifting shape dove into the kaleidoscopic patterning that surrounded them, lovers floating in a slow-moving river which surged and pulled and held them under, then tossed them into the air gasping. Talya travelled across a moving mountain range rising from a desert wasteland. A creature yelped and bayed its bitter desire as the earth swelled and heaved, revealing a cave with walls curved in a circle, shaping, holding generations. Like a mouth shocked open the cave gaped, then with a mighty sigh it closed on the creature, one with the pulsating universe. Talya twitched in her sleep as the hungry creature grovelled, filled with desire without the means to fulfil it; waiting at the open window, looking onto a bleak landscape, knowing it was the end of an endless existence; knowing that no one would ever come, yet crippled with eternal belief in face of the impossible.

Ruby raised her muzzle and licked Talya's hand, then she stretched out and rolled on her back, front legs pointing heavenwards, back legs splayed in abandon. She wriggled her body, swaying back and forth, nose and tail inching together, until she formed a red circle covering the pages of the big book, open at Plate 64; a drawing of the heart with covering peeled back and lungs flowering around it like petals, its volume depicted in darkened cross-hatching, the sturdy root of the vena cava rising above its eternal beating. Within the red circle of her body Ruby harboured a hunched creature dreaming a perfect world. A tear slipped from the corner of its eye, releasing the creature in baying bliss, circling the dog as rings of sound circle the spheres. The sleeping Ruby thumped her tail to the rhythm of the creature's black heart.

It was a dead man who ascended the steps of the aircraft, his wife sealed in her coffin in the belly of a monstrous bird. Nick heard nothing as the engines roared, felt nothing as they sped down the runway and were thrust into the sky. He sat insensible in his window seat, his grey temples beating with an enormous desire to return, to change the course of what had occurred.

The rain drove in horizontal lines, which were erased as they reached an altitude where everything evaporates and inspiration bursts the lungs. He dozed a while and sensed something floating, darkness tugging its shrunken mind in circles of longing to return to earth. *Once launched there is no going back*, he heard, a faint voice drawn away from him to a place where everything becomes its opposite. A cord tumbled, coiling on itself, shadows of rain-lines criss-crossing, erasing the sky which became a cave of paralyzing proportion, the blush of dawn creeping up its distant walls.

He was woken by someone shaking his arm as they came in to land at Pearson International. He had forgotten that he was alone and turned to Katya. When he saw a stranger sitting next to him a fresh wave of grief assaulted him and he turned his face shamefully to the bleak window and stared down at the rapidly approaching earth, veined with rivers curving underground through a gridlock of tiny streets lined with toy buildings. *Let us slam into them*, he prayed. *I cannot begin again. I cannot, I am caught, there's no way out.*

"Dad, you have to eat something."

"I never imagined I'd be coming back without her."

"Did you eat on the plane?"

"That garbage? No thanks." Nick poured himself another shot of Stolichnaya and plunked the bottle down on the kitchen table.

"I could order in. Haven't had time to get groceries. I've been working in Emergency at the General. They've given me a week's leave. Oh Dad, I wish I could have seen her, to say goodbye."

"We could arrange for the casket to be opened . . ."

"No, no, Dad, I mean before, when she was . . . I'm so sorry I didn't come."

"It's better that you didn't. She wouldn't have wanted you to see her the way she was at the end."

"I called Uncle Vassily. He's arriving early tomorrow."

"Riva?"

"Can't come."

"Thank god." He poured another shot of vodka. "You know, your mother and I, we had our own world. We didn't need anyone, only you, our blood."

"Uncle Vassily's blood."

"But I can't stand his wife and her snivelling kids."

"You haven't seen them for years. They've grown up. We must phone people, Dad, and tell them."

Nick shook his head. "I can't. I can't do it."

"Give me a list. I'll do it."

"I can't think."

"Just give me your address book and I'll call everyone." Her eyes shone with that strange animation that fuels people through crises. "Dad, the funeral's the day after tomorrow. There's no time to waste."

He fumbled in his pocket and handed over a tattered address book.

"The funeral home's arranging refreshments," Talya continued, heading for the hall, "And they're dealing with the notice. It'll be in the *Globe* and the *Star* tomorrow."

"Thanks, darling. I couldn't have coped with all those decisions alone," he called after her. *She's so like her mother, always coping. I was the weak one, the one who felt everything for both of us.* Moments later he heard her voice, a steady repetition which soon became unbearable. He poured himself another vodka to take upstairs. As he passed Talya in the hallway she glanced up and for a moment he thought she might hang up the phone and take him in her arms, then she turned her attention back to the long list of friends and acquaintances about whom he gave not a damn. He realized he had become a liability to his daughter, his only child.

As he reached the top of the stairs he had a wild hope that Katya might be sitting up in bed waiting for him, as though the whole thing had been a horrible nightmare and she would take him in her arms and they would laugh about it. He paused, savouring the possibility, almost believing he could make it happen with the power of his desire. He opened the door and a rush of cold air greeted him. His suitcase stood next to Katya's where he had placed them when they had come home from the funeral parlour in the afternoon. They had gone there straight from the airport, never thinking that it would take all day, that there could be so many hidden questions in dealing with one body, already embalmed and hermetically sealed in the presence of the Swiss consul. "You must conform with international policy regarding public sanitation on a public carrier," he had said in his lilting tongue.

Nick lifted the case gently and placed it on their bed. He snapped the locks and opened the lid until it gaped, bouncing on its hinges, an old-fashioned case. *Katya doesn't like zippers.* Each time he thought of her she still existed, then the dreadful knowledge of her passing countered him, his heart stopped, his breath froze, and he was suspended, a dead thing living. Nick sat on the bed and lifted out her garments. He slid back the mirrored door of the clothes closet and hung them one by one; garments folded and packed by Katya's hands, Katya's fingerprints all over them, all over him forever. Her perfume filled the room as the thin garments were unfolded, releasing their memory of the only woman who had ever worn them. Her sudden laughter shocked him. It was Talya, laughing on the phone, her laughter just like Katya's. Nick slammed the door and wept. He wanted more than anything to be alone, to continue his communion with Katya. He could not think of the future; it had been erased with her death. When he imagined the funeral and all the people, his brother, their friends, he felt sick. He buried his face in her nightgown, the one she had left under the pillow before they'd flown to Geneva with high hopes.

When Vassily arrived in a taxi Talya was at the door to meet him. She almost cried when she saw him, but she caught herself, rigid in his embrace as his hands gripped her ribs through the thin fabric of her blouse. The collar of his wool coat was rough and scratchy on her cheek and he smelled of cigarette smoke.

"Aren't you cold? It's freezing in here."

"I can turn the heat up. Uncle Vassily, you have to help me. Dad's in terrible shape."

"That's what I was afraid of. Where is he?"

"Upstairs. He's been up all night, drinking."

Vassily shook his head. "I'm so sorry, Talya. I feel . . . responsible somehow because I . . . "

"Uncle Vassily, I've learned enough about medicine to know that doctors are not responsible for everything."

They looked at each other a moment, then she stroked his face like a lover, a complicity between them.

"How about some breakfast?" he asked. "I'm starving."

"Scrambled eggs? Bacon?"

"Sounds good," he nodded and she disappeared into the kitchen.

Vassily walked to the foot of the stairs. "Nick?" No answer. He took the stairs two at a time and knocked on the door of the master bedroom. "Nick? Hey, Nicky, it's me, Vassily."

He knocked again and entered the room. Katya's clothes were strewn all over the bed and Nick lay under them, naked. Vassily walked over and shook Nick's shoulder. He stirred and grasped his head in both hands. Vassily sat on the bed, laying aside a black silk slip.

"This is her side of the bed. I'm trying to fill it," Nick said, his mouth dry and sticky, speech still slurred.

"It's going to take a while, Nick."

"Oh god, my head," he moaned.

"Come down and have some breakfast. Talya's cooking up some eggs." Vassily took hold of Nick's shoulders and propped him up with two big pillows. "C'mon, Nick. You can't wallow like this. How about a glass of water and a couple of aspirin?"

"Water is for washing. Stolichnaya for drinking," Nick said in a strong accent.

"*Dyédushka*."

"Yeah, old Gramps was right."

"He was a broken man full of pretensions."

Nick squinted as a wintry light brightened the room. He sat up slowly and swung his legs over the edge of the bed, holding his head as though it were a fragile object. "She died on me, Vassily. She died on me."

"I remember watching you two when you first met," Vassily said, his face solemn. "It was at one of those cocktail parties where you stand around with a glass in your hand, half listening to people, watching other people over their shoulders."

"I was watching Katya."

"And I was watching you and Katya watching each other. I saw you put your glass down and walk across the room. You whispered something in her ear and she laughed. I remember that, her head thrown back."

"Her beautiful white throat."

"Then she took your hand and you led her outside onto the terrace. I thought you knew each other. That's what it looked like, Nicky, as though you'd known each other forever, as though you were fated."

"Six months later we were married."

"What did you whisper?"

"'I'm your soulmate.' And she said, 'No one's ever thrown me that line before.' Ekaterina Vinográdova. Remember how she danced? She was always a wonder to me, Vassily. I can't believe she's gone . . . as enigmatically as she appeared. I lost her before her body went. Something kept on living in it, but she wasn't there any more. It was like an animal that wouldn't let go and I kept on feeding it."

"It takes time for the mind to catch up."

"I don't want to catch up. I do not accept what's happened. I kept her alive too long to stop now, Vassily!"

"She's gone, Nick. She's dead. Let her rest in peace."

Nick plunged his head into his hands and rested there a moment, then he raised it up and stared into Vassily's eyes. "They did a post-mortem in Geneva. And they found something very strange."

"It was a rare form of cancer, Nick."

"This was the rarest thing you'd ever see."

If only she'd agreed to have surgery. "Don't let them cut me, Nicky," she said. "Don't let them. I couldn't bear to be cut." And I protected her from that. If only I had . . . exerted my will . . . persuaded you to remove that thing . . . he lived the magical duality of unbearable grief.

~

Dai Ling threw a snowball at the bedroom window and seconds later saw Ray looming as she squinted up into the brightness. "I want to talk to you," she said urgently as he opened the window.

"Me too. Come on up. The door's open."

"Okay."

Ray's older brother, Wayne, was slouched in front of the TV. He was like a lizard, barely moving unless disturbed then he would jump up, surprising everyone, and in one smooth movement throw on his coat and slide out the door. Dai Ling crept past the parlour so as not to alert him, ran upstairs and along the corridor to Ray's room at the front of the house. His door was ajar. She pushed it open and burst in. "Ray, I've been wanting to talk for such a long time. Where've you been?"

"It's a long story, Dai Ling." He patted the bedcover next to him. "Come and sit down."

She hadn't been in his room for ages. The model aeroplanes were gone and movie posters had replaced the dinosaurs on the wall. "I have something wonderful to tell you, Ray," she said as she jumped onto the bed.

"I know. Congratulations! It's great news, Dai Ling."

"What d'you mean?"

"Your acceptance into the youth orchestra. Ma told me. Your Ma told her."

"Oh that. No, Ray, there's something else."

"What? Oh no, don't tell me. I think I can guess from the way your eyes are sparkling. Did you . . . did you . . . ?"

"Yes! I think I'm in love, Ray, but it's so complicated and . . . " She blushed and turned away.

"Don't be shy with me, Dai Ling. You're my best friend, after Wayne. But he's so grumpy since he dropped out of school again. Well, double congratulations, now you're lead cellist in the youth orchestra *and* you have a lover . . . like me."

"What!"

"That's what I want to talk to you about. I need your advice."

"You've got a girlfriend?" Dai Ling asked incredulously.

"A woman friend," he said solemnly, "An older woman." He waited for the news to sink in.

"Who is it, Ray?"

"You must promise not to tell, especially not your Ma."

"Is it Karen?" she asked, thinking of their shapely blonde neighbour who worked in the garden all summer in skimpy shorts and a bikini top.

"No! You don't know her. She's my professor at school. Her name is . . . Ana Lisa." He breathed the word as though it were a magic spell. "Professor Ana Lisa Tredicci."

"She's Italian?"

"Yes. Ma would kill me. First Mei Li then me."

"How did it happen?"

"I have a seminar with her on Japanese film and I always stay after class to talk to her about Ozu and Mizoguchi. She's been helping me with my research paper, suggesting books and websites. On Wednesday I was telling her about the Kurosawa Festival at the Bloor Cinema and we were talking so much that before I realized it we were at her office and she invited me in."

"Maybe she thinks you're Japanese."

"Dai Ling! This is serious."

Dai Ling bounced on the bed. "Come on, Ray, tell me more. I promise I'll be very serious" They sat cross-legged now, facing each other.

"Well, we were standing by her bookcase and she turned to hand me a book. She's tall, like me and our faces were very close. I could smell her perfume, kind of flowery lemony, then . . . then she kissed me. I took the book out of her hands and put it on her desk and I put my arms around her and I kissed her, Dai Ling, for such a long time. Then she said, 'Let's go to my place, Ray. We'll be more comfortable there.' 'But aren't you married?' I said and she said, 'He's away on a business trip, no worries.'"

Dai Ling was surprised by a twang of jealousy, like a lonely, discordant string. "She seduced you. How old is she?"

"Thirty-seven," he said with reverence. "She's so wonderful, Dai Ling. I can't stop thinking about her, but I don't know what to do because she's married and she's white. My family *really* wants me to go with a Chinese girl."

"I know. My Babá is the same. He thinks I'm going to marry you one day."

"How little they know of our real lives, eh? What would you do in my shoes?"

Dai Ling cocked her head to one side and looked thoughtful. "I'd go for it," she said finally.

"Really?" he leaned forward eagerly.

She nodded her head vehemently. "Life is short, Ray. We can't miss out because of our parents."

"But what if Ma finds out?"

"She'll realize you're a man and not a little boy any more."

She felt stronger now, bolder since she'd given Ray the advice she herself needed.

Don't tell them till you're sure. They'll get over it, Ray had said the last time they talked. She knew she couldn't live with secrecy for long. And now she was sure.

~

1552: Brussels

"BRING ME OYSTERS!" CALLED THE KING, and the chief steward hurried to relay the order to a page who ran to the palace kitchens. Charles V, ruler of the Holy Roman Empire, was an impatient man who demanded instant gratification of his appetites. Andreas Vesalius, in the spirit of his male ancestors, had settled into a life of service as court physician and field surgeon, applying himself to the wartime repair of wounded flesh and the domestic repercussions of the king's overreaching appetite. Charles was an impossible patient, demanding gross and gluttonous amounts of highly spiced food to tickle his numbed palate. In addition to his excesses he had a penchant for seafood, especially for oysters, eels and anchovies, which did not agree with him. He suffered from insomnia, so he sat up in bed and ate through the night, calling for capon and cold beer at three in the morning, oysters and mead at four, continuing through the daylight hours after perhaps a catnap at dawn. The emperor was plagued with gout, for which Vesalius prescribed moderation in his diet, to no avail.

"He won't listen, Anne! He sits at table with a dozen dishes before him! Great pasties, joints of roast meat, game birds and pies, all spiced to kingdom come. And he eats with his hands, the glutton, holding the plate beneath his jutting Hapsburg jaw. *Plus ultra* — yet further, a fine motto for an emperor, but not when applied to his girth. What am I to do?"

"Come to supper, husband. Cook has made a pie filled with wild boar meat soaked in brown gravy. We will eat moderately to make up for the emperor."

"I'm afraid for his health. What will happen if he dies?"

"You'll say 'I told him so,' and your reputation will be secure, I'll vouch for it. Then you'll dissect him and make a great pie of his innards." Anne laughed and slapped him on the behind. Vesalius grasped her wrist and pulled her to him. "We have troubles enough in our own house, Andreas," she said, slipping out of his grasp.

"What troubles?"

"Come and sit, my love. Be an example to our daughter. Come to table, Annie. Hurry up."

The child skipped around the table and sat herself down with a cheeky expression on her face. Vesalius stood at the head of the table, knife and serving fork poised above the pie. His face was a large question mark.

"We have no troubles," he muttered, for his mind was not on the domestic front. His home was a haven where he pondered on scientific dilemmas and on the emperor's health.

When I bleed him the blood swirls a moment in the bowl and then is still, and for a while there is relief, his florid complexion paling. As though the blood when it is let ceases its agitation of the body, for surely it must be in constant circulation responding to the emotions.

He saw Anne's face as she lay beneath him in their bed, a flush of pleasure beneath the delicate blue-veined skin of her breasts; her hips rising and tensing to meet him, her face suffused with the climax of her pleasure.

What emotion is it the blood responds to and what does it take with it from the body when it is let, leaving the patient peaceful? What causes blood to circulate through the body? Emotion? Or does the blood govern the emotions? Yes, surely, for with its letting emotion wanes. But the emperor's appetite does not wane . . . He felt his daughter's eyes upon him, and his wife's, questioning, as he stood poised like the conductor of a silent orchestra.

"Well? What troubles, wife? What troubles in our house?"

"The roof is leaking in the attic, and the parlour chimney bricks are crumbling."

"But the house is newly built."

"Not so new, Andreas. Eight years have passed and the house is settling nicely around us, but it needs attention in certain corners."

"We will deal with it when we return," he said, cutting into the pie and serving a healthy wedge for Annie.

"Are we going away with you, Father?" The child's eyes sparkled. Andreas nodded, spooning gravy onto his daughter's plate. "Where? Where?" the child chirped, bouncing in her chair and clapping her hands.

"Sit still, Annie," said her mother and turned to Andreas. "Where are we going this time?"

"To Nuremberg," he said, catching his wife's eyes with a smile. "The emperor is going on imperial business and we are to accompany him."

Their carriage rumbled through the night, wheels occasionally catching in the deeply rutted road, causing the coachman to jump down from his perch and urge the horses to pull harder. "Git on there, yer lazy nags!"

A crack of the whip and the carriage jolted free, waking Anne with a start. "What was that?" she exclaimed, clinging to Vesalius' arm, then, "Ah, we're on the road again. For a moment I thought I was in my bed and the earth was shaking." She turned to her daughter who was sleeping soundly, stroked her bonneted head and turned back to her husband. "There's been so much travelling in these years, sometimes I hardly know where I am."

She nestled into him, pushing her breasts hard against his chest as her hands began searching like blind creatures, manoeuvering their way through layers of woven fabrics and swaddlings. Vesalius, still half asleep, found the hard nuts of her nipples and twisted until Anne gasped. Honey poured into her generous loins as with a gliding movement she was on him, burying him to the pubis in her musky body. He gasped at her boldness, always taken by surprise, and sat passive as the rocking of the carriage assisted them in their transport.

When Anne opened her eyes on the darkness finally, Vesalius whispered, "The child?"

She glanced into the corner of the carriage, leaned across and caressed Annie's sleeping face, then she swung back into his arms and whispered in his ear, "Sleeping, my love, sleeping with the soundness of a seven year old."

Slowly, she raised her buttocks, like two great loaves of golden pan bread. She felt Andreas slip from her body like a spent fish, with a trickle of liquid, such as escapes the mouth of the newly dead.

"Oh, my husband," she whispered, barely audible, more of a breathing than a speaking, "Where have you gone? Where are you hiding? Something is missing that used to be there."

She knew he heard her because she felt his body stiffen. She had lost him again behind his wall of flesh and he would pretend he had not heard her, to save them both.

She busied herself with rearranging her clothing and their covers, then she linked her arm in his and nestled into him. Try as she might to maintain her natural abundance of spirit, she wondered and fretted at the slow retreat of her husband, as indeed Vesalius had wondered at hers when she had become a mother. He was proud of himself as he walked in his father's smaller steps, extending the stride, enlarging the print. *Here we are together in the carriage,* he thought, remembering his father's long absences. *My children will never look on me as a stranger* — his last thought as he drifted again into sleep.

But Anne was wakeful. Sometimes she thought she imagined the distance between herself and Andreas, but in her heart she knew he was leaving her, gradually, imperceptibly, like someone dying over a period of years. Lodged in her gut was a fear that even she could not face, that she and the child were somehow killing him with their love of him, their need.

While in Nuremberg, Vesalius was called upon to prescribe remedies against an outbreak of plague. It was thought to have come from Augsburg, seventy miles south, whence soldiers had carried it on their bodies, encrusted with disease from the battlefield. Vesalius assembled all his medicines to combat the pestilence — tormentil, snakeweed, absinthe, aloes, mastic, myrrh, dittany, balarmenico, water germander, amber, musk, oil of behen — and distributed them liberally amongst the emperor's retinue. He wondered at the delicacy of his practice with the tender leaves and liquids, remembering the deep incisions of his youth and the muscular exertion of his inquiry after the elusive Soul. But Vesalius was successful with his herbs, leaving behind only two plague-ridden patients, swollen with battlefield buboes, when Emperor Charles V ordered his retinue to make a swift return to the Netherlands before the plague took hold of Nuremberg.

What has become of me? Do all men experience this loss I feel in my heart with the accumulation of years?

Such were his musings as the carriage transported them, back the way they had come, the journey seeming faster and shorter now, with their return.

~

Katya Kulikovsky was interred at the Necropolis on Parliament Street, a stone's throw from Bloor and Sherbourne where Talya had first heard Dai Ling play cello. As the coffin was lowered into the earth, Talya stood rigid at the graveside, her mind filled with images of Vesalius digging in the Cemetery of the Innocents at Montfaucon, disinterring the bones of plague victims.

"Ashes to ashes, dust to dust," intoned the minister. "In the sure and certain hope of the resurrection to eternal life."

The wreaths of flowers which had covered the coffin were placed on the ground now, piled by the gravesite. Talya felt enclosed by a wall of glass that threatened to shatter; only the warmth and solidity of Dai Ling's hand reassured her. Nick threw the first handful of earth. It hit the coffin lid, crumbling. Talya stooped and tried to grasp the earth but her fingers would not move. She saw the earth filled with bones, rivers of flesh teeming with creatures, places hollowed in the earth where lovers had lain for millennia — the shape of their absence. Mountains of bones tumbled together in mass burials — bones of the Romanovs, bones of her ancestors, the shining bones of Andreas Vesalius. She saw bones rocking in the darkness of the ocean floor, sea creatures swimming through the sockets of empty skulls. *The earth is filled with the dead. They hold the earth and feed its creatures.* Katya in her garden, kneeling, digging in the earth. *The hands of the living sort the bones of the dead.* She felt the long slow turning of lovers to each other, the miraculous movement born of desire, the power of the Soul to guide the body. Dai Ling's grandma, tired of waiting, her body sinking into the earth she had turned, spade in hand, beside her only lover.

When Dai Ling squeezed her hand, Talya opened her eyes and turned to her in surprise. Then she took hold of Nick's hand and walked with him and Dai Ling, past crowds of mourners, to a waiting car which drove them to the funeral parlour. Her memory of the reception was like being in the still centre of a blizzard, a blur of white chatter all around her, rain lacerating her face, frozen in a smile.

Dai Ling entered her father's clinic and closed the door quietly. She heard his voice behind the wall of his consulting room and sat down to wait. On the wall opposite was a poster of the human form marked with acupressure points, next to it a chart showing the interaction of the five elements — fire, earth, metal, water, wood — and underneath a diagram of the yin-yang tidal flow of rhythm. On the low end of the curve where midnight winter solstice was marked Dai Ling saw the words Death, Emptiness, Yearning, Germination, and there were tiny drops of water falling outside the circle of life. She thought of Talya's mother lying in her coffin under the earth, and wondered what might germinate out of the emptiness of her death. She remembered her own burial, the panic when she thought that Ray and the other kids had forgotten her, the relief of gulping fresh air as she sprang from her grave. Dai Ling regretted that she had so narrowly missed meeting Talya's mother, who might have shed some light on her extraordinary daughter. Nick had barely responded when she'd shaken his hand, as though he wasn't really there. Now that she was Talya's lover she felt responsible somehow for her well-being. She could not imagine how she had ever doubted her own feelings. It felt so right. She was determined to tell her parents tonight, first Babá, then he would help her break the news to Ma.

Jia Song smiled when he saw her. "My beautiful daughter, what are you doing here?"

"I'm on my way home from school, Babá. We can take the streetcar together."

"Yes, yes, of course. Just one minute, Dai Ling."

Jia Song began measuring out herbs for his patient, a middle-aged Caucasian man who was bending over, putting on his winter boots. Dai Ling watched her father's careful preparation, pouring dried leaves and twigs into little packets, sealing them. After the patient had paid for his treatment and left the clinic, Jia Song sat next to Dai Ling and put his arm around her.

"It's our celebration dinner tonight, Babá. I'm sorry about the other night. Ma went to so much trouble with the dinner. And she'd just given me Grandma's jade bracelet. I felt so bad. Did she say anything?"

"She was disappointed, but she understood. When someone dies in China all the village comes to help. You were right to stay with Talya. She should not be alone at a time like this. Anyway, it was more food for me and Ma," he laughed. "What has happened to you, Dai Ling? You are radiant," he said, stroking her face.

Dai Ling blushed and looked down at her bracelet, circling it around and around her wrist. She'd never had to keep anything from her parents before. How could she tell her father when it was still so new to her? In his presence, she felt unsure again, as though everything that had happened was a crazy dream.

"You must guard this jade and carry on the traditions for us. You're all the family that we have now."

"Don't you have any mementos of your parents?"

Jia song shook his head. "I was young, only five years old, when I went to live with my aunt in Beijing. Many children lived with their grandparents, but mine had died during the great famine, a year after I was born. The old people went without food so we younger ones could survive. Auntie told me that my father was a writer. 'You can be proud of your parents,' she said. 'They're good Communists, working to feed the people.' After working in the fields all day he would sit at his desk and write, late into the night. I was so proud. I used to brag about him at school, about the books he was writing."

"Did you look for my grandparents before we left China?"

Jia Song hesitated a moment, turning his wedding ring as Dai Ling often saw him do when he was considering.

"I went back to the village to look for my Ma. Nobody knew where she was. They said she'd left when my father was taken away to a labour camp for re-education. He had 'counter-revolutionary ideas.'"

"Things are different in China now. Can't we try to find them, Babá?"

"No use in looking," he said, shaking his head. "No use in talking about this."

"But what about my uncle? Couldn't he look for them?"

"I no longer have a brother."

"What happened? You never talk about him, Babá."

"We had a political disagreement," he said curtly, standing up and reaching for his coat.

There was a hardness in his voice that she had rarely heard. She wanted to ask him more, to push open the door in him that had closed so quickly, but she sensed the pain behind that door and she remained silent. Somehow she had missed her chance of talking to him about Talya. She felt relieved. *It's better to wait awhile*, she thought. *See what happens. Invite Talya over so they get to know her better.*

Just as they were leaving the clinic the phone rang. It was Xian Ming.

"Yes, yes, we're coming," Jia Song said, "Dai Ling is with me. Yes, yes."

"What did she say?"

"She wants us to buy oranges at Cai Yuan."

They took the elevator to the ground floor and walked out onto Danforth Avenue.

"Better take the streetcar," Jia Song said, "Your Ma is waiting."

He put his arm around Dai Ling as they walked west to Broadview station, trudging through the late January slush.

~

Nick sat in his study, feet on the desk.

"To you, my beloved Katya," he said and drained the glass in one shot. He welcomed the burning in his throat and belly, like fire cleansing him. Alone in the house, he threw his head back and let the ugly sounds rip from his throat. "I'll be fine, darling," he'd said. "I have to get used to this. Can't be a wimp." But in truth he knew he would never get used to it. He felt damaged and abused as though his spirit had been tampered with by a capricious God.

He blew noisily into a large handkerchief and walked over to the window. Snow was crusted in the corners of the window frame, dirty-looking, persistent. *This is when we would have gone somewhere warm,* he thought . . . *Mexico, the Caribbean* . . . He was back from his daily pilgrimage to the Necropolis where he had laid fresh red roses on Katya's grave. He had relived the moment of her death over and over, tunnelling the finality of it deeper into himself, as though he could one day believe in it.

When his old buddy, Bill Cameron phoned, he'd put him off. "Taking a short sabbatical, Cam. I need some time."

"Bay Street isn't the same without you, Nick. Keep looking across at your empty desk each day, thinking you're gonna be in. It's piling up with mail. But don't you worry, we're taking care of your clients' portfolios . . . me and Carla." Cam's habitual laugh, the gravelly force of it. Carla, their assistant with her willing smile and bottom-tilting heels. "Look, I didn't have a chance to talk to you at the funeral . . . "

"You were there?"

"Of course I was there, Nick. You . . . "

"Sorry, Cam, I didn't . . . "

"It's okay, it's okay, I just wanted to tell you, Bud, I'm real sorry about Katya."

There had been a long pause, Nick unable to speak. What did people expect him to say? "Well Nick, I guess I'll let you go. Uh . . . Pop down for a drink at lunchtime, why don't you? We'll be waiting." That laugh again, grating on him.

Vassily phoned regularly from Montréal, the tea-swilling, sandwich-eating funeral crowd left messages on his phone with invitations to dinner, the wives of business friends left casseroles and cookies at the door. Truth was he didn't want intruders in the house where he lived still with his Katya. He wanted to be alone with the warm shadow of her, wooing her back to their secret life together.

Across town Talya lay on the sofa in the darkness of her Brunswick street apartment. The Vesalius *Illustrations* lay on the coffee table in front of her — Plate 42 an array of primitive surgical instruments — knives, scissors, curved needles, pliers, saw and mallet. She'd just come off night duty and her curtains were drawn to keep the daylight out. Candles burned at intervals around the room, a bank of them illuminating a photograph of Katya on the mantel, but all she could see was Lily's face, Lily who could have been her mother, Lily who sang to her with a heavy heart, who lifted her with longing arms and laughed so that she wouldn't cry. Above her bed Lily had taped a drawing sent from the Philippines by her daughter, Carrie. In the picture Carrie held the hand of her small brother and with their free hands they waved. Behind them was a figure in the sky with closed eyes, flying away on big wings. 'Mine,' Talya would say, 'mine,' throwing her arms around Lily, trying to pull her away from the drawing.

A sliver of pale green glass lay in Talya's palm, carrying within it the memory of its form. As she drifted into sleep she saw herself climbing out of the shattered ARTwomb, trying to embrace Lily, but she kept floating away, waving to her, weeping. And when she floated back her face was Katya's and a red tide rose in Talya, a fury at the cruel trick of her mother's dying before she could tell her that the glass monstrosity was finally gone. *It's too late, it's too late.* Her hand clenched and she woke to the sharp pain. Blood welled in the palm of her hand and she watched it from a great distance as she felt the river of her blood pulling from its banks, a peaceful ebbing. Then she heard the door, familiar steps, and she sat up and wadded a bunch of kleenex into her palm.

"We finished orchestra class early and I couldn't wait to see you." Dai Ling knelt by Talya and kissed her. "What's wrong? Are you okay?"

"Mmm, I just dropped off to sleep."

"What's wrong with your hand? It's bleeding."

"It's nothing." Talya tried to pull her hand away, but Dai Ling held on and lifted the kleenex. Underneath was a maze of little nicks criss-crossing her palm, with a deeper cut in the fleshy mound of her thumb.

"You have so many cuts! What did you do?"

"Don't make a fuss. I'm okay," Talya said angrily. "They're superficial."

Dai Ling picked up the sliver of glass and held it above the candle where it flared briefly, a brilliant orange, then turned pale aqua. "Is this from the ARTwomb?"

Talya squirmed. "You'll think I'm stupid . . . "

"Come on. Tell me."

"I had to save a few pieces . . . to show my mom."

"But why were you holding it?"

She shrugged. "It was an accident. I was half asleep and my hand must have clenched. It woke me up. Sometimes I feel like I'm behind glass and nobody's there . . . "

"I'm here. I love you."

"Do you? Sometimes I don't know what's real."

Dai Ling took Talya's face in her hands and looked at her for a long time. Then she kissed her mouth, soft and yielding. "This is real," she said, holding Talya's shoulders, gazing into her eyes. She raised her arms and reached behind her neck, undid the clasp of her necklace, and dangled a small jade pendant in front of Talya. "This is for you," she said, "to remind you. Jade is for power and protection. In China it's prized more than gold, more than diamonds or silver."

Talya held the pendant in her hand, staring at it.

"When I was little Ma used to take me to the Chinese temple downtown. It was filled with flowers and big bowls of oranges. Ma lit joss sticks and candles for Quan Yin, the Goddess of Mercy, then she knelt in front of her statue and prayed for Grandma in Beijing. She always cried, then wiped her eyes and took my hand. 'Come on Dai Ling,' she'd say, 'Now we must send a prayer into the fire for your grandma. These papers are our wishes.' She took the bundle of gold and red papers that the candles and joss sticks had been wrapped in, then she pulled a very thin needle from the lapel of her coat and pricked her finger and squeezed a drop of blood onto the paper. We took our paper wishes to a big iron bowl in the corner and Ma laid them in the bowl and set fire to them. I watched her blood burning. It was my blood too, she said, and Grandma's blood."

She stood, still talking, and walked to the mantel where one of the candles next to Katya's portrait was spluttering. "Afterwards we'd go eat pork dumplings, my favourite, and buy sweet dried plums and chew them on the streetcar going home." She pressed her thumb into the warm wax, shoring it up, and turned to Talya. "My parents have invited you to have dinner with us for Chinese New Year — February first, Year of the Ram."

"What does that mean?"

"I don't know. I'm Canadian," Dai Ling laughed. "You'll have to ask my dad."

"Do they know?"

"What?"

"That we're lovers."

"I'm scared to tell them. I can hardly believe it myself. Please don't hurt yourself again."

"All those things I told you about my birth . . . they're not true."

"The ARTwomb?"

Talya nodded and stared past her at the candles, her mouth tight. Dai Ling moved quickly and sat close to her, cradling her wounded hand. "Tell me," she said, and Talya took a deep breath.

"Uncle Vassily told me it was just a piece of art. I was flushed out of my mother and they were going to reimplant me in a surrogate, but she wanted me back, so I *am* a product of reproductive technology but . . . I don't know why I thought that lump of glass was so important. It really had nothing to do with me. When I was a kid I used to sit and stare at it for hours. It was something about the light . . . it reminded me . . . "

"I don't care where you came from or how you got here, I only care about now."

Dai Ling leaned forward, her eyes wide open, and pressed the softness of her mouth against Talya's lips. She felt herself rising, spilling over, a surfeit of pure pleasure. Nothing was like this, only the music — but she was awake, and it was real, and her astonishment filled her with unaccountable joy for her good fortune.

The jade slipped from Talya's fingers and landed silently by the green sliver of glass. Sputtering candles cast shadows that leapt across their bodies and soon they were in darkness as the flames died and Katya's face disappeared.

"You'll have to tell them, you know," Talya said sleepily as she nuzzled into the sweet hollow between Dai Ling's shoulder and collar bone.

~

1555: Brussels

Vesalius frowned, his body hunched, head bowed over sheets of manuscript. He was preparing to publish a second edition of the *Fabrica*. Twelve years had passed since publication of the first edition and there were changes to be made, changes of course to his erroneous assumptions concerning the foetal sac, for which he had excused himself in writing, publishing the *Letter on the China Root* in 1546 after his opportunity to examine the foetal sac of the indigent woman. But the changes which preoccupied Vesalius now were of a subtle nature, and more peripheral than central to the mapping of the body's bones, veins, arteries and islands of vital organs floating within – perhaps, one might say, changes concerning diplomacy rather than accuracy.

Vesalius shuffled in his seat and loosened his collar. He was sweating. He had grown fleshy within the daily round of his private practice, his home, his lecturing. He felt like a caged animal pacing a ritual path which narrowed daily, although in truth he travelled frequently, accompanying the king and his retinue as court physician. *A feeling, merely a feeling*, he thought, *with no foothold in reality*. He struggled with the widening gap.

An image flashed through his mind of the Galgenberg hill with its wooded slopes ascending to the gallows. Inside his sedentary body a small boy raced toward it, the wind rushing through his hair, everything on the periphery blurring as he swept past, up the mountain, craving to touch the magical instruments.

Vesalius shook his head, trying to clear it of the past. He rose from his chair and paced the room for several minutes, measuring his steps, and when he returned to his desk he scored firmly through the name of Dr. Lazarus de Frigeis. Vesalius had studied Hebrew with him in the old days. *Just another language*, he thought, his pen poised over the page, *one must at least learn Latin, Greek, Arabic and Hebrew.* He scored through the remaining lines concerning his close friendship with the Jewish physician. "Peripheral, peripheral," he muttered, but the truth of the matter was that it was advisable not to be known to have Jewish friends, even in one's past. And Vesalius had grown increasingly circumspect as his wealth and reputation had increased. No longer did the passion of youth and early success enliven him; he was pale and soft like a grub feeding on carrion in a dark place. He had lost his magnetism. He was forty years old.

This is what happens, he thought. But in truth he heard Anne's whispered words echoing inside his head, "Something is missing that used to be there.'"

"I am building a new house for her," he muttered, "a veritable palace."

"Andreas, a new house is uncalled for," she'd said, "I merely asked for refurbishments."

"Oh, my never-to-be-sufficiently-praised wife, you will walk the halls of your domain with a fine set of keys clinking at your waist. There'll be no more leaking roofs or crumbling chimneys."

"I want a big room, Papa, with a window where the sun comes up! Can I? Can I?" Annie had danced around him, her blonde ringlets bouncing, tugging on his beard and teasing him, winding her arms around his neck.

"Of course, my little Annie." He'd kissed her cheek. "You shall have whatever your heart desires."

She's growing, she's growing, and where is my son?

"And how will we afford all this, Andreas?"

"The king has confided to me that when he abdicates later this year I will be granted a lifetime pension with permission to join the court of his son and successor, Philip II. There will be no shortage of money, my sweet Anne, to furnish and drape our rooms. Am I not a good husband, a good father, an ample provider? What more do you want?"

A drop of sweat splashed onto the manuscript, smudging the defaced name of Lazarus. Andreas brought his fist down on the table with a crash. "I'm doing my best and everyone is against me!" He sprang to his feet, grabbed his quill pen and stabbed it into the inkwell, splattering ink over the careful pages. He began scoring through lines of text.

"I will delete your names, all of you who have quarrelled with me," he rasped, slashing at the pages. "John Caius, you who shared my quarters in Padua, debating feverishly into the night. We fed off each other for eight months then you broke with me over my rejection of Galen's outmoded theories!

"Colombo, you were a mere student and you dared to criticize me behind my back and hinted devilishly that you'd found something 'unknown' to me, knowing that you would drive me mad with your impudent insinuations about the seat of the Soul. I curse you! I curse all of you who have plagiarized my work, I curse you to hell! All you who have accused me of murder and body theft, I challenge you to prove it in a court of law!"

His face now florid, he parried and stabbed, scoring out references to grave robbery. He erased the passage about a skeleton he'd acquired as a student, with the help of Gemma Frisius, from a roadside stake outside the walls of Louvain. He cut out the 'beating heart' documented in the first edition, remembering accusations of 'a living human experiment,' and carefully rewrote that part of *Human Vivisection*, describing the heart of a man killed in an accident and that of an executed criminal. Then he slumped back in his chair, exhausted.

"I have so much to lose now. The accumulation of my life. I feel the weight of it."

The sun streamed through the window and bathed him in gold for a moment in its rapid sinking, or was it the earth's turning? Purged by the light, Vesalius turned to more mundane thoughts.

"I will dedicate this edition to the emperor," he said, penning *Dedicated to My Emperor and Benefactor, Charles V* on a fresh sheet of paper. *Plus Ultra ad Humani Corporis.*

"I would have liked a son," he mused. "I wonder why Anne has not conceived another child. I would have liked many more children." He remembered tumbling down

Hell's Lane with brothers Nicolas and Franciscus, little sister Anne running behind.

~

"We were sorry to hear about your mother's death," Xian Ming said.

"How is your father?" Jia Song asked gently.

"I think he'll be all right, but it's early days yet." Talya's quick glance took in the dimensions of the room, so much smaller than the living room of her family home.

"Does he have help?" Xian Ming asked. She wore a creamy blouse with an apron over it, and blue polyester pants. She smelled of hot oil and ginger.

"Oh yes. Everyone wants to help. There were so many friends at the funeral. My mother was very popular."

"You will miss her," Xian Ming said.

There was an awkward silence, broken by Dai Ling's entry with a tray of appetizers and a pot of jasmine green tea. Dai Ling poured the steaming tea into little cups. Their hands touched as Talya took her cup and she looked up quickly and smiled.

"These are deep fried peanut cookies," Xian Ming said, "And those are rice crackers and seaweed wafers."

Talya bit into a tiny peanut-flavoured triangle.

"Babá, Talya wants to know about Chinese New Year."

"Oh, I thought we would resume our talk about medicine . . . east meets west," Jia Song said, his face creasing into a smile.

"Well, it's a long evening," Talya said.

"Indeed. What would you like to know?"

"Chinese New Year is on a different date each year, isn't it?" She wanted somehow to impress Jia Song, but didn't know if that would be possible. His calmness seemed impenetrable.

"Always on the second new moon after winter solstice. And tonight is New Year's eve for us. Traditionally it's a family affair with a big meal. We're honoured to have you join us."

"I've been cooking all day," Xian Ming said, "Many dishes — dumplings, noodles, tofu, fish balls . . . "

"We always have fish for New Year," Jia Song said. "It's a symbol of abundance, always more fish in the ocean."

"And of course, rice," Talya said.

"In the south they eat rice," Xian Ming said. "We're northerners from Beijing. We eat dumplings and noodles. All this talk about food makes me hungry. I'll dish up then we'll eat." She said something to Dai Ling in Mandarin, a quick exchange, then went down the hallway to the kitchen.

"When I was little my parents gave me a red and gold envelope with a coin in it. All the children get New Year's money," Dai Ling said. "On New Year's day we used to have a big dinner with our neighbours, the Lees, didn't we, Babá? And we'd all go to the dragon parade in Chinatown. Now everyone's too busy."

"In China the festivities go on for two weeks," Jia Song said. New year is part of the spring festival. People give something to the doctor to keep them in good health. If they're rich they give a big fish. If they're poor they give a fish head. You give what you can afford. If you're very poor you give a salty fish head," he said, laughing.

"What did you think when you first came here, Dr. Xiang?"

"Oh please, you call me Jason."

Talya smiled and began to relax. She'd been nervous, not knowing what to expect, wondering what Dai Ling's parents would make of her, but Jia Song made her feel at home. When Xian Ming called them to the table and they were all seated, Talya remarked on the variety of fragrant dishes and sauces.

"This one is soy sauce, here is vinegar and this is sesame oil," Dai Ling said. "You can pour a little of each in these dishes and dip the dumplings. And you must try this chili sauce, very hot and spicy. D'you want a fork?" she asked, seeing Talya fumbling with her chopsticks.

"What's wrong? You cut your hand?" Xian Ming asked, seeing the cuts in Talya's palm.

"No, it's nothing, just a scratch," she said, balling her fist to hide it."

"My first impression of western medicine was in China," Jia Song said, balancing a dumpling on his chopsticks. "TCM practitioners must have a solid grounding in allopathic medicine, because when our two systems work in harmony we have the ideal balance. TCM is best for treating chronic cases, and for prevention. Allopathic is for acute cases."

"Dai Ling says you're a doctor already, working in the hospital," Xian Ming said.

"Oh no, I'm only in my third year. I have another year of training then three years residency before I'm fully qualified. But I'm working in the hospital now on a clinical clerkship team. We rotate six weeks in each discipline – pediatrics, obstetrics and gynecology, family medicine, emergency, psychiatry, and surgery. Right now I'm in Family Med. It's a relief after working in Emergency."

"Always in a crisis situation, eh?" Jia Song said, reaching with his chopsticks for another dumpling. "In TCM we're trained to cultivate wellness so that the crisis doesn't occur. In China the doctor is a gardener, in the west a mechanic. The gardener doesn't make the garden grow, nature does."

"But the gardener must turn the earth and weed it and prune the roses," Xian Ming said.

"And here we replace parts that don't work, like a car mechanic," Talya laughed.

"Sometimes this is necessary," Jia Song said. "When you work in Emergency you see accidents. If a man comes in with his leg crushed you must amputate; no amount of herbs will cure such an injury. This is not about either/or, it is about harmony and balance."

"What do you think about reproductive technology?"

"There is a desire to profit by treating symptoms instead of seeking the source of the problem and treating it. The basic difference in medical philosophy between east and west, Talya, is partly economic and partly influenced by spiritual and cultural belief. In China, chemical drugs are expensive so we have continued our age-old tradition of herbal medicine. It has the same effect and is easier to find and inexpensive."

"You want a fork? Get her a fork, Dai Ling," Xian Ming said.

"No, no, I can manage."

"But you eat so slow."

"I'm not used to chopsticks, but I want to learn."

Jia Song leaned over and took Talya's hand in his. "Like this," he said, arranging the chopsticks, raising them to her mouth. She grinned with her mouth full of dumpling and Jia Song smiled and nodded as he continued, "After the Maoist Revolution in 1949 the doctors of TCM we called 'barefoot' doctors were able to move around the countryside and treat the people. All they needed was needles and herbs. It was the missionaries who brought knowledge of western medicine and we were very impressed, but the Revolution brought an understanding of the economic advantages of traditional methods. Taosim has for centuries shaped our minds to a holistic view of the world. We understand the world as a living body, and we study the human body as a microcosm."

Talya felt Dai Ling's hand on her shoulder as she leaned over to pour more tea, and she smiled up at her, seeing her now in a different light as she listened to her father.

"Western medicine is based on anatomical studies of the cadaver — a fixed environment. But the living body is a dynamic environment where relationships of one part to another are always changing within the context of the whole. The human being is only a small part of a larger system. In North America, people believe in individualism and the way medicine is practised reflects this philosophy. It began, I believe, with the American Revolution and the declaration of independence which says that any man can be a millionaire, any man can be president of the United States," he finished with a wry smile.

"And look what we have to the south of us," Talya said, "A nation that terrorizes and punishes any country it chooses, waging war for no valid reason!"

"Ah, but war is profitable," Jia Song said calmly. "And western medicine is profitable. All heroic measures are profitable."

"What about passion?" Talya said. "You have to feel passionate about humanity to want to be a doctor."

Dai Ling watched Talya and her father closely. She heard them like a duet, her father loud and clear, Talya watching him, following the shape of his thought, interjecting with questions to keep his voice flowing, point and counterpoint.

Xian Ming brought another dish of steaming tofu and fish balls and served some to Jia Song before she set it on the table.

"We had an ancient ruler called Shen Nung, known as the Red Emperor or the 'Divine Husbandman', because of his knowledge of agriculture and plants. He tested the plants on himself and he was poisoned many times and recovered. From what he learned he wrote the oldest book on herbal remedies, the famous *Ben Cao*, and for this he is acknowledged as the father of Chinese pharmaceutics. Some people say he was like a god because he was poisoned so many times and came back to life, but eventually he died of poisoning. Herbal medicines were his passion."

"In Western medicine Andreas Vesalius is considered to be the father of anatomy. He . . . "

"Father? What is all this husband, god, father?" Xian Ming snapped. "Without us women there would be nothing."

"Oh, I know," Talya replied quickly, her hand on Xian Ming's arm. "I agree with you totally, but we can't rewrite history. Vesalius lived during the Renaissance when it really was a man's world, and his passion was to map the human body. Thank goodness we live in a more balanced society now."

"Do you have a boyfriend, Talya?" Xian Ming asked.

"No," she said quickly.

"Talya is . . . " Dai Ling began.

"I'm much too busy. There's just no time. The only people I see are the students on my clinical team . . . and my friend, Elliott, he's a fellow student."

"You like him?" Xian Ming asked.

"He's my best friend. He's gay."

Xian Ming frowned, questioning, and was about to speak when Jia Song said, "Passion means sacrifice. One day you'll marry, Talya. Family is the most important, work comes second, but for a physician sometimes there is no separation."

"Dai Ling's the same, a career girl," Xian Ming said matter-of-factly. "But one day she'll marry, maybe someone famous like Yo-Yo Ma, and our grandchildren will all be musicians."

"Oh Ma, will you quit!" Dai Ling laughed, swiping playfully at Xian Ming.

"Okay, let's clear the table. You have to excuse my rude daughter, Talya."

"Can I do the dishes?" Talya asked, jumping up.

"No, you're our guest." She said something to Jia Song in Mandarin, calling him Zhuzi, and he nodded. "My husband will take you into the parlour while Dai Ling and I clear up. You two got a lot to talk about."

"How do you make your diagnoses?" Talya asked when she was settled again in the parlour, staring at the orchid's delicate petals which, due to an intensity of golden light from the setting sun, seemed to grow out of Jia Song's head.

"There are twelve pulses, Talya, three on each side of each wrist, two levels, half are deep pulses, half surface pulses. And the tongue, the eyes, body posture, so many things to notice, Talya. TCM is empirical, everything based on observation. It is a physical, not an intellectual practice."

"You must have studied for many years."

"The light is in your eyes," he said, getting up. "I'll close the blinds."

"Thank you. You're so thoughtful."

"You're Dai Ling's friend, and you will be a doctor," he said, smiling, as though that were explanation enough for his solicitousness. In fact he was delighted to have the opportunity to talk with this young medical student. He detected in her a dynamic mixture of energies which reminded him of his own youthful struggles in China, trying to balance his passion for learning with his political activities, the one expansive, the other reductive — trying to tear down an old regime. And it appeared to him that for Talya, too, her family was important. "My training was interrupted when I came to Canada."

"Did you speak English?"

"I learned at the university in Beijing, but when I arrived in Canada I realized how bad my English was," Jia Song laughed. "It was very difficult in the beginning. My wife was homesick and I didn't know how to start our life here. But I was lucky to meet Doctor Wu our first week in Toronto. He took me on as his assistant and I finished my training with him. We worked together for five years, then I started my own practice, here in this house for the first seven years. This room was my clinic."

Without thinking, Talya confided, "I'm going to specialize in surgery. Really vital cases. It's more important to me than anything. I've seen so much unnecessary surgery."

"You want to do the kind of surgery that saves people's lives, like in the movies and on TV?"

They both laughed, and Talya, surprised at the ease she felt with this man, continued, "I made my decision after my first post-mortem. I don't want to deal with death any more."

Jia Song looked at her and nodded slowly. "You've been through a lot with the death of your mother." He saw that Talya might cry and that she didn't want to, so he continued, "TCM and surgery are good companions. The best way to prepare a patient for surgery is to treat him with herbs, massage, acupuncture — a tuneup so the body is ready for the surgeon — and afterwards, to help with a fast recovery. We think of the body as two energies mixing, yin and yang like two banks of a river, one in the shade, one in the sun; yin is the desire that creates beauty and yang is the satisfaction that creates power. A surgeon who knows some of these things is a valuable doctor, Talya. There is also what we call the *qi* — the energy, the breath in the body. Man is himself a form of *qi*. His energy affects everything around him; the environment of the earth is affected, and the universe in turn is affected by the state of the earth. It is both simple and complex."

"Like DNA."

"Yes, like DNA. Talya, I will be honoured to share with you anything you want to know. You can visit my clinic."

Talya was about to thank him when Xian Ming entered with another pot of jasmine green tea.

"Did you hear, Zhuzi? Dai Ling says Sylvie wasn't accepted by the youth orchestra."

"The pianist?"

"Yes," Dai Ling said, following Xian Ming with a stack of tiny cups in her hand. "She waited all this time and they only told her this morning. She's so disappointed. But Christie got in. We'll be rooming together on tour."

Talya rolled her eyes at Dai Ling as she set the cups down and Xian Ming poured carefully into each one.

"Now we'll make our wishes for the New Year," Jia Song said. "This is the year of the ram in a flock of ewes, like me, a position of good fortune, surrounded by females," he laughed.

"So what does it mean?" Talya asked.

"It means that behavior must be appropriate. The ram is in the fifth direction, in the centre, very visible, and must avoid the taking of sides."

They raised their cups and sipped the fragrant tea. Talya's eyes were on Dai Ling. She smiled as she wished, most fervently.

~

Talya saw him as soon as she walked into the restaurant. He had his back to her, a glass in his hand. His shoulders were stooped. He looked old. He turned suddenly as though he'd felt her eyes on him, and when he saw her he waved and tried to stand. *Oh God, he's drunk already*. She walked rapidly across the carpeted floor, weaving her way between tables.

"It's okay, Dad, you don't have to get up." She leaned down to kiss him as he flopped back into his chair.

"Talya, you look tired. They're working you too hard in that hospital."

"Par for the course, Dad. That's what med school is all about, pushing you into an altered reality."

"Your mother would've been so proud of you." A bitter smile hovered at the corners of his mouth.

"Did you order?"

"I was waiting for you."

"Sorry I'm late."

"What will you have to drink?"

"Red wine."

"We'll have a bottle of Valpolicella, shall we? Waiter!" He waved his arm in the air, swivelling his head, searching.

He was never like this, Talya thought as she busied herself with her coat, draping it on the back of her chair, *he's wrecked*. A waiter appeared with menus. Another waiter came and took the drinks order. Nick ordered a double vodka and a bottle of Allegrini La Grola.

"Are you back at work, Dad?"

"Oh yes, back in the saddle."

"Are you busy?"

"Uh-huh, the TSE index is recovering, investors coming out of the woodwork. I'm busy, yes, I am," he blustered. "They can't seem to manage without me."

He's shrunk. His tie is askew. She leaned across the table and straightened it, then she took his hand and his eyes filled with tears.

"I miss you, Natáshenka."

"Want me to come home for a while?"

"No, no, I have to do it alone." He downed his vodka. "I'll be fine. But would you take the dog?"

"Ruby? Sure." Talya grabbed a breadstick and crunched on it.

"She mopes around the house all day, whining. I can't stand it."

"I can take her, no problem. And I could come home in the summer if you like, Dad. I get a couple of weeks off in August."

"It's a big house. I may downsize. On the other hand I could get the stables going again. Get us a couple of horses, like the old days."

"Sure. I loved our riding days."

"That was our time, eh, Natáshenka? Remember Corky?"

Talya laughed. "He was my Pegasus."

"Remember the jumps I set up for you by the orchard? You won some ribbons, *moya dochka.*"

"They're still on my bedroom wall."

He looked at her vacantly, his jaw slackening.

"How about some food, Dad? I'm going to have the lasagna. What about you?"

"Your mother wouldn't eat pasta. Afraid of losing her figure." He gulped the last of his vodka and picked up his wine glass. "Here's to . . . here's to us, darling."

That's what he called Mom. Talya smiled and raised her glass. She watched his mouth moving, the shadows under his eyes, the deadness in them as he seemed to recede, his voice getting fainter. She grasped the jade pendant at her throat. "Yes," she heard herself say, "We'll have an Easter breakfast. I'll make *koulitch* and *paskha.*" She saw the frosted *koulitch* bleed where it was sliced, a red egg baked in its centre, red bug eyes around the table — Riva, Sandra, Nathan, Vassily — "Oh Natáshenka," Katya's voice as she cracked an egg, doused it with salt, bit into it . . .

"Remember the big pots of pussy willow we had all over the house?" Nick said, his eyes alight with memory, "And the eggs she dyed with cochineal, piled high in a dish, for life, for hope, for resurrection!" He gulped his wine. "We ate them with salt and washed them down with *Stolichnaya.*" His speech had become slurred, his voice louder. The people at the next table were looking.

"She wanted you there in Geneva with us."

She saw red eggs clustered in a bowl, a bowl of blood swimming in her eyes, Nick drinking cold vodka to clean his mind, then everything lost its form and merged into the bloodbath, bundles of pussy willow drinking it in. "I couldn't, Dad! I was on overload!" She heard her voice rising. "Work, exams, looking after the house . . . "

"She talked about you a lot when we first arrived. We had dinner in a restaurant much like this. Of course it was Swiss, not Italian, and we were at a window table, looking over Lake

Geneva. We were very happy that night, full of hope. She said how much she loved you, Natalya. How she wished you'd been . . . closer."

"I wish we had been too," Talya said eagerly. "Did she say anything about why . . . ?"

She was interrupted by the arrival of their food, the waiter hovering, asking if they'd like more wine. Talya shook her head and waited for him to leave.

"Remember the family reunions in Montréal, Dad? That summer when I turned twelve, at Uncle Vassily's house, she danced with you to some wild Russian music. She was so beautiful and I was jealous. You and Mom lived in a world where I didn't belong."

She watched her father picking at his lasagna, pushing it around the plate, his mouth and chin quivering. *Oh no, please don't cry, I can't bear it.* Talya could see that he was struggling to control himself, but tears spilled from his eyes and coursed down his trembling cheeks.

"Come on, Dad, I'll take you home. Where's your coat?"

"I hung it in the lobby, with my hat." His voice was gruff.

Talya helped her father on his unsteady course across the restaurant. People stopped eating and turned to stare. She struggled to keep control. What if she fell with him? She felt like a puppeteer, manoeuvering him from a great distance, placing her hand carefully under his elbow, an arm around his waist. She couldn't even feel him, though she sustained the bulk of him. Then the waiter came running across the room, wanting to know if there was something wrong with the food.

"No, no, my father's not feeling well. The bill please. And could you call us a cab?"

Ruby's bones shone in a perfect circle as she curled at the foot of Talya's bed. She slept, her nose quivering, a wet black circle whorled like the surface of earth seen from the Heavens. Ruby conducted electrical fields of immense complexity with her nose; she called in a universe of planets spinning as she raised her snout to the sky in a hunter's dreamscape. The moon silvered her bared teeth, her whiskers quivered, meteors singed her fur as they hurtled by, and her paws twitched in the ecstasy of pursuit as she scented her prey. She dreamed of wild places and hungry nights, of the one-minded pack which howled on the dark. Her breath, hot with the chase, came in spurts and whimpers as her body hurtled forward, laced with blood lust. The snow turned red as the pack downed a deer, anointing their tongues as they nosed into the convulsing body, long teeth tearing, exposing bone for the first time to the full moon.

Talya rolled over when she heard the door open. She watched Dai Ling undress in the shuttered moonlight, shedding garment after garment until she was naked and slipped into bed beside her. Then she gathered her in her arms, murmuring, "Mmm, and I thought you were going home to mom and dad."

"Can't stay away from you," Dai Ling said. "I'll tell them rehearsal ran late and I just had to sleep over." She laughed and rolled on top of Talya. "How was your dad?"

"Not so good. I took him home." Talya's long legs stretched to the foot of the bed and she ruffled Ruby's soft fur with her toes as she found Dai Ling's mouth in the darkness. "I'm so glad you're here. Ruby's here too. We're all together again."

Dai Ling ran her tongue down the inside of Talya's arm, tracing the veins to the palm of her hand. The scars were barely discernible now, even to her tongue. "The moon is full," she whispered. "I saw it rising."

Talya wriggled from under her and sat up in bed, the fragility of her neck revealed when she swept her hair onto one shoulder, the long curve of her back fluid as she moved to the window and stood there, parting the venetian blinds. "It's so bright, almost like day."

Dai Ling gazed at the luxury of her; eyes burning in the pale oval of her face, skin blooming with an unusual beauty; the swell of her shoulders, breasts, hips.

"Come back to bed," she said, her voice husky, as she reached out her arms.

"This is what it must be like to have a twin," Talya said as their skin touched and she was home once again, her grief at bay even as it sought her out in this most intimate place. With all her casual lovers she'd never had to take such risks. Dai Ling delighted and challenged her in a new way. She'd felt protective of Dai Ling, but who in honesty was looking after who? Talya was flying without wings, in a dream where she rose magically into the sky to survey the world beneath from a new perspective. But she knew that if she thought about it she would fall.

"Are you coming to Europe with me?" Dai Ling asked.

"Depends on Dad. I promised to spend my vacation time with him. You know I want to, especially to be with you in Italy." She twirled Dai Ling's hair around her fingers, thick silky strands. "I keep thinking about Palazzo Del Bo in Padua where Vesalius and Galileo lectured. I dreamed I was there last night. I walked across the courtyard into a hall where one wall was lined with skulls of the deceased faculty. There was a blank space on the wall with a plaque underneath and a coat of arms with three weasels, one on top of the other. Then someone called me and I crossed the courtyard to another hall with steps leading to a circular pulpit. An old man stood inside it lecturing to a group of people. He had white hair and a long beard . . . "

"Was it God?"

"No," Talya laughed, "I don't believe in God."

"We're doing our last concert in Padua, after Milan. You have to come."

Dai Ling kissed her eyelids and covered her ears with her fingers. Talya's scalp began to tingle and she felt herself pulled back slowly, sinking into the soft cave of Dai Ling's mouth as she kissed her . . .

"*We must separate the construction of the universe from considerations of Holy Writ*," said the old man, "*I, Galileo Galilei, have demonstrated with my telescope the truth of Copernican theory. The planets, including Earth, do indeed revolve around the Sun. And the turning of our planet Earth on its axis, as it revolves, accounts for the apparent rising and setting of the stars.*"

He was silenced by a hammer hitting the table. A dark mass clustered around him as cloaks, lifting like wings, obscured the old man.

At first she appeared a child, then it was clear to see that the slight figure, drenched in sunlight, was a woman thinned into middle age. She laid a dish of honey cakes in the shadow of a shuttered window and began treading grapes in the sunlight, crushing them to make wine for her father's homecoming. The childlike woman disappeared as a darkness fell over everything, the cloaks again, lifting and flapping, the Florentine inquisitors darkening the light ablaze in Galileo's house. And from his house issued the screams of the tortured echoing down five centuries. Smoke billowed from the shutters flung back, the wine spilled across the courtyard, and there was a sharp smell of burning flesh – heretics, witches, inventors, scientists, geniuses . . .

When Talya woke the earth had dipped to meet the moon, flanked by a million stars pulsing. The Galilean moons circled Jupiter slowly, their motion, not apparently centred on Earth, noted by a crazy old man with a telescope; Jupiter, sometimes called Jove or Zeus, ruler of the Gods, largest planet of the solar system, 300 times the size of Earth, sailing brightly across the sky, a white swan coupled with Leda, who gives birth to Helen, the woman whose beauty catalyzes the Trojan war and launches a thousand ships . . . and on it went, unreeling in Talya's mind, one story leading to another, and another, until everything in the universe was connected, caught in a web of impossible intricacy, too great for any mind.

Talya turned and Dai Ling stirred and reached for her. *My skull in her hands.* Her mind was flooded with exquisite music, something she'd never heard before. She wondered if Dai Ling heard it too in her sleep, or if it was she who played it.

~

1559: Brussels

Despite the efforts of his physicians the Emperor Charles' gout at last overwhelmed him, and on October 25th, 1555 he entered the great hall of Brussels, where members of the Golden Fleece were gathered with nobles and deputies of all the provinces, many of whom wept unashamedly as the popular king officially declared his abdication. He ceded his majesty to his son, the cold, stiff-necked Philip II of Spain, and in parting he granted many indulgences, including the pension promised to his diligent physican, Andreas Vesalius, together with permission for him to enter the service of the new ruler who, being more Spaniard than Netherlander, favored a move.

"King Philip is moving his court to Madrid."

"And you, Andreas?"

"I must go as court physician. You and Annie will come with me, naturally."

"Oh, husband, travel is one thing, but am I to move my entire household? What about our beautiful house, newly built? What about your private practice here in Brussels?"

"Questions, questions! These details will be taken care of, Anne."

"But I don't want to move, Andreas." Anne's face was troubled, her head bowed as though burdened by her thick golden hair.

"Of course, if you do not wish to accompany me . . . ?"

"You know I would go anywhere with you, Andreas, but . . . "

"But what? What is it, my love?"

"Of this journey I am not so sure." Anne fretted at his sleeve, her fingers twisting the burgundy velvet. "Annie is to be fourteen, a delicate age. The journey will unsettle her, such a long voyage . . . "

"Twaddle! It will broaden her mind. You spoil her, Anne. She needs to burst forth."

"It is you, Andreas, who needs to burst! You're all buttoned up these years, moving further and further away and now you take us to Spain when you have already a fat pension, a fine home, and all the patients a physician could want."

"Damn you, Anne Van Wesele! When did you become a shrew?"

"When I lost *you*!" She stared at him a moment, hands on ample hips, then buried her face in her hands and sobbed.

Vesalius gathered her in his arms and stroked her weighty hair. A muscle twitched in his jaw as he felt her heart beating against his. She looked up finally, blew her nose on her sleeve and faced him squarely.

"I'll go with you, Andreas, but I beg you let me be . . . *with* you. I cannot share my bed with you each night and pretend there's nothing amiss as the distance between us increases."

Vesalius clenched his fist and marked the blood pulsing through his veins. He felt his face suffused and kept silence until the choleric flood had ebbed.

"How long do I have to settle my household?"

"We were to sail on the eighth day of August in the king's retinue, but this foolish Nostradamus, with his threats of tempests and shipwrecks has put the sailors in great fear, so we are delayed. You have sufficient time, my dear, to arrange your household goods as you please."

Anne sniffed and patted her damp cheeks. "I'll break the news to Annie. She has attachments here, Andreas, friendships built over her whole life."

"She's a child."

"No longer. As I said . . . a delicate age."

"Anne, why have there been no more children?"

She blushed and looked down. "I have not wanted . . ." her breast heaved and she looked up at him suddenly, her words tumbling. "I have not wanted to lose you further, my husband. I had thought to fill our house, but it has not been so. I'm sorry, I had thought . . . " A guilty uncertainty rose in her, but she took a deep breath and gathered herself. "We've been blessed with our daughter and must be grateful for that. Thank the Lord."

"Indeed," he nodded curtly.

Anne walked towards the door, then she turned, her face solemn. "It is not my choice to go to Madrid, Andreas, but we will make the best of it. Perhaps it is a blessing, a new beginning for us."

"Let us hope," he replied, a dry and humorless response, for he failed to understand what it was he hoped for.

They sailed from Flanders finally, on August 23rd, 1559. Vesalius spent many solitary hours on deck staring into the churning waters of the ship's wake. Sometimes he had a violent urge to throw himself overboard to combat his great fear of drowning in that moving body which seemed to cover so much of the earth's surface. But he was more troubled by a subtle and persistent feeling, a nameless tugging within him which he took to be the echo of Anne's dissatisfaction. It was to continue long after they landed at Laredo.

After the lengthy treck overland, trunks and chests piled atop their carriage, rocking precipitously with each turn of the wheel, the family settled, nestling into each other, seeking familiarity in that new land. Vesalius was glad to be landlocked again, secure in Madrid after several weeks adrift on treacherous waters. For a while he seemed his old self, passionate and immediate. *Such is the influence of travel*, he thought, *shaking us out of our complacency, repatterning us into a new aspect.* But the strictures of Spain gradually tightened around him. There was not a bone to be had in Madrid, not a skull, a femur, not even a simple rib. The aftermath of the Inquisition, together with the harsh sun, bore down on the Van Weseles, accustomed to a liberal life in a damp climate. Anne and her daughter only grew closer with the move, while Vesalius shrunk once again into himself, a guarded place where Anne could not reach him.

~

"What a morning." Talya slumped over the cafeteria table.

"God, I thought it'd never end. That manic-depressive . . .

"And you told him he was drinking too much coffee!" Talya burst out laughing. "Elliott, what's wrong with you?"

"I had a sleepless night."

"On call?"

"In heat."

"Oh no, you're not in love again?"

"Lust! You know I never fall in love, dear."

"Who is it this time?"

"Daniel, a delightful young vampire I found in the blood lab last week when I went to get my test results."

"See, you don't have to rely on the bars. You can cruise at the General."

"Think we should add it to the Gay Guide?"

What happened to Lawrence?"

"The way of all flesh. Boredom."

"Seriously, Elliott, haven't you ever been in love?"

"Don't expect the whole world to be in love just because you are, sweetheart. I'm sure Dai Ling's awfully cute, but really."

"Aren't you afraid of . . . you know . . . ?"

"I'm protected by a dark angel. Didn't I ever tell you, I was lovers for two years with a man who had AIDS? And here I am, clean as a whistle, not even a carrier."

"What happened to him?"

"He died."

"And ?"

"Life goes on."

"But two years, Elliott?"

"An exception to my rule. Really we can't *all* get overwrought. Look at you." He took hold of Talya's hand and opened her palm, cross-hatched with tiny white scars. "Tearing yourself up, silly girl. Didn't help, did it?"

"I told you, Elliott, it was an accident. I fell asleep and . . ."

"Oh, come on, we're all sleep deprived, but really, bloodletting went out with the Victorians. Drink up your coffee and get real."

"What if I turn manic?" she teased.

"I'll send you for shock. Fifteen cups of double espresso."

"The big controversy in Vesalius' time was whether to let blood on the affected side of the body or on the opposite, until he introduced an entirely new element — the concept of direct observation."

"Vesalius again? Tal, you're obsessed."

"But listen! Bloodletting used to be standard procedure before Harvey's discovery of the circulation of blood, and it was Vesalius who led him to it. Following from the results of his dissections and observation of the venous system . . ."

"Is this how you seduced Dai Ling? With historical discourse? Myself I prefer intercourse."

"Come on, Elliott, I'm serious, nobody *really* understands blood, despite all our scientific knowledge. There's always more to discover, and the thing about Vesalius was his hands-on approach. That's what led Harvey to appeal to the body rather than relying on abstract concepts . . ."

"And led to the discovery of the venous valves — *voila*! — the key to unlock the secret of circulation!"

"But that's not the point! The point is, Elliott, that Vesalius changed the course of medical history by insisting on following his nose. Have you ever watched a dog hunting? It becomes so focussed that it's oblivious to everything but the scent. It doesn't hear, it doesn't see, it's in passionate pursuit."

"Like sex."

"Yeah, kind of like sex. You always bring me down to earth, don't you."

"Give your brain a rest, have an orgasm. Haven't you noticed? Everyone in this hospital's screwing like rabbits. Sex is a stress-induced behavior to get the endorphins going so . . ."

"So we don't have to think?"

"Or feel. Can't afford to have feelings, Tal. Why d'you think they run us ragged with sixteen-hour days and overload us with information? So we'll stay in our heads and never venture out because we're emotionally exhausted. I'm numb."

"And my brain's fried."

"Mmm, delicious. Sweetbreads Chez Hannibal Lecter. How's your dad doing?"

"We had dinner the other night . . . he's drinking too much."

"And you? How're you doing, Tal, behind your 'True Love Finally' euphoria?"

"You're one to talk. You've just come out to me as a survivor of a two year relationship with a lover who died of AIDS and all you can say about it is, 'Life goes on.' Now you want *me* to bare my soul?"

"Sweetheart, I know you didn't get along with your mom, and I know you wanted that to change, so all I'm saying is . . .

"I know. But not now. Give me a break, okay?"

"Our break's over," he said, looking at his watch and raising one eyebrow. "Can I borrow your palm pilot? I have to do prescriptions this afternoon and I can never remember the dosages on all these psyche drugs."

"Sure." Talya reached out and put her hand on Elliott's. "Ellie, d'you think we're going to make it?"

"I have to make it, Tal. I've wanted this ever since . . . "

"Ever since what?"

Elliott hesitated a moment. "I've wanted it all my life," he said with conviction.

"Me too. My life depends on it now."

~

"Heading west?" Christie asked as she and Dai Ling met at the lockers after practice.

"East. You too?"

"Uh-huh. Had a fight?"

"We don't fight."

"Really? Everybody fights."

"We don't."

"Just wait."

Dai Ling laughed. "Don't be so negative, Christie."

"So why are you going home?"

"We don't spend *all* our time together. Talya has clinical evaluations tomorrow. She has to study, and I'm taking my cello so I can practise at home. I'm free till the afternoon. It's my library day. Anything else you want to know?"

They swung through the glass doors of the Edward Johnson building, out into the sun and started walking up to St. George.

"Isn't it great that we both made the orchestra? And the very year they decide to tour Europe instead of Canada!" Christie said, beaming. "You heard about the private donation?"

"Yes, our scholarships will be increased."

"Eight and a half thousand dollars! I've never had so much money."

Christie's teeth were uniformly white and perfectly aligned in identical squares. *She's like an instrument with all her workings exposed,* Dai Ling thought, looking at her gel-spiked hair and sharp jaw line. "Sylvie seems to have gotten over it," she said.

"Well, no wonder. She's fallen in love with that hunk of a guy. We'll still room together, won't we? I've never been to Europe. I'm quite nervous to tell you the truth."

"But you're so brave, Christie. You hitchhiked across Canada all on your own last summer."

"That's different. Everyone speaks English. I'm quite shy really, you know." She dropped her token in the slot and entered the revolving door.

"I can't! My cello!" Dai Ling shouted. She'd forgotten, caught up with Christie's chatter, that she was at the wrong subway entrance, so she walked on to the main subway, the one with turnstiles instead of revolving doors. She expected

Christie to be gone by the time she reached the platform, but there she was, still beaming.

"You'll need a *really* good case for travelling," she said. "I've heard the planes are rough on instruments."

"Unless the NYO buys a seat for my cello."

"I don't think so. It's not as if it's a Guadagnini."

Dai Ling's parents could never have afforded such a cello, or indeed any cello. When she'd grown big enough for a full-sized instrument her teacher had found a benefactor, an elderly lady who owned an Enrico Rocca, a modern Italian cello worth $40,000. She'd listened to Dai Ling play and afterwards she'd said, "It's yours, my dear, on permanent loan. What good is this beautiful thing sitting silently in my house? You bring it to life."

Christie stood with her head to one side, her lower lip pushed out, staring at a billboard on the far wall of the platform. A cute young woman was talking on a smart new cell phone — to a textbook-handsome guy grinning at her from the next billboard. *Keep in 'touch' with him*, the ad said.

"D'you think we'll be rich and famous one day, Christie, playing all the great concert halls of the world, making CDs and giving master classes?"

Christie whirled around and their laughter was drowned by the noise of an approaching train. Dai Ling pushed her way in, protecting the cello with her body, and stood in the corner, wedged between the door and a glass panel, her legs straddled for stability. As the train rattled east, Christie leaned into her.

"I never knew for sure you were a lesbian till I saw you with Talya. If I'd known . . . "

"I didn't know myself."

Dai Ling grabbed her cello as the train lurched and Christie fell against her.

"Sorry," she said, laughing. "You're so mysterious, Dai Ling. Would I stand a chance when it's over?"

Dai Ling saw her reflection in the darkened glass of the subway door, and when she spoke it was as much to herself as to Christie. "It won't be over," she said quietly.

Sitting in her bedroom much later that night Dai Ling was startled to see her father standing in the doorway.

"Babá! I didn't hear you come upstairs."

"In my stocking feet," he said. She jumped up and reached to hug him. "We don't see enough of you, Dai Ling. Always downtown rehearsing with the orchestra," his intonation almost a question.

"What about you? Working late at your clinic? Sit down, Babá." She indicated the chair next to her bedside table with its pool of light, and curled herself up on the bed.

"Ah, everybody's sick. How can I say no?" He sank into the chair. "We were worried about you last night."

"But I called Ma."

"She told me, you stayed over with Talya?"

"Rehearsals ran late."

"So many nights now you don't come home to sleep," he said sadly.

"Sometimes it's just easier to stay downtown with my friends." She busied herself arranging the sheet music scattered on her bed. "I'm so tired after rehearsals."

"When you were small I used to watch you sleeping. Every night I stood in your room and listened to your breathing. Sometimes I sat by your bed, touched your face, stroked your hair. When I left the room I would close the door quietly, not to wake you, secure in the knowledge that you were our future. Now you're growing up it feels as though you're moving away from us."

"No, Babá, it's only for the youth orchestra," she said, leaning forward intently. "They've received a big private donation, so they've increased our scholarships. It will cover all the costs, tuition and master classes too," she said proudly. "I'll go on a spending spree in Paris and get presents for everyone. Maybe I'll even convince Talya to come with us to Europe."

"Talya? Why would she be going to Europe?"

"I only said she might come. She's a really good friend."

"She came to visit at my clinic, full of questions. She's a smart one. I lent her some books, and she made an appointment for her father. You stay often with her downtown when you're practising late?"

"Yes."

"Does she have a nice apartment?"

"Uh-huh."

"You're sure it's not a secret boyfriend you stay with?" Jia Song teased

"No, Babá! But in a way you're right because . . . Talya is becoming . . . more than a friend."

"What do you mean?"

Her palms were sweating, her mouth dry. "We're . . . getting . . . close."

There was a moment's silence, then Jia Song said, "It's good to have close friends. Like Karen next door is to your Ma, talking in the garden, working together in their rose beds."

"No, it's not at all like Karen. This is different."

"What are you trying to say, Dai Ling?"

"I think I'm . . . I'm in love with Talya." Her face flushed.

"In love with a girl?" His brow furrowed fiercely. "You're confused, Dai Ling. It's friendship, that's all. Friendship is normal."

"I told you, Babá, it's more than friendship. I'm . . . I'm a lesbian."

A look of confusion crossed Jia Song's face and he reared up in his chair. "What is this craziness? This Talya, she's a bad influence on you, gives you crazy ideas. You must not see this girl again." He stood abruptly, knocking the bedside table, almost toppling the lamp. Dai Ling caught it and she stood too, facing him.

"Please don't be angry with me, Babá."

"I'm afraid for you, Dai Ling. I'm your father. I must protect you," he said stiffly.

They hovered, neither able to close the short distance between them.

"Don't do this to me, Babá."

"Your Ma and I, we don't understand everything that happens in this country, but . . ."

"Please don't try to stop me from doing what I want."

"What you want?" he barked. "To be unnatural? To make a bad choice that will ruin your life?" He turned his head away, fists clenched, then turned back, his face red. "Remember the blood of your ancestors, the traditions you carry in your blood."

"Yes, and remember Grandma, a part of me that's Canadian, like Ma. Grandma changed everything for us."

A swollen vein pulsed in his neck and his jaw trembled. "I've heard enough of your insults."

Dai Ling felt the hot prick of tears behind her eyes and bowed her head. She felt a swoosh of air, heard her father's footsteps as he left the room, closing the door behind him, the soft footfalls on the stairs. She ran to the door and opened it, stood there hesitating, then a wave of anger swept over her and she slammed it shut, threw herself on the bed, and wept.

"I knew when that girl came to our house. I had a feeling," Xian Ming said. "Oh, Jia Song! What are we going to do?" They sat at the kitchen table facing each other. "Maybe I shouldn't have pushed her so hard. Now she rebels . . . like my Ma. And look what happened to *her.* She died all alone in China. I have a lot to answer for."

"If we had stayed in China she would have had something real to rebel against," he said bitterly. "She doesn't understand what it's like for us, living two lives. She doesn't know what her life would have been if we hadn't brought her to Canada." He dropped his head into his hands and muttered to himself, as though unaware of Xian Ming. "Wu-Li crushed by a tank . . . Jiang-Gang shot in the head . . . Fang Li and Wu Fat rotting in prison, tortured so badly that they've lost their minds. They don't know their families when they come to visit. If we had stayed . . . "

"They could have thrown *you* in prison too, Zhuzi and left me like a widow. Or for sure we would have lost you in the massacre on Tiananmen Square. How can Dai Ling ever understand the suffering you endured?"

"She wants us to accept everything she does. She doesn't know how to be an honourable daughter."

"I'll talk to her." She stood up and started for the door, but Jia Song caught her hand.

"No! Give her time to think about her foolishness. Tomorrow she will apologize."

Xian Ming shook her head. "Since she was a tiny girl she's been determined to have her way. Music, music, it's always been about her music, until now."

"And for us it was the promise of change." A spasm of pain contorted Jia Song's face. "We've worked so hard for it and now we are betrayed again."

"We must have patience, Zhuzi. This will pass. I know Dai Ling. Music will be her life long after she has forgotten about this Talya."

"It's time for our daughter to know the truth about her grandfather . . . humiliated before his family, forced to kneel on broken glass in the hot sun, forced to eat the pages of his own book. They sentenced him to twenty-five years of re-education through labour, but he didn't even last ten years. They starved him to death. In the end he hadn't the strength to eat the half ladle of noodles they gave him each day." Jia Song bent his head and wept.

"Zhuzi, you must forget this. It will destroy you."

"I will never forget that betrayal. My father. How can a man betray his own father?"

"He was a child. He didn't understand the consequences." She stood behind him, cradling his head, smoothing his hunched shoulders.

~

Talya knelt on the floor, chin in hands, surrounded by Jia Song's books. She was studying a mandala pattern of the Five-Phase Relationships: *Fire engenders Earth, Earth engenders Metal, Metal engenders Water, Water engenders Wood, Wood engenders Fire.*

Her dark hair swung as she turned the page to a diagram of the Restraining Sequence, each element representing a vital organ and its relationship to another organ. *Fire restrains Metal by burning and melting it. Earth supports Metal by forming minerals and bringing them to the surface, but controls Water by damming and absorbing it. Metal vitalizes Water by permeating it with refined substances that enhance its life-giving properties. Metal restrains and inhibits Wood by cutting it*

She was comforted by the memory of her conversation with Jia Song. It was almost as though he were in the room with her, sharing his knowledge.

Just as Water nourishes Wood, within the body the Kidney Essence can be understood to generate the Blood stored by the Liver. As Wood feeds Fire, the Blood of the Liver can be said to nurture the spirit of the Heart by providing the mind with its basis. As Fire generates Earth, the Heart supports the Spleen by providing the warmth and metabolic energy (oxygenated blood) necessary for the transformation and assimilation of food.

Her lips moved as she read, a visceral sense awakening in her, marrying with sparks of memory.

As Earth gives rise to Metal, the Spleen supports the Lung by raising Food Essence upward to be combined with Air Essence, forming the pure Qi that circulates in the channels. And just as Metal vitalizes Water, the Lung nurtures the Kidney by precipitating its moist Qi downward to be collected and stored as Essence by the Kidney.

She leaned back on her heels and sighed. She was beginning to get a sense of a different way of learning. It went beyond her learned response to reading and she opened to it like a lover. She heard Jia Song's voice, and saw his face, the shadow of his daughter living there within him. She imagined Vesalius delving into the body, mapping it, searching in a distinct and limited environment. In his *Illustrations* each figure stood within a background of nature. Had he searched there also? Had he thought of the elements of Nature which mirror the workings of the human body? In her first post-mortem Talya had felt overwhelmed by a sense of revelation, as though the inner body revealed all the secrets of the universe. She remembered hiding out in the garden as a child, at one with the earth, the trees, the sky – larger and yet smaller than herself, a living paradox with no separation between self and the natural world.

She thought again of Jia Song as she hunched over and continued reading, the solidity and the lightness of him.

She resolved to talk further with him when she returned his books.

In the Lung, the Qi of Heaven (air) joins with the Qi of Earth (nutrition), forming the Qi that vitalizes human life . . . The newborn's first breath ushers in its separate individual existence. The activity of respiration drives the Qi throughout the body. This continuous bellows-like pulsation of the chest and abdomen sets the basic rhythmic pattern of all functions in the organism.

There was a pivot within her, turning her way from Katya's death and, as it turned, Talya's emptiness filled with desire. She read the epigraphs in the opening pages, quotations chosen to reflect the essence of the book.

Heaven, Earth, and I are living together, and all things and I form an inseparable unity. Chuang Tzu

The organic pattern in Nature was for the medieval Chinese the Li, and it was mirrored in every subordinate whole . . . Li signified the pattern in things, the markings in jade or the fibres in muscle, like the strands in a piece of thread, or the bamboo in a basket . . . Talya rubbed the smooth surface of the jade at her throat . . . *it is dynamic pattern as embodied in all living things, in human relationships and in the highest human values . . . Li, in its most ancient meaning, is the principle of organization and pattern in all its forms. Joseph Needham.*

The *Illustrations* lay open behind her at Plate 63. She swivelled on the hardwood floor and faced a flayed man suspended, limbless, on the white page. His breastbone was peeled back, forcing his bearded face onto his shoulder. A cut rope was still looped around his neck, the frayed ends snaking into space. Stubbed ribs grinned like buck teeth revealing his lungs folded inside his body, bloodeagle wings, soft and white. The cadaver's stomach bulged over its truncated breeches, the genitals bagged in an incongruous codpiece. It was a beautiful drawing, like an abstract piece of art. It evoked in Talya an unaccountable sadness for the poor tortured man who housed the world within him, a desecrated landscape.

~

1563: Madrid

"Come, Andreas, let us go to our rooms."

His head was buzzing as they left the Banquet Hall, Anne on his arm, steadying him, their daughter following behind. He had consumed numerous goblets of well-aged Tempranillo, drawn from oak barrels in the Royal Cellars."

"Come outside with me, wife, and look at the stars."

"The Inquisition frowns upon star-gazing. Remember, we are in Spain." She leaned into him, her lips touching his ear. "We must see Annie safely to her chamber. I fear she may be followed into the night by that young blood who was eyeing her across the table."

"I saw nothing."

"Never fear, I watch for us both," she whispered. "Come along, Annie, it is time for us to be abed."

"But Mother, how can I sleep on a full belly"

"A full belly?" she laughed. "Child, you eat like a bird!" She wrapped her arm around the girl's thin waist and tickled her ribs. "Come on with you, I'll race you to your room."

Vesalius was left standing unsteadily in the Great Hall, amazed by his wife's nimbleness as she sped up a wide flight of curving stairs, Annie at her heels, to the first level of the king's palace. He was about to follow when he felt eyes upon him. He turned slowly, his head heavy with the wine, and glimpsed a figure receding into the shadows. Vesalius lunged, his own shadow lurching grotesquely on the walls of the marbled hall. He stopped and listened, holding his breath. Nothing but the sputtering of candles above, burning in a monstrous chandelier, a dark ring of wood. *A wheel to break a body on*, Vesalius thought, looking up, remembering the torture instruments of Galgenberg Hill. He shook his head to clear it, stumbled in the dying light and made his way outside.

There he gulped the night air like a drowning man and gazed up at the stars. After a while he looked about him for a sign of the silent intruder. *It must be that fellow who's sniffing around my Annie*, he thought. *We must find her a husband, a good Fleming, here at court, I will speak to Anne.* The thought of his wife roused his blood or, more particularly, the memory of her indiscretion, which Vesalius had put from his mind until now. Loosened with wine, the memory bloomed in him. Rounding a corner in the labyrinthine palace two days past, he had chanced to see in the distance a parting embrace. Or was it? His mind played endless tricks these days. Perhaps it was a simple exit from the room, of a single woman, but he swore he glimpsed an arm around her waist, a large hand covering her hip, and the woman's form so like his wife's as she closed the door and bustled away down the corridor, jiggling her body as she rearranged her parts, patting her burden of hair with that achingly familiar gesture. *In meeting and parting our lives exist*, he thought, *all in between pales.* He remembered his father's homecomings, the excitement in

Hell's Lane as his carriage rumbled through the mire. The children threw themselves upon him, clinging like limpets while their mother stood in the doorway beaming, but all too soon he was gone again and the light went from her blue eyes. Young Andreas had sworn that when he was a man he would not be parted from his family.

Perhaps I imagined it, the poor light, the unexpected nature of it. Why would Anne betray me? Our bodies have a life of their own and are joined frequently in the utmost desire. I have been loyal and she has never refused me, but once, in more than eighteen years.

When he opened the door the room was in darkness with barely a glimmer from the new moon. He smelled a recently extinguished candle. Anne must still be awake. He crept across the room, steadier now with his lungs full of fresh air. He undressed and slipped silently under the heavy brocade of their winter cover, carried all the way from Brussels. Anne did not stir as he ran his hand over the heavily-fleshed wing of her pelvis. She lay on her side, facing away from him, swaddled in her nightgown.

"Wife, oh wife of mine," he crooned in her ear, his hands slowly pulling up her gown and caressing her ample thighs. He felt her body tauten the instant before she rolled sharply onto her back.

"I cannot perform this empty ritual with you, Andreas," she said in a voice fraught with emotion. "It is too painfully at odds with our daily lives. It is driving me to . . . " and here her voice caught and silenced her.

"Empty?" he echoed, "What do you mean, empty?"

Anne sat up in the darkness, hunched over, hugging her knees. "I have lost you long ago, Andreas. I had hoped to win you back, I have lit candles, I have prayed, but you are not there as you once were."

"Here I am, feel, full of desire for you, my beloved wife."

"Ah, you always say the right words, Andreas, but you make a fool of me. There is a deficiency that you do not acknowledge. What is this . . . this . . . perversity in you?"

"Perversity? What nonsense you speak, woman! I am a most attentive husband."

"I don't deny it."

"I've always kept you and Annie beside me on my travels. Rarely have we been apart but for my spells of field surgery in times of war and then I had only your safety in mind. I have provided you with a fine house, with money and means."

"I know, I know." She rocked, almost sobbing now.

"Then what? Of what am I accused?" he blustered.

"Look to your heart," she said, softly. "The heart must grow with the body, husband. In all these years of our marriage I am diminished by the repetition. Our soup lacks flavour," she offered, struggling to explain her innermost pain, "It is the activity of the heart I require, Andreas." With this she lay down, far over on her own side, and turned her back. Vesalius lay naked, trembling with anger.

"Is the danger at court to our *daughter's* virtue or to your own?" he snapped.

He felt the tremor of Anne's silent weeping which only increased his conviction that she had betrayed him. Swollen with anger he pleasured himself noisily, there in the bed next to her. She did not move and when it was over Andreas felt emptiness where he had hoped for vengeance and the humiliation of his unwilling wife. He lay in the stickiness of his drying seed, wide awake. Over and over Anne's words echoed in his head. Over and over he reviewed the years of their marriage until he could no longer think. But sleep would not come, so he dressed and crept to the open casement, where the cold night air cleared his mind. He looked over his shoulder at the bed and saw Anne's sleeping face, a pool of light in the darkness, and he felt a pang of regret and cursed the complicated emotions of this woman who plagued him to find in himself that which he lacked. He began to list yet again his accomplishments as husband, father, provider, but a wave of exhaustion overcame him and he hardly had time to stumble back to bed before he fell asleep, drugged with repetition.

Vesalius woke quite suddenly in the night from a dream which escaped him, but left him floating in a sea of nostalgia for the academic life he had enjoyed in Padua under Venetian governance. *The company of learned men*, he mused, *the sweet leisure of letters, the operating theatre where I performed my dissections with row upon row of eager faces awaiting my incisions.* His heart throbbed with longing and tears welled in the corners of his eyes, open on the dark.

In the ensuing weeks he had much occasion to ponder. His wife and daughter made themselves scarce, strolling outdoors in a rare winter warm spell, while king and courtiers enjoyed unusual health. Philip had not the gluttonous appetite that had been the downfall of his father. The court physician had time on his hands. He shunned human contact and, instead, sat in his study, his head, weighty with thoughts, supported in his hands. Unopened books mounted in piles around him while his thoughts lost focus and drifted into the past. In his mind's eye Vesalius walked the colonnades of the University of Padua, footsteps ringing on the ancient stones.

His hand reached out and came to rest on a small volume, *Observationes Anatomicae.* Gilles de Hertogh, a fellow physician from the Brabant, had arrived in Madrid two years previous and presented him with this gem, written by Gabriele Fallopio. Vesalius had recognized Fallopio as a kindred spirit.

Anne had barely a word out of him over the next four months as he first devoured the work and then composed a lengthy reply, his *Examen*, dated 17th of December 1561, which he had entrusted to Paolo Tiepolo, Venetian ambassador to the Spanish court.

The *Observationes* was dear to his heart on two counts. Firstly, it was a brilliant work of anatomical quest and discovery in which Fallopio acknowledged Vesalius' *Fabrica* as the guide and inspiration for his studies. Secondly, the work made frequent reference to "*the divine Vesalius*," rendering acceptable to Andreas the intelligent criticism and challenges to his work. With no facilities to research the innovative anatomical observations recorded, he had eagerly awaited a reply, but eighteen months had passed and there had been none. Vesalius wondered at the silence and imagined Fallopio firmly ensconced in the chair of Anatomy in Padua, "*the most worthy school in the whole world*," he had written, "*where for almost six years I held the same chair you now occupy.*" He felt the old yearning for discourse with men such as Gabriele Fallopio, intelligent men who shared his occupation and understood him.

~

"Where's Babá?" Dai Ling stood in the kitchen doorway, her eyes red and puffy.

"Sit down. We must talk," Xian Ming said brusquely.

"Where is he?"

"Gone to the clinic. He was up at six. You want eggs, toast?"

"I'm not hungry." Dai Ling headed for the back door, but Xian Ming blocked her way.

"No running away, Dai Ling."

"I'm not. I'm going to see Babá."

"Your Babá is too angry right now. Sit down."

Dai Ling sat reluctantly and Xian Ming placed a cup of steaming green tea in front of her and sat down next to her. She ran her hand across Dai Ling's eyes. "You've been crying. Everybody in this house is unhappy."

"Did he tell you?"

"Of course."

"You can't stop me seeing Talya. I love her."

"Drink your tea. Do you remember China, Dai Ling?"

"What's that got to do with anything?"

"You were already two years old when we left. Tell me what you remember," Xian Ming insisted.

"I remember Grandma Geneviéve," she said, shrugging, sulky. "I remember sitting on the grass, a big expanse of grass, everything golden, the sun warm on my skin . . ."

"Sounds like Zizhuyuan Park by the Beijing Zoo . . . "

"There were no animals. There was water, a big pond, lots of kids screaming, huge trees reaching into the sky."

"Ah, Riverdale Park. I took you there every day. There was a little girl you liked to play with, splashing each other in the water. She had a nanny from the Philippines. When we left the child would scream because she wanted to come home with us."

"I wish I'd been born here!" Dai Ling burst out angrily. "I hate it that I can't remember where things happened!"

"If you'd been born here you wouldn't have known your grandma. She used to worry. She said, 'You'll end up like me, a political widow. Find a good Communist boy.'"

"You mean she didn't want you to marry Babá?"

"He was too involved in the political struggles, Dai Ling. It was dangerous for us. And we thought it would be a better life for you in Canada, more opportunities."

"I would still have been a musician if we'd stayed in China."

"But you wouldn't have had freedom. Here you can play with any orchestra you choose, you can travel with the youth orchestra. Don't destroy your career after all your hard work. This Talya is a crazy girl."

"Ma, I love Talya. Please don't insult her. You don't know her."

"I know enough. I won't invite her to eat in my house again."

"Then I won't eat in your house again!" Dai Ling shouted, sweeping her tea cup onto the floor where it shattered.

"Dai Ling!" Xian Ming exclaimed. "Have some respect for your parents. You are our daughter, the only one. What about our grandchildren?"

"I can't believe it," Dai Ling said, on her feet now. "I tell you I'm a lesbian and all you can think about is grand-children and my career! As if lesbians didn't have careers and children."

"What?" Xian Ming's eyes were wide with bewilderment.

"Lots of lesbians have children, naturally or by donor, or even by adoption."

"But you are all that we have left, Dai Ling," Xian Ming said, her voice thick with emotion. "Don't make your Babá throw you out."

"Don't worry about it. I'm moving out anyway!" she said, and the back door slammed behind her.

Maybe our difficulties are just beginning, Xian Ming thought, *in this crazy country where my daughter is blooming like a hybrid. What happened? Where did we lose her?*

The girls stood in the hallway of the Brunswick Street apartment, arms around each other.

"It's okay, Dai Ling, they'll get over it, you'll see . . . "

"They won't. You don't understand, Talya . . . "

"But they adore you. They'll have to accept your choice. Just give them time. You can stay here."

"Can I? Can I really?"

"Of course. It's time you moved away from your parents' house anyway."

Dai Ling flinched slightly, but decided to ignore Talya's remark. She felt both excited and trapped, but without her own money she had no choice.

"Can I bring my stuff over tonight? I have classes all day, but I'll go home at dinner time and I'll . . . I'll tell them."

"Congratulations on coming out," Talya said, leading her into the living room. "You're very brave. It's probably the hardest thing you'll ever have to do. Come on, I'll make coffee."

"Well, I didn't exactly. My dad kind of guessed. I mean he was suspicious and . . . "

"It doesn't matter how it happened. You told him. I'm so proud of you. Why d'you think we have Pride Day? We have to be proud of who we are because there's a million people out there ready to trash us as freaks."

"Oh my god . . . "

"What is it?"

"I can't believe this is happening. I never imagined having a fight with my parents."

"I told you, they'll get over it. You have to be patient."

"But it hurts." Dai Ling began to cry, bent over, sobbing. "I love Ma and Babá."

"Come here," Talya said, cradling her. "Tell you what, I'll go and talk to your dad if you like."

"No! You can't do that. He'd refuse to speak to you. I know him."

"Not if I go to his clinic. I have to return his books anyway. He's a professional. I think that will be stronger than his homophobia."

"My dad's not homophobic. He just doesn't understand."

Talya laughed. "Come on, here's your coffee."

"I feel like I'm being swallowed," Dai Ling said, sitting on the sofa and placing her coffee cup on the table in front of her.

"It's claustrophobia, like when you were buried in Ray Lee's garden."

"You think so?"

"Of course, you're perfectly safe here. Tell me the story," she said, sitting next to her.

"But I've told you before."

"I never get tired of hearing it. Each time you tell it the story becomes more vivid." Although Talya was staring directly at Dai Ling her eyes had a faraway look, as though she were searching for something in the distance. "These are the stories that have made you, Dai Ling. They're like paintings with layers and layers of colour and glazing. Some colors are so deeply embedded that they appear only as a faint hue shining through the surface like blood under the skin. You know it's there, but you never see it unless . . . "

"They say you can see the ancestors' blood circulating inside the funerary jade." Dai Ling took Talya's jade pendant between her fingers and touched it to her own bracelet. "It's buried with the dead to help them safely to the other side, then we dig it up for the next generation. I didn't even know my great-grandmother who was buried with this bracelet around her wrist."

Talya closed her hand around Dai Ling's hand which held the pendant. "This is my power and protection," she said,

"And your good fortune. Look," Dai Ling said, opening her hand, "There are two words engraved on it."

"What do they say?"

"Catch luck."

"I caught you." Talya laughed and kissed Dai Ling. "I bet your parents would rather Ray Lee had caught you."

"You're right. I can't imagine them ever getting used to us being together."

"Don't they have gays and lesbians in China? Elliott told me . . ."

"I don't know what they do in China. I'm Canadian!"

"Okay, okay, I'm sorry. Tell me the story again so I can see you clearly."

Dai Ling began, pulling forth the dark ribbon of her story, unravelling in scarlet words edged with gold, transforming as she spoke into the long line of a charmed life stretching before her. When the story was finished she opened her eyes and found Talya staring at her.

"There you are," Talya said. "That's who you are."

Nick lay curled in the centre of their bed, his hands clenched, nails digging into his palms. His stomach growled but he had no appetite and alcohol no longer affected him. There was nothing to draw him from the bed . . . except Talya. Nick had entered the whiteness of this void many times since Katya's death, and had returned, pulled back by the thought of his daughter, by their weekly dinner dates, by her telephone calls. But his deepest need was still for Katya, for her touch, her hypnotic eyes, for the cradle they had woven to hold each other in the world. It wasn't fair. They'd had an agreement. She had stood between him and the world and then she had abandoned him. He felt like a surviving Siamese twin, half of himself severed in the separation.

Nick had tortured himself with photographs. He had stood in her closet and inhaled the faint perfume that lingered there. He had crouched in a corner, his face buried in her rose silk blouse. When his old friend, Bill Cameron came to the house Nick had stood like a ghost, unable even to invite him in. "Hey, Nick," Cam's gravelly laugh, "It's been too long, Bud. What's happening?" He'd punched his shoulder, "Got a game plan, Nick." Leaning in conspiratorially, he'd said, "Couple of girls lined up, dinner reservations, a few drinks, dancing . . . Are you on?" When Nick shook his head Cam had said, "Aw, c'mon, Bud, do you good, do us both good. I'm on my own now. Jenny left me, took the kids, the furniture, everything. All I got is the TV."

"I'm sorry, Cam. I'm so sorry. I just can't . . . "

Cam had shrugged and pressed his lips together. At the bottom of the steps he'd turned back and said, "Call me, Nick. Call me when you're feeling up to it, okay?"

Nick had watched him sloping down the driveway, his big feet crunching on the gravel. He walked as though he were still wearing football tackle. They had been in college together, graduated to Bay Street, same brokerage company, Cam's desk across from his. He would always put his feet up on the desk, lean back with his headset on, winking at Nick as he talked his clients up, all the while gesturing with his big hands. No wonder Jenny had left him. How many women had there been? And Cam had always ribbed him about his fidelity. "Katya got you by the balls, Bud? What's her secret?"

That night Nick had pushed the living room furniture back, poured himself a tumbler of vodka and danced to their favourite songs. *Heaven, I'm in heaven, and my heart beats to that I can hardly speak . . .* His voice had cracked. He'd taken a gulp of vodka and resumed his lonely waltz, arms embracing the air, holding the empty shape of his Katya. *I seem to find the happiness I seek when we're out together dancing cheek to cheek . . .*

She'd loved the old songs. She always sang beside him in the car, watching him at the wheel, her eyes sparkling. *Blue skies shining above, nothing but blue skies for my love . . .* He uncurled himself slowly and reached for the phone. He dialled and waited, his fragile body pulsing to the useless beating of his heart.

"Natáshenka . . ."

"Dad! Where've you been? I've called you so many times."

"Will you come home, Talya?"

"Of course, Dad, of course I'll come. But I'm on duty in an hour. How about tomorrow morning?"

"I want you now."

"I can't, Dad. I'm on duty at Mount Sinai till midnight, then I'll have to get some sleep. I'll come over as early as I can tomorrow."

"Promise?"

"Yes."

There was a pause and then he said, "I can't go on."

When Talya spoke her voice was tinged with fear. "What d'you mean? . . . Dad?" She heard him sobbing at the other end of the phone. "Oh, Dad . . . stop. Please stop."

"Talya, please . . . you're her flesh and blood."

"Look, I have to go now. I'll see you tomorrow."

Talya shivered as she replaced the receiver. She felt strangely removed, as though the conversation had happened a long, long time ago. She busied herself preparing for her shift at the hospital, gathering her stethoscope, her palm pilot, stuffing a white coat into her pack.

Nick was waiting for her in the living room, watching from the window. He met her in the front hall as she walked in the door. "Natáshenka. I didn't think you'd come." He staggered towards her, arms reaching.

"Oh, Dad, look at you." He was unkempt. He smelled. "What's wrong? Are you drunk?" He shook his head. "You're so thin and . . . you've been neglecting yourself. Come on, let's get you into the bath."

"I want to talk to you," he said.

"First a bath." Talya took his hand and led him upstairs. She turned on the hot tap and poured a stream of her mother's rose essence bubble bath into the swirling water.

"Can you manage?" she asked curtly. "I'll fix you something to eat while you're bathing. Here's the shampoo. And a towel." She found a slab of rose-perfumed soap in the bathroom cabinet and unwrapped it. "Here, Mom's soap. You'll smell like her."

"Talya?" Nick was sitting on the edge of the tub, scrunching his toes into the pile of the bathroom mat. "Will you scrub my back."

"Sure." She waited while he undressed, fumbling with buttons, slowly pulling off his shirt, letting it drop onto the bathroom mat. She heard his pants zipper and felt a tremor as he almost lost his balance. His underpants hung pathetically around his hips. Talya tried not to look. She was embarrassed to see her father's pale flesh. Finally he peeled off his socks and climbed into the steaming tub.

"Watch out, Dad! You'll burn yourself." She lurched forward and shut off the hot tap. "Oh look, you're turning red!"

"It's all right. I don't feel it. I'm a white Russian."

They both laughed as she turned on the cold tap, gently swishing cool water around him. She held the soap in her left hand, rinsed his back and began soaping it vigorously. His hair straggled in damp curls, neck bent forward, his back curved like a very old baby.

"Remember how we'd bathe together when you were little?"

"I remember Lily bathing me."

"No, but we bathed you, your mom and I, when Lily was gone."

"I missed her."

"We wanted you to ourselves. Ouch! You're scrubbing too hard," he whimpered.

"Sorry, Dad. I'm not exactly nursing material."

"No, you're going to be a doctor." He looked up into her face, his eyes wide. "I'm proud of you, Natáshenka."

"Thanks, Dad." She took his bristly face in her hands and kissed his damp forehead. "Come down when you're done. And don't forget to shave."

Talya left the bathroom quickly and closed the door. Standing in the corridor she licked her salty lips. A shiver passed through her. She moved like a whirlwind, ripping soiled sheets off his bed, running downstairs, throwing them into the washing machine with gobs of soap powder, setting the dial. She stacked dirty dishes in the dish washer, cleaned out the fridge and threw all the rotten food into a garbage bag. She gathered empty vodka bottles from the living room and piled them on the back porch with the garbage. She called Molly Maid and asked them to send a team over the next day, then she opened some cans and laid out a meal of sorts — pickled beets, artichoke hearts, olives, tuna, and crackers. She picked fresh herbs from the overgrown kitchen garden where skeletal lupins were barely visible above tall grass surrounding the tennis court. When she returned to the kitchen Nick was standing in the doorway, a lopsided smile on his face, his hair curling damply around his ears.

"You look much better, Dad, but you do need a haircut."

He was like a half-dead plant plunged suddenly into warm water. Talya put her arms around him and laid her head on his shoulder. She felt the delicacy of his spirit, barely hovering, absorbing her life force. "Come and eat." She took his hand and led him to the table.

"In the kitchen?"

"Why not?" Talya pulled out a chain for him and walked around to the other side of the long wooden table.

"Katya would never eat in the kitchen."

"Come on, you're half starved." Talya began filling his plate with small portions of the makeshift meal. She found a bottle of white wine in the fridge, opened it and poured them each a glass. When she returned to the table Nick was bent over his plate eating like a hungry child.

"I want you to take her clothes."

"I have plenty of clothes, Dad."

"Please. I can't bear to see them hanging there."

"I'll call the Salvation Army."

"No. I don't want them to go to strangers." He took a swig of wine and wiped his mouth with the back of his hand. "Wouldn't some of your friends like to . . . " he trailed off as he caught her eye. "We did our best, Natáshenka. I don't know how we failed you."

Talya drained her glass, set it on the table and twirled the stem.

"She wanted you so desperately. You can't imagine the joy we felt when you were born."

"I guess Mom was relieved after all that time bed-bound."

"You don't know how wonderful she was. You never allowed her to show you."

"Oh, please!" Talya pushed her chair back from the table, scraping the tiled floor.

"Don't waste your life hating her, Talya."

"I don't hate her! I . . . "

"You're just like her. You're the very best of her — bright and quick and witty — so sensitive and easily hurt." He stared at her, willing her to meet his gaze, but she wouldn't. "It was a terrible blow to her, all those miscarriages. With each one she felt more inadequate. The fifth time she miscarried it was already four months and the foetus was perfectly developed." He wiped his mouth again, searching with his tongue for a morsel lodged in a molar. "It happened in the morning. She called me at the office. I came home right away and she took me upstairs to the bathroom. There it was between two sheets of paper torn from a magazine. I'd never seen a foetus before. It took me out of myself somehow . . . I can't explain, but Katya understood. She felt the same. We hadn't seen the others. It'd always been too early and whatever remains there were the doctor whisked away." He caught her eyes now as she glanced up, and he held her there. "The baby was like something from another world, dark and wet, and we wanted it to be alive. 'My heart is pierced,' Katya said, and I knew what she felt because that tiny thing had pierced me too. Three inches long," he held up his index finger, "stuck on a glossy page — an ad for computer software — with a cord trailing from the centre of it. 'I'm going to a specialist,' she said. 'I'm going to bear our child, Nick, even if we have to resort to technology.' She thought of nothing else until you were born." He bowed his head. "Then we burned the foetus."

There was a long silence.

"You haven't noticed, have you?"

"What?"

"The ARTwomb."

"What about it?"

"When you were in Geneva there was a storm. It shattered. Vibration of the thunder, I suppose." She stared at her plate, pushed the olive pits around, formed a circle with them.

"D'you remember when I broke the blue vase on the hall stand, sliding down the banisters?"

He nodded.

"It was an accident."

"We didn't blame you," he said. "We never punished you."

"You didn't need to."

Nick sat, head in hands, hair curling around his thick fingers.

"I was just a little girl, Dad! I had to get my comfort from Lily."

"We gave Lily the money to go home to her own children."

"You sent her away because I loved her!"

Nick jerked his head up and looked at her, his handsome face sagging and defeated.

"Oh, Talya. We were sorry for her, that's all."

"She was supposed to be my surrogate mother," she said accusingly.

Nick nodded, his eyes inscrutable to Talya as she stared into the deadness of them.

"There was a post-mortem in Geneva," he said. "Inside your mother's tumor they found a dead creature. I saw it. It was like that foetus from twenty-five years ago, but it was ancient — a homunculus with long strands and tufts of hair — monstrous, like something deprived of light, a rotten potato forgotten under the sink, long tubers sprouting from it. It had claws like a dog, Talya, yellow horny claws grown out of proportion to its tiny hands." Nick's voice was hoarse. "The face was distorted. One long tooth pierced its lower lip. I can't believe that creature dwelt in my Katya all these years."

"My twin."

Nick shook his head. "No, my darling, a monster. A pathetic little monster." He pulled a large handkerchief from his pocket and blew his nose. "I'm sorry, *moya dochka*, that I haven't been the father you wanted."

Talya's mouth quivered into a bitter smile, as though she might cry. But instead she reached for Nick's hand across the table and clasped it, digging her nails into the fleshy mound of his palm. Her body began to shake. There was blood in Nick's palm when she pulled her hand away and covered her face. "I'm sorry," she chanted, "I'm sorry, I'm sorry."

Another sweltering summer passed at the court in Madrid, another winter, and with the coming of spring in the year 1564, Anne Van Wesele began to feel like a dumbshow before the glazed eyes of her husband, her every attempt at discourse failing in the wake of his retreat, further and further into the distance. Finally, in the privacy of their bedchamber one afternoon as she came upon him at the open casement, she took him by the shoulders and shook him.

"Andreas! You must talk to me! What ails you, husband?"

"I was remembering . . . Padua . . . the golden days."

"Not Brussels? Not our home in the Brabant?"

"No. Padua."

Her lips betrayed a tremor, then she braced herself. "*I* have been remembering Brussels. A return to our home would be timely and advantageous. Annie is eighteen years old and she must be married. There will be suitors aplenty for her in Brussels."

"I do not wish to return to Brussels."

"Nor do I expect you to."

"Nor can I."

"Of course not."

Vesalius was alert now, and suspicious. He had tried to forget the glimpsed parting at the door, tried to persuade himself that he'd been mistaken.

"How do you propose to get there?"

"I'll travel overland."

"I will accompany you."

"It won't be necessary."

"As far as the border."

Anne seemed about to protest, but she held her tongue and nodded. "We'd like to leave within the month."

"We?" His eyes narrowed.

"Annie is agreeable. She desires a suitable match."

"And you? What do you desire?"

For a split second, in which the air around her turned white and cold, Anne stood with held breath, eyes locked on Andreas, uncertain of her reply. "To go in peace," she heard herself say, and time moved on.

Vesalius turned away. "I'll speak to the king about a letter of free passage." He heard the door close.

Vesalius was quick to form a plan. He couldn't bear the helplessness of his situation. Although he wouldn't name it he knew his marriage was finished and the tugging within him demanded, finally, that he follow where it was pulling.

Something irresistible pulled him forward. *Something is lost*, he thought, *something must be retrieved. Jerusalem. I will go on a pilgrimage to clear the way for a new beginning.* He found himself leaning forward, poised at the edge of his chair, his beard jutting, his blood racing. Vesalius sprang to his feet and headed for the king's chambers.

Jia Song was waiting for her. When Dai Ling entered quietly through the back door Xian Ming looked up from the stove. "Your father is in the parlour."

They had argued. "Don't send her away," she'd begged. "You're at work all day, but my life is here at home. Dai Ling's comings and goings are what I live for. We must be patient. This will pass." But a door had closed in Jia Song. He was determined. As Dai Ling entered the parlor he stood abruptly, knocking the table where the orchid rested, causing its petals to tremble. They stared at each other, then he spoke, his speech curt and cold.

"Have you thought about what I said to you last night?"

"Babá, please don't cause a fight. What about Ma?"

"Answer me."

"I'm moving in with Talya."

"I will not allow this."

"You can't stop me."

"If you leave my house I will disown you."

Dai Ling stared in disbelief. "You can't do that. I'm your daughter."

"You are no daughter of mine. You are unnatural."

"Babá! No! Please listen to me, I . . . "

"I've heard enough. You must obey me. I am your father."

"But you're cruel. You've never been like this . . . " She trailed off, suddenly afraid as she realized that she couldn't reach her father. Their shadows chased silently around the room, Jia Song puffing like a dragon, Dai Ling running, running, laughing, *I'm in love with you, remember?* She began to cry, wailing like a child. "It's like my uncle, isn't it? You're going to banish me like my uncle!"

Jia Song lunged forward, his hand raised and, as Dai Ling cringed, he stopped, frozen. Then he turned suddenly, threw on his coat and overshoes in the hallway, and left by the front door, banging it behind him.

Xian Ming found Dai Ling standing like a ghost. When she saw her mother she began to wail again and Xian Ming took her in her arms. "Your Babá is right. You must do as he says, Dai Ling. Forget this silliness."

"No!" She wrenched free of Xian Ming's arms. "I'd rather give up the cello than give up Talya! This is *my* decision, *mine*, Ma. I'm twenty-one years old. Stop treating me like a child."

She ran from the parlour and up the stairs, leaving Xian Ming standing alone amidst her trembling plants. As Dai Ling threw clothing and shoes, books and sheet music into a suitcase she tried to still her mind because she couldn't bear to think of what was happening. It was unbelievable, shocking. When the case was full and she was struggling to close the zipper she looked up suddenly and saw her *shui pao* hanging, a gift from her Babá. She hesitated a moment, then she grabbed it from the back of the door and laid it on top and closed the case. As she left the room she turned back, standing in the doorway. *I've slept in this room all my life. I never thought to leave like this, never.* She looked at her narrow bed, the bedside table with the soft pink light she'd read by — biographies of Jaqueline du Pré and Yo-Yo Ma, *Lives of the Composers* — the half-empty closet with dustballs in the corners, the window overlooking Xian Ming's garden.

Her mother would not look at her as she passed by the parlor door. Dai Ling saw her from the corner of her eye, hunched over, face in her hands.

Candles burned all around them on the deck, flickering, throwing shadows on the melting snow. In Dai Ling's hand a bulbous glass glimmered darkly with wine. A freakish warmth had lured them out into the night; Talya had insisted — "We must celebrate," she'd said. "It's spring, a new beginning." But it was only the beginning of April. Dai Ling knew there would be more to come. Ma never planted her garden until May 24th.

They toasted each other, their chairs pulled close together, Dai Ling's feet in Talya's lap. She felt she'd lost everything and was adrift in the sky, a place much larger than she'd ever imagined, absorbing her, so small in the scheme of things. Even though she felt like crying, she knew it was all right, because it was like the music, how she lost herself in it, but then she could always lay down her bow and return. She stared into Talya's eyes, searching there. Talya leaned forward, her mouth full of wine, and Dai Ling parted her lips to receive it, letting the liquid trickle down her throat, her chin, drizzling a dark path between her breasts.

An early band of meteors showered the sky, spraying ancestral patterns on the darkness of Earth's revolution.

Dai Ling heard a whining, sharp and insistent, then Ruby's cold nose pushed at her face, rooting, trying to raise her head. She knew Talya was gone even before she reached into the empty space beside her. As her feet hit the floor she threw on her *shui pao*, the crane swaying on her back as she ran towards the door, her motion sliced by bars of moonlight through the blinds as though the bird were trying to flap its broken wings. Talya might be sleeping on the couch, but no, she wasn't there. Through the kitchen window Dai Ling saw their empty wineglasses, the deck bathed in moonlight. Everything had an eerie quality, as though there had been a party and everyone had gone home leaving her there alone. Ruby was at the door now, scratching and whimpering to get out.

Dai Ling shivered as she stepped onto the deck and stood there listening. An occasional swish of tires on the wet street, slush melting into the gutters, the scream of an ambulance in the far distance, whining to a crescendo, stopping suddenly. *Where is she?* Dai Ling's heart pulsed a slow beat, all the threads of her body interwoven with Talya, taut. A sound in the night, no more than a drip soaking into the earth, but she heard it. Then Ruby's snuffling from across the garden, the flag of her tail waving in the darkness.

Dai Ling ran across the sodden grass and gathered Talya in her arms. She was like a large doll, her limbs flopping. In her right hand shone a bright blade of light and down her left arm a jagged gash oozed darkness. There was a ripping sound as Dai Ling tore at her *shui pao* and began to wrap Talya's arm, pushing Ruby away, but the dog kept on lapping at her arm until Dai Ling shouted at her, then she slunk away. She tore another length, ripping off the crane's feet, binding them around Talya's arm. Something dropped from her hand — the jade pendant, a broken chain.

"I'm sorry," Talya whimpered. "I'm sorry, I'm sorry," her voice so faint.

Dai Ling pushed her body forward to support Talya's back and wrapped her arms tightly around her. The bandage was darkening at the crease of the elbow and in the centre of her forearm. "Talya, we must go to the hospital. You need stitches."

In the first grey light of dawn she saw Talya's face emerge.

"No, not the hospital . . . not the General . . . or Mount Sinai . . . " Her voice was barely audible.

Dai Ling tightened the bandage and pressed hard with her thumbs on the dark, wet places. "Why did you do it? Why didn't you wake me?"

"Couldn't bear it . . . had to feel . . . "

She opened Talya's other hand, took the green shard and flung it into the bushes.

"I can watch the cut heal," Talya said, her voice surging, "Then I know I can win the battle."

"What battle?"

"'Gainst my devil twin. Pain so big . . . couldn't feel till I cut."

"Shhh. Come on, we're going inside. It's too cold out here." Dai Ling eased Talya's head back till it was resting on her shoulder. She placed the pendant in Talya's palm and closed her fingers around it. "Hold onto that."

"The stars are fading," Talya said, gazing up at a grey sky as Dai Ling lifted her, "But they're still inside me. I could go blind with pain, but they'd still be inside me."

They hobbled together into the apartment, Dai Ling almost weeping now. She was shivering again and wished that she was home in her own bed. *What have I gotten myself into with this crazy woman and her devil twin talk? Maybe Ma and Babá were right.* But Dai Ling was a girl who'd survived death and resurrection.

"Come on, Talya, help me. Sit on the sofa while I get some hot water and disinfectant."

Ruby sat alert at Talya's side, licking her hand persistently.

By the time the ambulance came Talya was only semiconscious, leaning into Dai Ling, murmuring unintelligibly, something about St. Mike's, Women's College —hospitals, Dai Ling supposed, but the situation was out of her control now.

As they sped through the empty streets with the siren screaming, Dai Ling felt the universe spinning crazily, her body throwing out lines to anchor itself. She felt Talya's soul in staunch alliance with her body, vowing to keep on; her sweet on and on, wise and incorruptible, keen as a wet-nosed animal. *All I ever wanted was to hear the music and I find myself trapped in a nightmare, rooted in hope.* Her throat ached with unshed tears as she was torn between feelings of anger at Talya for what she'd done, her own pain at the shocking loss of her home and family, and an instinctual knowledge of something larger. She thought of all the lovers in the world, loyal to each other, all the souls singing in their bodies. The nightmare of the Brunswick Street garden would stay with her always — a memory of blood and life and risk.

Talya lost consciousness as they pulled into the General. Everything moved so fast it was a blur of white light through which Dai Ling moved painfully slowly. The next thing she remembered was sitting beside Talya watching a bag of blood dripping into her right arm. The other arm was stitched and bandaged. A stocky, dark-haired doctor bent over her and whispered something which caused Talya to smile faintly as she opened her eyes.

"Ellie," she said, "Thank Heavens you're on Emerg. Must be all the stars inside me."

He put his finger to his lips. "Don't talk, Tal. Save your strength. I'm sending you home to rest. You'll feel way better after this transfusion."

"Elliott, don't tell . . . "

"No worries, sweetheart. Why d'you think I'm getting you the hell out of here?"

Elliott introduced himself to Dai Ling and kissed her cheek. "Give her a couple of these when you get her home," he said, pressing a vial of tablets into her hand, "And take a couple yourself, why don't you. They'll help you sleep."

Talya wouldn't let Dai Ling call Nick. "What's the point in worrying him? I'm okay now, I promise. It was just the details about Mom's . . . tumor that unhinged me. I'll be back at work tomorrow. Problem is I won't be able to hug you for a while," she laughed. "Go to your orchestra practice, please. And don't look so serious."

But Dai Ling skipped practice and took the subway to Broadview, the streetcar south to Gerrard, and walked east . . . to Ray Lee's house. She half expected to see her Ma on the street and was disappointed when she didn't see her amongst the bustle of ladies shopping at Cai Yuan.

"I'm lucky to get some of your precious time, Dai Ling. Never see you now that you're in the National Youth Orchestra *and* in love," Ray teased as they headed for Withrow Park.

"Have you heard the news?"

"Now what?"

"Your Ma didn't say anything?"

"About what?"

"My Ma didn't talk to her?"

"Come on, Dai Ling, spit it out!"

"I've left home, Ray. My dad has disowned me."

Ray's grin was quite inappropriate, but Dai Ling knew that it meant he was scared for her.

"You told him?" he asked.

She nodded and began to cry. Ray gathered her in his arms and held her for a long time while she sobbed out her story. Then he gave her his handkerchief. "That's enough, Dai Ling. Peeeeople will saaaaay we're in looooove," he crooned.

Dai Ling laughed and hiccoughed as she dabbed at her eyes. "What are you so happy about? Did you get over your heartache?"

"Oh sure. I knew it couldn't last. Ana Lisa's fifteen years older than me."

"*And* married. So you have another girl now?"

Ray leapt at an overhanging branch and set the whole tree trembling, releasing a shower of drops from the overnight rain. "Remember Dee-Dee Chong?"

"Of course. She moved to Willowdale years ago."

"Well, I found her."

"Where?"

"She came into the bookstore looking for a book on Eisenstein. She's studying History of Film. Isn't that amazing?"

"You'll have to show her all your boring Ozu films, and Mizoguchi, and Kurosawa."

"Hey!" he protested. "But seriously, this one's for real. Wait till I tell Ma. She'll be over the moon. She always loved Dee-Dee. Oh sorry, I didn't mean . . . "

"It's okay. We can't all have perfect lives."

"But you're in love with Talya, aren't you?"

"Ray, I feel like I'm just beginning to get to know her. It's a crazy roller-coaster ride. And I've lost my Ma and Babá."

"Don't lose hope, Dai Ling. This is a different country. They have to learn from us."

"But what if they don't come around?"

"It's a risk. You must be brave. When you're an old lady and you look back on your life you'll say, I remember that day in Withrow Park when Ray Lee told me to be brave, and he was right."

Dai Ling tried to punch him but Ray ducked just in time and started running. Dai Ling chased him until she caught up and grabbed his sleeve so hard it ripped. They both laughed.

"I know you're right, but there's a part of me that's so scared."

~

Talya entered the morgue with an image in her mind of a small bent creature, hardly human, begging for its life. She felt polluted by the knowledge of her mother's tumor, somehow responsible. Everything had come too late. *Too late, it's too late, too late.* Too late for what? It made no sense. She took a deep breath and held it high in her chest.

"Stage fright?" Elliott was at her side. He touched her hand, his eyebrows questioning.

"I'm fine."

"That's my girl."

He gave her the thumbs up and Talya closed her mind and approached the cadaver. A shiver passed through her as she picked up the scalpel. Stage fright, yes. *And I'll dare and dare and dare until I die!* She was Joan of Arc standing in a pool of light, star of the school play, Nick and Katya sitting front row centre. The play was over, they stood and cheered, their hands a blur of applause. Did that creature live in her then?

The pathologist pulled back the sheet. It was a male. Talya saw everything in a flash; shrunken genitals, injury to the neck, blackened face, hair matted on the pale chest, waxen hue around the half-moon of the nails. She glanced at the pathologist, who nodded. Talya slid the scalpel into the soft place under the rib cage and pulled it downward to the pubic bone. Her good arm. So easy. Like gliding through water, the generous body opening itself to reveal its shocked organs.

Talya heard a sigh and she didn't know if it was her own breath, one of the students, or a posthumous sound from the traumatized body. She laid the scalpel down and proceeded now with both hands, as though they were independent of her, removing vital organs, weighing, dissecting, until the torso was an empty cavity. Then the pathologist stepped forward with a skill saw and buzzed through the breastbone. There was the heart, pale and shrivelled. She wished the man was alive so she could see the beating of his organs, hear the symphony of them. All her desire in that moment was to witness the harmony of the living body's fabric, the mysteries of its perversion.

Afterwards, in the cafeteria, she was elated. Elliott congratulated her. Then he turned on her. "I'm really mad at you, cutting yourself up like that."

"Fuck off, Elliott."

"Goddam it, Tal, if anything happened to you what d'you think I'd do?"

"What d'you mean?"

"I love you for chrissakes! Don't you know that?" he asked angrily. "Can't keep a lover for more than a few months, but I've been in love with you since the first day I set eyes on you in the Med Sci lobby. In a brotherly way of course."

"I need a brother. Promise me you'll always be here."

"Gimme five! Other hand, silly," he said as Talya lifted her throbbing left arm. Dai Ling had helped her to dress it that morning, the skin puckering, pulled by a scab already closing over her long wound. It mortified her to know that Elliott had done the stitches, but at least she could trust him to keep it quiet. The whole thing had been kind of like gambling, something driving her — humiliation or death by bloodletting, risking the end of her career. But she hadn't intended to cut so deep and she felt stupid now, although better somehow, cleansed. She took a gulp of coffee and set her cup down, staring at Elliott.

"You *did* have a lover for more than a few months. In fact, as you confessed to me in a caffeine-manic moment, it was two years. Isn't that right, Ellie?"

"So?"

"What happened to you when he was dying?"

"None of your business, nosy bitch."

"Come on, tell me."

"I went through hell," he said, gesticulating dramatically to undercut his words.

"What was his name?"

"Joe."

"Where'd you meet?"

"Montréal, Pride Day."

"And . . . ?"

"Oh, Talya!" he exclaimed impatiently, and then continued, resigned. "He was an artist, the most beautiful man, like a wild creature surprised in the forest. Green eyes, long graceful limbs, and a kind of Pan-like quality — with an erection to match I might add. Being with Joe was another reality, like nothing I'd known before. We lived on Amherst in the Gay Village, right in the thick of it. We'd stay up all night, doing our thing, you know," — he caught his lower lip between his teeth and narrowed his eyes — "At Aigle Noir, a leather bar we liked . . . at Adonis . . . Stud . . . Then we'd cruise over for breakfast at our favourite greasy spoon and watch the sun come up. It was a helluva life until Joe got sick." He looked up at Talya, his eyebrows raised. "I lived with him till the end, Tal. I looked after him." He shook his head. "Nothing could ever match that time, not the bars, the multiple S & M partners, the . . . "

"Not even med school?"

Elliott smiled. "Kind of like that, really intense, but with one patient." With a quick hand gesture he resumed his customary flippancy. "Now there are lots of patients and legions of lovers. I trust in non-monogamy and my own magical immunity against all harm, against cancer, AIDS, ALS, Crohn's, against all forms of disease, viral and bacterial, against accidents and coincidences, against flesh-eating disease and mad cow and bird flu and . . . "

"Elliott, Elliott, stop! What happened when Joe died?"

He stared at her, and his jaw began to quiver. "They put him in the hospital at the very end, and they barred me from visiting."

"The family?"

He nodded.

"Oh Elliott, I'm so sorry."

He bowed his head, unable to speak. Talya reached for his hand and he held onto her tightly, his shoulders trembling.

"Oh sorry, is that your bad hand?" he said as she winced.

"No, it's the good one!" They both burst out laughing. "Sorry, Ellie, but you were holding so tight."

He wiped his eyes and blew his nose with a large white handkerchief. "That's why I support gay marriage, Tal, stupid though it is — a ridiculous institution which goes against everything we stand for, right? But it's the only way to claim our basic rights. Some guys get beaten to a pulp, some are murdered, then there's the invisible crime — family privilege. They wouldn't even tell me where he was buried. But I found out and we had our own private funeral," he said proudly, "with champagne and cheesecake — that was Joe's favourite. I ate it all for him then I got a pain in my gut. I'm lactose intolerant," he said, laughing.

"So *that's* why you went into med school. It's a true passion."

"You know it is. I want to make people better, I want to help . . . "

"You'll be a better doctor with your armour off, Ellie. I'm trying really hard to get rid of my own. Can we do this together . . . this . . . disarmament?"

"So, what are you armoured against, sweetheart? What's in there fighting to get out with all the bloodletting? Aside from systemic homophobia, internalized oppression and the frozen need for a textbook mom waiting with chocolate chip cookies when you come home from school?"

"Shut up!" Talya glared at him.

"Come on, Tal. Hannibal and Starling, remember? I tell, you tell, true confessions."

Talya sighed, leaned her arms on the table, then winced and pulled back. "Dad told me about a grotesque little foetus they found inside my mom's tumor, a shrunken thing. It freaked me out, because I've always believed until recently . . . well not exactly believed, but held it like a personal mythology . . . that I was gestated in an artificial uterus."

"What?" Elliott's mouth dropped open in mock surprise.

"Ectogenetic gestation to term *is* technically possible, Elliott, there's been billions of dollars of funding poured into the research for decades. Aldous Huxley wasn't dreaming — a decanted infant *is* possible — the only thing stopping the research from perfecting the ectogenetic environment and carrying a foetus to term has been the IVF and stem cell laws. We've done it with animals, but not with humans. I know you'll think I'm crazy . . . "

"I *know* you're crazy, sweetheart, and so am I to be having this conversation with you. Go on, this is fascinating."

"There's a doctor at Cornell University, in the Center for Reproductive Medicine and Infertility — she's pioneered the development of an artificial womb by removing cells from the uterine lining, then, using hormones, she's grown layers of these cells on a modelled uterus. When the model dissolves we're left with a new, artifical womb that continues to thrive. Within days of being placed in the artificial environment embryos attach themselves to its walls and begin to grow. At this point she has to terminate her experiments to comply with IVF laws."

"She could go work somewhere else where those laws aren't in place"

Talya nodded and continued. "There's a synthetic amniotic fluid that could save premature babies. It's a breathable liquid made of perfluorocarbons — liquids that carry more oxygen than air. It's been tested on lamb foetuses not yet capable of breathing air. The only reason it's not being used on humans is lack of funding."

"Oh my, won't the Right to Lifers love this!"

"Well yeah," Talya shrugged, "It *will* redefine the abortion debate eventually."

"No kidding."

"At Juntendo University in Japan an artificial womb has been created. It's an acrylic tank filled with synthetic amniotic fluid and attached to a machine that acts as a placenta to bring oxygen and nutrition to the foetus. Goats have been successfully gestated and delivered with it."

"So, your personal myth is scientifically based." Elliott's eyes narrowed. "That's important to you isn't it Tal, to be right?"

"Not any more. What's important for me is to understand about my devil twin. I've been here a number of times, Elliott. I have memories of almost entering the world – my mom had miscarriages – I think that either I kept on coming, determined to be somehow fused with her, or maybe I had a twin who never got born . . . or a part of me that split off from a miscarried pregnancy. I don't know. I could never make sense of it, so I developed my own story when I was a kid, and because it was a secret it grew stronger and somehow warped in the darkness, like that devil foetus they found in her."

Elliott waved at someone behind her and Talya turned to look.

"Who's that?" she asked.

"My young vampire."

"Hmm, handsome."

"But shallow. Dai Ling, on the other hand, is a keeper. Cherish that girl, Tal."

"I do."

"Sorry, I interrupted, but I couldn't ignore him."

"Of course not. I was just going to say . . . Maybe I created it, Elliott, that creature. What if my imagination was so strong that it took root in her and killed her? I don't believe I ever really separated from Katya. We couldn't get along. We fought all the time, so the real bond, the part that was determined to hold us together, took root in her body, like a shadow from the past that created itself out of some . . . perverse desire."

"You know what Tal, there's no answer to this, no way of knowing. You're a crazy wonderful woman. I love you, Dai Ling loves you, your dad loves you, and I know your mom loved you — why can't you just accept that?"

Talya stared at him across the table, challenging him. Elliott whipped out his palm pilot and said, "See, I remembered mine today." As she continued to stare, he said, "You're too damned smart for your own good. Maybe you should go into psychiatry after we graduate — only three more years of study."

~

Annie sat between her parents in a state of subdued excitement as their carriage rumbled along interminably. Vesalius had started out in good cheer, encouraged by the king with a sum of money for travel expenses and a letter of diplomatic immunity to hasten matters at the several customs posts to be crossed, but they'd been travelling already for five days and he was wearying.

"We'll soon be in France, Annie," he said, "and at Cette we will be parting."

"Oh, Papa, I'll miss you!" She threw her arms around his neck and kissed his beard.

"The next time we meet, my little Annie, you will be married. I trust your mother to make the right choice."

"I'll wait for you to return from the Holy Land. You will come home to Brussels, won't you, after your pilgrimage?"

"The king wants me to resume imperial service at court directly upon my return."

Anne heard the false note in his voice and turned from her endless staring out of the carriage window. "You will return to Madrid?"

"I've been given no choice."

Anne turned away to hide her own secret. Happiness tugged at her conflicted heart, mixed with the sadness of this long, drawn out journey. The carriage lurched to a halt and an official tapped on the glass. Vesalius opened the window and handed over his letter. "Andreas Vesalius, physician to the court of Philip II," he said proudly.

The man glanced at the letter and handed it back. "Fifty miles to the frontier. You should be there by nightfall," he said and waved them on.

By the time they reached the customs crossing at Perpignan Vesalius was tired and hungry, and his head throbbed to the rhythm of the wheels. His little Annie was asleep, her head on Anne's slumbering shoulder. Vesalius handed over his letter and waited, slumped in the shadows of the carriage until, through a haze of weariness, he heard the official clearing his throat. He looked up to find an outstretched palm thrust in his face.

"What is it, man? What do you require?"

Again, the fellow cleared his throat, tilting his head suggestively. He grinned, revealing bad teeth.

"Where is my letter?" Vesalius demanded.

"We don't deal in letters here," the man whined. "We require a little gold across the palm."

His face was so close that his foul breath caused Vesalius to flinch.

"I will not pay a bribe!" he shouted, waking his wife and daughter. "This is a legitimate journey with legitimate papers from the king to prove it. We are to be given safe passage into France!"

"Oh no, sir, you're mistaken, sir. You must pay thirty francs to cross this frontier."

"Damn you!" Vesalius sprang from the carriage, cracking his head on the door frame and nearly knocked the wheedling official off his spindly legs. He snatched the letter from the man's hand and spun around in the darkness. "Who is in charge here?"

"I'm in charge, and I tell you this carriage cannot pass until you pay the customs fee."

An argument ensued in which the customs official was backed up by five silent men of increasing size who emerged from the darkness one by one like skulking dogs and menaced the little group with their presence. The carriage driver refused to drive on as Vesalius urged him and Vesalius refused to give in and pay the levy as his wife bid him.

"Come, Andreas, it's a paltry sum for our liberty to pass. We're cold and tired and it's late. We've been journeying already many days and have many more to go."

"It is not the sum, it is the principle." Vesalius dug in his heels and thrust his chin out. Anne knew that gesture. He was not going to back down.

"Then let us take lodgings for the night and get some sleep."

She trusted that the light would bring a change of heart, or of border officials. The five thugs closed in and would undoubtedly have injured Vesalius had Anne not taken her husband's arm and pulled him into the carriage.

"Turn back, driver!" she called from her window. "Stop at the first inn."

Nineteen days later Vesalius thrust the king's letter, emblazoned now with dirty thumb prints, under the Judge's nose. His case had finally come to judgement in the local court after nearly three weeks of waiting in the border town of Perpignan. The ordeal had brought Anne to the end of her patience. She had humoured, wheedled, wept, bullied, and finally lost her temper with Vesalius.

"Why are you in such a hurry?" he'd asked. "Our daughter won't lose her marriageable charms over a few weeks' delay."

"We must be in Cette as soon as possible. We're already late."

"Late for what?"

"It's none of your business. You no longer have a say in my affairs."

"While I pay for your keep and your carriage I do."

"You're leaving us to go on a . . . a . . . pilgrimage." she spat.

"And you? Where are you going in such haste? Is it your own charms you're afraid of losing with this delay?"

"Damn you, Andreas!"

"Ah, I've hit home."

"Damn you and your stubborn perversity. Annie and I will take the carriage and leave without you. I don't know why I have endured so long. I must be a fool."

"It is I who am the fool, to have wasted my life in providing for you. And now you will leave, on the eve of my hearing, when I've extended myself financially and exercised the utmost patience to save us the indignity of paying this bribe?"

"Yes, I *will* leave! I'll leave you to enjoy your moral victory. Give me money for the crossing, Andreas."

"I'll give you no money. You'll wait for me and for safe passage with our letter."

"Damn the letter! I've a mind to burn it. This journey, you will remember, is not for me, it's for our daughter and you must provide for her until I find her a husband."

Vesalius was trembling, his fists clenched bone-white. "Who is waiting for you in Cette?"

"Give me the money."

"Who is it?"

"You've spent a fortune keeping us here during this delay. You've ruined the journey for Annie. How will she remember you?"

His face blanched. "You speak as though I were dead."

"You *are* dead. Your heart is dead and unfeeling. You have worn me out with your unwilling heart." Anne bowed her head and wept noisily. Vesalius dropped his head in his hands, weary suddenly beyond all measure.

"You've found someone better than me," he stated calmly.

"Yes," she sobbed.

"And he will meet you in Cette."

"Yes, and he'll come home with us to Brussels."

"Home?"

"Cornelius is Flemish. He has left the imperial court and wishes, like me, to return to his homeland."

"To lie in *my* bed and enjoy *my* wife!"

"Oh Andreas, don't make this more painful than it already is. You said you'd let me go in peace. I thought you knew."

"Go!" He threw a purse full of coins at her feet. "Go and rut in the pigsty with your Cornelius. You're a disgrace to the Van Weseles."

Anne, her face a white mask, stooped to pick up the purse. She pulled herself upright and stared at Vesalius, but he avoided her eyes.

"I will send our daughter in to bid you farewell," she said, then she turned and walked stiffly to the door, opened it and turned back to him. "I want my freedom. When you return you will grant me a divorce. And if you never return I will presume you dead and marry Cornelius."

These were her last words. Vesalius maintained his composure until Annie, tearful and confused, had taken leave of him, then he curled under his bedcover and fell into a fitful sleep. He dreamed that his body was tossed on rocks, thrown up from the deep and cast ashore in a foreign land

and he wept inconsolably, because he knew that he was dying and could do nothing to save himself.

~

Bloor Street was busy with night-walkers; lovers sauntering arm in arm with brightly colored scarves wrapped around their necks, worshippers emerging from Evensong, weathered people who lived and slept on the street sheltering in darkened doorways with their shopping carts piled with junk. Dai Ling walked west through the Annex, past brightly lit bookshops, cafés and restaurants, longing, like everyone, for the coming of spring, discouraged by the promise of sudden warmth only to be broken by yet another freak snowfall which melted overnight and then froze. She was dressed in layers, ready to discard her skins. She missed her Ma, she missed her room in the row house on Gerrard Street where she had lived all her life. It had been a cocoon which held her and now that she was out in the world she felt raw and exposed. When she came home to Brunswick Street the apartment was often empty, like tonight. She'd eaten a sandwich standing at the kitchen counter and afterwards had picked up the phone to call her Ma. When Jia Song answered her throat thickened so that she couldn't speak and she had replaced the receiver quietly.

Now, as she stood in front of Bookworld, gazing absently through the window, a familiar voice chirped in her ear.

"Dai Ling! What are you doing here? Isn't this your night at the library?" Christie leaned across her and picked up a copy of *EYE* magazine.

"I've applied for a transfer to the Spadina branch."

"Ah, closer to home. How's it going, living with Talya? Is the honeymoon over yet?"

"What d'you mean?"

"Oh, you're such a baby dyke," she laughed. "I hope it works out for you, I really do. What do your parents think about you moving out?"

"D'you want to have coffee?"

"No, I have a date." Christie rolled the magazine into her pack and adjusted her bicycle helmet. "Elise. She's new in town. I met her on the west coast last summer. She's a sound techie. We're going to the late show at the Bloor—*The Red Violin*." Christie winked at Dai Ling and laughed.

"That's great, Christie. I can't wait to meet her."

"She's coming to sit in at rehearsal tomorrow. What are we starting with?"

"The Schubert."

"Oh, don't you love the opening? Like a waterfall bringing us into the piece."

"Your runs are so clean. And your choice of fingering gives you that light touch and speed."

"Thanks," Christie grinned, flattered. "I especially like our tumbling violin figuration that follows the wind chords in the first movement."

"My favourite is the *Elgar*."

"Well, of course, it's your solo! You're brilliant, Dai Ling. I wouldn't be surprised if you get a recording contract out of this tour."

"No one follows Jacqueline du Pré."

"Oh, I don't know, your interpretation is quite unique. And it seems effortless. How d'you do it? You should teach."

"I don't want to teach. I just love to play."

"Well I must run. Don't want to keep my date waiting. See you at rehearsal tomorrow. I'll be playing my best, inspired by the movie." Christie swung her leg over the bike and cycled down the sidewalk ringing her bell at pedestrians.

When Dai Ling opened the door Ruby jumped up, her tail wagging. She scratched her ears absent-mindedly and went to look for Talya in the bedroom, Ruby following her, licking her hand. No one home. In the living room the message machine blinked. Three blank messages — a silence and then the dial tone, each one shorter than the last, like a series of deaths. *It's Ma. I know it's Ma. She wants to talk but Babá won't let her.* Then the phone rang and she jumped, scared suddenly. She lifted the receiver, her blood racing.

As the taxi turned the corner she saw the flashing red light on the roof of the ambulance. The taxi pulled up behind it and Talya paid and jumped out. As she ran up the path she saw a man in a rumpled suit standing on the steps wringing his hands.

"Thank God you're here!" He offered a thick hand. "I'm Bill Cameron, call me Cam, old friend of your dad." He laughed, a sound like a bucket of gravel spilling. His breath smelled of alcohol.

"Where is he?" Her eyes locked on his florid face as he stumbled for words.

"It's been . . . it's been . . . a terrible shock. I dropped by — home alone on a Friday night. We're bachelors now, me and Nick. My wife . . . she left, you see, took the kids . . . "

"Where *is* he?" Talya shouted.

"I saw him through the window," Cam waved his hand at the open front door. "He's okay now, no worries," he called after her as Talya ran into the house and entered the living room.

He lay on the sofa, his eyelids fluttering as a couple of medics worked on him.

"Dad, it's me, Talya. What happened?"

Nick tried to speak, a mumbled, garbled sound, his head rolling back and forth.

"He's gonna be okay. We've given him an antidote," the young medic said. His face was pale, Talya thought, anaemic.

"Is this what he took — Diazepam?" She picked up an empty bottle lying on its side on the coffee table. Next to it was an empty bottle of Stolichnaya. "Tell me what you gave him. I'm a med student."

"Intravenus Flumazenil," the other guy said, his voice deep and authoritative. "He's responding well. Pulse almost normal. We can take him in if you like, but . . . "

"No, I can take care of him," Talya said quickly. "Will he need more?"

"Are you okay with injecting?"

"Of course. I'm in third year at U of T Med School. I work at the General and Mount Sinai."

"Fine. We'll leave you a couple of vials. He had the first at 10:05. Give it half an hour and if he's still drowsy . . . "

"Yeah, yeah, I know," Talya said impatiently.

"Just sign here," the pale young medic said, coming forward.

"You look exhausted. You should go home and rest," Talya said.

Both guys laughed. "We have a long night ahead of us," the one with the voice said.

As they left Cam hovered at the door. "Is he gonna be okay? Anything I can do?"

"He's all right, Cam. Thanks for raising the alarm. He'll owe you a few after this. You saved his life."

"What are friends for? Poor old Nick, it's been a rough road . . . "

"Look, it's late. Why don't you go home. I can take care of him now."

"Oh, I could stay and help. Got nothing to go home to, I . . . "

"Really, you've done enough." Talya rose and walked him to the door. "Thanks a million, Cam. I'll get Dad to call you when he's back on his feet."

Cam nodded and started down the stone steps, his body swaying from side to side.

"How did you get my pager number?" she called after him.

"It was right there on the telephone table," he said, turning hopefully. "Natalya – beautiful name. Nick always talks about you."

She closed the door and leaned against it. A red tide was rising in her, she felt it, the level dangerously high. She clenched her jaw and tried to control the raging. *Dai Ling,*

Dai Ling, I don't want to contaminate you with this, you're the only pure thing in my life. I wonder what TCM can do for suicides? No, it's an allopathic issue. It requires heroic action. Elliott — I'll call Elliott — no, I have to deal with this myself.

She entered the living room and tried to rouse her father. When she tried to lift him he was a dead weight, although his color was good and his pulse steady. She checked the time and gave him another shot of Flumazenil, then sat with him, stroking his face, the skin damp and clammy. She ran her hands through his freshly cut hair. The other night she had spread newspapers on the kitchen floor and snipped away with Katya's kitchen scissors, then dropped his dark curls, flecked with silver, around the white rose on the terrace. "Good for the garden, Dad."

She looked now through the french doors onto the terrace; thought she saw a figure there. *Cam, spying on us. Weird man, gives me the creeps. No, something else. Something dark in here, something hungry.* She threw the doors open and walked across the terrace, stood a moment in the darkness, then she stepped onto the grass and moved silently around the side of the house to the rose garden. She froze as she saw a white figure hunched by the arbour, then it was gone, so quickly that she wasn't sure she'd seen it. But she smelled Katya's perfume. "Go away! Leave us alone!" she screamed. "You have to let him live."

A waxing moon shone brightly, turning everything an eerie white, yet the grass looked like a lake of blood. Talya turned and started walking towards the stables. She felt the dew splashing her ankles as she walked and she felt contaminated. She found herself in Limerick's old stable, crouched once again in the corner under the belly of the ghost horse. She wanted to get up and pace, to escape the ghosts of the past, but she couldn't move and suddenly the words poured from her, as though she were vomiting.

"I've had enough! I can't go on!" She saw her arm rise up in the darkness, the jagged scar appearing as her sleeve fell back. "You dropped that devil twin on me and let it creep into my body and swim in my blood, I had to cut myself to let it out! Filthy horn-toothed monster, get off me, get out of me! I'll cut your claws and rip you out, I hate you, I hate you!" The words spewed as though someone else were speaking and she listened aghast. "Oh Dad, where are you? Help me, please! Everything was you and her, no place for me. She was your keeper and you let her do it. I miss her too, but she's dead! Don't make me be like her. I don't even know who I am. I feel like some kind of clone . . . artificial and broken, I can't . . . oh no . . . let me go . . . make it stop . . . " She was breathless, sobbing, her shoulders trembling, then it began again, gripping her. "I had to bathe you and feed you and clean up your shit. For Christ's sake, I can't do it any more. I can't protect you from the world while you lie in this bloody mausoleum. I want you . . . " she began to sob afresh, deeper and deeper, "I want you to be my daddy, let me in, help me, Daddy or I'll kill you, I swear it . . . "

As she struggled to get up she remembered bringing Dai Ling there in the fall, soon after they'd met, expecting her to understand, to inhabit her past. *But this is my place*, she thought. *No one can share this with me. No one should have to.*

She closed the stable door, mumbling to herself, "Must give him another shot. What a dumb thing to do. Thank god for Bill Cameron and his miserable failed marriage."

She made her way back to the house, staggering across the wet grass like a drunk, her legs tingling and weak. She looked at Nick, who was still sleeping, then picked up the phone.

"Dai Ling, I'm at Dad's. I have to stay over. There's been a problem here. I'll explain later."

"Are you okay?'

"Yeah, I'm fine. Where were you?"

"Did you call before?"

"Three times."

"D'you want me to come?"

"No, I'm exhausted. I'm going to sleep. Dai Ling? You're the best part of my life, d'you know that? I love you so much."

"I love you too, Talya. I miss you. It's so quiet here without you."

"I'll be home tomorrow."

She knelt beside her father and watched the slow rise and fall of his chest — the lungs carrying oxygen to his brain, the drug coursing through his veins, cleansing his blood, his heart, of the overdose. One drug to counteract another. She lifted one of his sleeping eyelids then covered his eyes with her hands, and wondered at this man who seemed more than ever a stranger.

"You're going to be all right," she whispered as softly as though he were a sleeping child, then she went upstairs and took Katya's clothes out of the closet, one by one, laying them on the bed. She folded them carefully and packed them into a large suitcase, and when it was full she took another case and filled it, until the closet was empty. Then she went downstairs and sat beside him. When she'd been little he'd sometimes read to her from *The Magic Book of Fairy Stories*. "Snow White" had been their favourite, and he would always tease her as he closed the book and kissed her forehead . . . "Mirror, mirror on the wall, who's the fairest of them all? *Moya dochka!*" A bitter smile spread on her face as she recalled how she had refused to eat red apples into her early teens for fear that her mother had poisoned them and placed them amongst the other fruit to trick her. *What a fool I've been,* she thought, *believing in all that improbable magic.*

Talya roused her father and as he woke he smiled at her, a winning smile, and she embraced him, burying her face in his neck.

Talya phoned in sick the next day, then she called Dai Ling but there was no answer, so she left a message, and went upstairs to put clean sheets on Nick's bed.

"I don't want to go upstairs," Nick said. "In fact I don't want to go on living in this house. What d'you think about selling, Talya? Making a fresh start?"

"Your call, Dad."

"Will you help me?"

"Maybe you should get Uncle Vassily down here for a few days. There's so much old family stuff in the house."

"I've been looking at the photos."

"Of Mom?"

"Childhood snaps of me and Vassily." He handed her a thick white envelope and she took the photos out, one by one, examining them, spreading them on the table.

"I've never seen these before, they're amazing. Which one is you?" she asked, lifting a tattered photo with serrated edges. "You look almost like twins."

"That's me, on the left," he said, pointing. "We were on vacation at Owen Sound, up by Lake Huron. I was learning to swim, but Vassily wasn't allowed, he was too young. He screamed so hard that I tried to pick him up and carry him into the water. Got a good spanking for that. Our dad was strict."

"Is that him with the funny swim suit?" Talya asked.

"No, that's *Dyedushka*, our grandpa Nicholas. He was a colonel in the Russian army. I was quite young when he died, but I remember him. And there's *Babushka*— Olga, his wife"

Talya looked up. "We *are* related to the Romanovs, aren't we?"

"Of course, you know that, Talya. Olga, your great-grandma, was sister to the Tsar."

Nick pointed to an old-fashioned portrait. "Here she is, the Grand Duchess Olga Alexandrovna Romanov. She married Nicholas Kulikovsky, the one with the swim suit, and they had . . . yes, here they are, two sons. The one on the left, Yuri, was my father and his second wife, Helen Gagarin, was my mother. You won't remember them, they died before you were born. They'd left Europe in 1950, the year I was born—I was conceived in Copenhagen, born in Toronto—we came to join my grandparents who'd left Denmark after the war."

The photograph became a blur as Talya listened to her father. There was something new in his voice, something that took her back to childhood, the way he'd been sometimes in their snatched moments. *This is who I've been missing,* she thought. *This is him.* She only half-listened to his words, all her attention caught by the tone of his voice, animated, like the whirring of a camera as the movie unreels, projecting onto a vast screen. And she was there, a small child staring up through a dusty stream of light, entering a magical world of flickering shadows.

"When *Dyedushka* died *Babushka* moved in with a Russian couple, in an apartment above a barber shop. Dad took us there to have our hair cut, then we'd go upstairs to see her. She kept the samovar displayed on the living room sideboard and she'd always point to it and say, 'This will be yours one day, Nicholas. You are the first-born son.'"

Nick turned to his daughter. "Look, Talya. Look." He pointed to the sideboard.

She turned away from him, following with her eye the direction of his finger. "That's it? *Babushka's* samovar?"

Talya got up and walked over to the sideboard where the Artwomb had been displayed. As she cupped the bulging samovar in her hands a slow smile began to spread on her face.

"Oh, Dad, you're such a joker," she said, turning to Nick, laughing.

"It's yours, *moya dochenka.*"

"It's beautiful. I love it!" She ran back to the sofa and sat beside him, hugging him. "Thanks, Dad."

"You're welcome." Nick bowed his head and busied himself with the photos. "Look, here's a photo of you splashing in the pool."

"Lily must have taken it. Who's that little girl? She looks kind of familiar."

"And here's your first birthday, reported in the *Globe and Mail.*"

"'*The miracle child,*' it says."

"You *were* our miracle."

"Really? I've always felt that you didn't need anyone but each other."

"Oh, Katya was determined to have you. She had this thing about mixing royal blood with blood of the peasantry."

"But she was from a wealthy family."

"The Vinográdovs made their money in Canada."

"Ah. How come you've never talked about the Romanovs? It seemed as though you had no history until you met Mom."

"I've had . . . mixed feelings about our heritage, Talya. We're a displaced family, five sub-clans scattered around the world, with no home to go back to. Russia no longer exists."

"But we exist. How can we know the truth about our family, about our blood?"

"Science. The claims of Anna Anderson were finally discounted on the grounds of DNA testing. You know that the Tsar had an unusual condition called heteroplasmy — his DNA was a mix of two types." He gathered up the photos as he spoke, putting them back into their envelope. "The bodies had disappeared but years later a grave was discovered near Ekaterinburg in Siberia where the Tsar and his family spent their final days in exile. They took a sample from the remains of his brother, Georgij, and found the same mix, so that was conclusive. We'll have to get an album, put these photos in together."

"Yes, Dad, let's do that."

"Anderson was dead by then, but they used a sample of her tissue, removed and fortunately preserved during surgery she'd had in the US, and the results ruled out her claim conclusively."

"The body as proof? Do you believe the body tells the truth?"

"Can't argue with genetic sequencing. It's given us the ability to read all the information stored in our genes."

"The history of the universe encoded in our cells? But it's still a mystery. Some things are true and not true at the same time, mysteries that can't be solved."

"Your mother and I were fated from the moment we met. We were meant to be together. I never thought it would end, you don't when you're happy, you think it's always going to be like that. Happiness excludes all other possibilities, that's the nature of it, until we fall." He sighed. "It must have been difficult for you, Talya, to find your place in this house. I'm sorry." He took a swig of water from a plastic bottle. "Got a terrible thirst."

"That's what happens when you OD," Talya said. "Oh Dad, I'm so glad you're safe." She took him in her arms and held him close.

"Me too," Nick said, his words muffled by her hair. "Guess I owe Cam. Have to buy him a big bottle of Glenlivet."

"Why did you try to kill yourself? I did everything I could, but . . ."

"Oh *moya dochka*, you're not to blame. It was a selfish thing I did, but I can't be sorry. I had to take action. And it's set me free. I went on a journey; you were at my side."

He put his hand on her knee and patted her, then staring out front, reaching with his other hand, he said, "I saw a glimmer of light in a rich darkness which has surrounded and held me in a tender embrace since I first saw Katya. I can hardly grasp it yet, but I've seen it, a tiny particle and so elusive, but . . . let me try now, yes . . . some part of her which has taken root in me," he crossed his hands on his chest, "which has grown in me and which I mistook for her when all the while it was myself. She was so grand with her quick energy, her bright ideas, her powerful spirit. And she attached herself to this part of me, transfusing herself into me, vibrant and alive, causing me to feel complete for the first time in my life."

He turned to Talya and took her in his arms, holding her close as he spoke. "When she died — well, you can imagine perhaps how I felt. I don't know how you've taken it, Talya, you've been so . . . sensible, looking after me, my dear daughter."

"Not so sensible, Dad. This is how I feel." She pulled up her sleeve and showed him her arm, the jagged scar scabbed over, pulling her skin tight.

"Oh, Talya! An accident?"

She shook her head and looked down, avoiding his eyes. "I cut myself to let the poison out. We're not so different, Dad. If you'd died I don't know what I would've done."

"Who took care of you?"

"My girlfriend. My lover. She lives with me. You met her at the funeral, but I don't suppose you remember. You were hardly there yourself. She's kept me alive through all this."

Nick nodded slowly. "I can understand that you'd turn to a woman. I haven't been a proper father to you."

"Oh Dad, it's not that. I'm a lesbian. It's the way I live."

"And my generation," Nick said, "that's how we think, that everything has a cause and effect."

"Well, Dad, if that's the way you want it, you've been a great model of romantic obsession."

They both laughed, then Talya stretched and yawned. "Oh god, I'm exhausted. D'you want some breakfast?"

"I'd like to take you out, but . . . "

"No, no, you must rest."

"A big glass of orange juice would be good. No, a jug of orange juice. I must be dehydrated," he said, smacking his dry lips and mouth."

"Are you really going to move?"

"I thought . . . maybe a condo . . . two or three rooms, that's all I need. What d'you think?"

"What are we going to do with all this stuff?"

"Sell it. Get the house on the market. Cam's sister is in real estate. I'll give her a call."

"Let's get Uncle Vassily down. We can do it together like a family. Will you keep the samovar for me?"

Nick smiled and took her wounded arm. He pulled the sleeve back, bowed his head and kissed the length of her scar, gentle kisses she barely felt because the skin around the scar was still numb, but she saw him, his lips brushing her recently opened flesh.

Vesalius did not stop in Cette. He bid the driver race on to Marseilles where he took passage on the first boat to Genoa. He could not look back for fear that his heart might break. How could he not think of Anne? She was part of his body, interwoven with him, ever present. She came unbidden at all hours, torturing him with the timbre of her voice, the weight of her breasts, her hair, the musky hot smell of her. Vesalius dropped his face into his hands and closed his eyes tight, protecting himself with a hard shell of anger.

From Genoa he travelled overland towards Venice, a distance of some 130 miles, but when they stopped en route, in Padua, he climbed down from the carriage at Del Bo and dismissed his driver.

It was night and the city streets were deserted. Vesalius walked across the hallowed courtyards of the university, drinking in the silence of the stones, and entered the operating theatre. He stood in the centre looking up and around him at the tiered balconies, seeing there the floating faces of eager young men, desirous, like himself, of uncovering the mysteries of the human body. His ears filled with sighs and whispers, the clash of metal on bone, a trickling of liquid followed by a steady drip. A wave swept over him, an undertow of memory dragging him into the glory-days of his youth. He threw his head back.

"This is my world," his voice boomed, shocking him in the darkness. "This is where I belong!" He raised his arms high and shouted, "I am home! I am home! I am home!"

He danced on the dais where the corpses were dissected, a crazed, broken-hearted man paying homage to the dead. A wind rushed in his ears and spun him in circles like a dervish until he lost himself and fell to the floor. There he lay for some minutes in the windowless theatre until a gathering of energy pulled him to his feet and led him through the dawn light of the adjoining room and out to the courtyard.

His footsteps rang clear and sharp, increasing in pace as he walked the quadrangular colonnade. He heard someone descending the wide stone steps from the upper level and waited in the shadows until a cloaked figure appeared, jangling a bunch of keys.

"Antonio?"

The man peered from under his hood. "Dr. Vesalius! Is it truly you, sir, or am I seeing an apparition?"

"Yes, it is I, Antonio." He embraced the old man, whose familiar form had welcomed many a weary-eyed dawn as Vesalius had emerged from the operating theatre. "Back from Spain, Antonio, and on my way to the Holy Land."

"Ah, Dr. Vesalius," the old man nodded. "We haven't seen you in many a year."

"I am in search of Dr. Fallopio."

"Dr. Fallopio is dead, sir, a year and a half gone with quinsy."

"Dead?" He felt nonplussed by the word. How could Fallopio be dead? He was there to see him. With a long slow gesture he stroked his beard, clustering his fingers around the point of it, releasing his hand into an inquiring gesture. "And the chair of Anatomy?"

"Vacant, sir, quite vacant since Dr. Fallopio's passing."

"Ah." He gathered his coat around him. "I must away to Venice. You have helped me greatly, Antonio." He pressed a coin into the old man's hand and was gone before Antonio could form the words to thank him.

Appointments to the university were made by the Venetian senate. Vesalius wasted no time in renewing his acquaintance with several influential Venetian families he had known during his professorship. He dined in the elegant banquet hall of the Contarinis where he conversed at length with a group of senators and rapidly secured the chair of Anatomy at the University of Padua. Then he booked passage for the Holy Land, confident in the knowledge that his spring pilgrimage would fulfil at least part of his promise to Philip of Spain and that he would be back in Padua in time to settle into quarters before commencement of the new academic year. He could hardly believe his good fortune as he emerged from the morass of his final year in Madrid, the gruelling weeks in Perpignan, his parting with Anne; it all faded as he, Andreas Vesalius, flared again.

The day before his voyage, on a fine April morning distinguished by that liquid, golden light peculiar to Venice, Vesalius entered the premises of Francesco dei Francesci, publisher and bookseller, where he was greeted warmly by Agostino Gadaldino, Andrea Marino, and several other distinguished physicians. The conversation turned to Gabriele Fallopio's demise and his legacy of the *Observationes*. Vesalius told them of his long treatise, the *Examen*, written in response to Fallopio's manuscript.

"I entrusted my letter to Paolo Tiepolo," he said. "Did he deliver it, I wonder, into Dr. Fallopio's hands?"

"Ah," exclaimed Marino, "Tiepolo was delayed many months in Catalonia due to the civil war in France. He only arrived in Venice after Fallopio's death. He must have your letter still."

They agreed to track down Tiepolo, retrieve the letter and have it published by Francesci under the title, *Andreae Vesalii Anatomicarum Gabrielis Fallopii Observationum Examen*.

Vesalius' heart swelled to fill his barrel chest as his friends lauded him in anticipation of another great work of anatomical scholarship. He felt the harvest of his life, so long fallow, springing in golden sheaves around him. "I must take leave of you, gentlemen," he said, overcome with emotion. My voyage . . . tomorrow . . . I must prepare."

He burst out onto the cobbled street and walked rapidly through a narrow alley to the Piazza San Marco. From there he headed for the water and hailed a boat.

"La Chiesa della Salute," he said and the gondolier started his leisurely circular motion.

A scattering of souls knelt in their pews, isolated islands of humanity, while circled before the altar were four priests in robes of white damask edged with purple and gold. The mosaic floor was strewn with light refracted through the stained glass windows. Vesalius dipped his fingers in the font, bobbed on bended knee and crossed himself, then he knelt and gave thanks to the Virgin for smiling upon him on the eve of his pilgrimage.

"I will honour you in Jerusalem," he whispered as he lit candles for Her, for Saint Jude Thaddeus, and for Christ.

The Latin liturgy flowed from the priests' mouths, a river of sound echoing through the domed church, setting Vesalius' soul quivering. He stood motionless in the shadows, barely breathing, and marked the music playing his body. He felt his organs tremble and spin, his body attuning as the voices entered and travelled the pathways within him. The priests dipped their faces, one by one, into a golden wine goblet, communing with the blood of Christ.

Talya speeds across the Don Valley bridge where workers are putting the final touches to suicide barriers — 10,000 stainless steel rods and bow-string masts — a luminous veil across the bridge. She imagines people throwing themselves hopelessly at the mesh, like panicked birds caught inside a glass house, banging their bodies against the windows over and over, unable to believe the divide between experience and vision. Her thoughts race as she cycles past Parliament Street, remembering Katya interred in her dark coffin at the Necropolis, past Sherbourne where she'd first seen Dai Ling, past Yonge and Bloor — *involuntary muscular contractions, chorea, chorea, chorionic membrane, St. Vitus dance, disorder of the nervous system, double snakes, systems entwining, double helix DNA strands, lovers creating figures of eight fissioning through eternity* . . . She pedals over the visioning place — Toronto, where the First Peoples gathered, fished, hunted, before the Europeans. The sky holds her as the earth spins, turning, turning.

"I'm winning," she whispers as she flirts with the paradox of her double vision, trying to recapture it and run from it simultaneously, pedalling hard, speeding away from herself, muscles aching, spirit wrestling, a creature floating on a long cord stretched taut across the city, father to lover to clinical rounds, immersed in the body, her slim fingers examining the flesh, kneading it like Easter bread. She studies Vesalius' maps and Jia Song's charts as her hands memorize the perfection of Dai Ling's body, a landscape of joy she is learning to travel.

A gate opens onto a winding path protected by an arbour of twisted vines. Collapsed in the surrounding beds are the dark sticks of last season's blooms, new shoots piercing the earth beneath them. In a corner of the Brunswick Street garden snowdrops quiver, white and fragile, nourished perhaps by Talya's blood. She leans her bicycle, wheels still spinning, against the shed and runs into her apartment.

Dai Ling plays, her life moving through her, a musical score, playing her, the player. Her body trembles with the vibration of her strings, a constant desire — for Talya, for reunion with her family, for refuge in the music. She has awoken from a dream drenched with the redness of a silken robe, and she rises shivering and covers her naked body, the shredded white feathers of the crane whispering to her the story of the Crane Maiden, which Ma used to read to her, about the bird-girl who wove a fine cloth out of the feathers of her own body; how she transformed herself and flew away.

Ruby stretches her dog's body after the long night curled in a circle, and licks Dai Ling's toes.

Everyone waits for the brief Toronto spring. When it comes, tulips shoot from the earth overnight and stand sentinel in the city, sap coursing through pale stems, coloring their bright helmets. Sap rises through the trunks of trees, forcing them into leaf. Lilac clusters in tight buds; peonies remember their roundness. Sap bubbles through sewers, spills onto streets, it rises in the air and perfumes the dreams of streetwalkers. It trickles and gushes, a deluge flooding the city, once again, with hope.

Three gardenias float in a bowl, scenting the air. Talya lies naked, her eyes green slits as Dai Ling rises above her, a many-petalled flower opening. *She loves me, she loves me not, she loves me, she loves me . . .* Outside, voices swell and fade, people passing on the street, a distant ambulance screams. Dai Ling's coppery hair tumbles like a live thing as she swings her head back and forth. Higher and higher they rise until they are above the moon and everything slows, slowing, slowing to a point of stillness where height becomes depth. They are a long, long way from Earth, embedded deep within it.

~

Xian Ming turned the earth with her spade, a steady rhythm, broken each time she bent to shake the weeds free and toss them into her wheelbarrow. When she was half-way down the first bed she stopped, leaned on her shovel and looked up at the sky. She still caught herself imagining that Geneviève might one day walk through the door, her red hair flaming, hands moving in quick gestures, punctuating her latest story. When she was a child Xian Ming had been embarrassed by her mother. All the children had laughed at her, and they'd resented Xian Ming and her Ma because they were exempt from Party criticism — they were foreigners. She'd done everything she could to fit in and to disassociate herself from Ma. Was that how Dai Ling felt about her and Jia Song, ashamed of her immigrant parents? She began to dig again, her spade opening the reluctant earth, packed tight against winter's cold.

She'd stopped feeling guilty when Ma died; the grief had cleansed her of everything. After that she'd been able to see her wild French-Canadian mother in Dai Ling, condensed and distilled, her flamboyant gestures reined in. She remembered the deep rich sound of the cello floating from Dai Ling's bedroom window. Xian Ming had loved it when she'd brought her cello home to practise. Mrs. Jordao, her first teacher, had said, "You must take her to concerts, Mrs. Xiang. Dai Ling has talent, but it must be encouraged if she's to flourish." She remembered their first concert, at the Toronto Symphony Hall, Yo-Yo Ma playing, and Dai Ling, six years old, on Jia Song's knee, hardly moving except for the fingers of her left hand playing the air. When the music ended and everyone applauded, Dai Ling had been quite still. It was a minute before she had turned to her parents, her face filled with wonder.

Xian Ming knelt and filled her hands with earth. She closed her eyes and crumbled it between her fingers, feeling for temperature and moisture content. She had learned about the earth from her Ma, about how to place and feed a plant until it bloomed and bore fruit.

"Ma?"

She opened her eyes and saw Dai Ling standing at the gate.

"Isn't it too early for planting?"

"I'm preparing the beds."

"Is Babá here?"

"He's at work. You know that. You coming home?"

Dai Ling shook her head. "I miss you, Ma."

"I miss you too. Very quiet around here."

"Is Babá okay?"

"What d'you think? You are his life."

"Can't you talk to him, Ma? Ask him to forgive me?"

"Your Babá doesn't talk. He's a different man since you left. When I try to talk to him we fight."

"I've invited Talya to come on tour with us."

"Dai Ling! This is not a vacation. It's a big chance for your career."

"I know, Ma. Don't worry. Nothing can interfere with my music."

"Something strange about that girl," Xian Ming said, "Something missing."

"There's something missing in all of us, Ma. Isn't that why we're here, to find the missing pieces?"

"Too much trouble in that family. Sick mother, crazy father."

"Remember how sad you were when Grandma died? You should have gone to see her, Ma."

Xian Ming looked up abruptly and stared at her daughter. She seemed about to speak but stopped herself, her hands gripping the top of her garden fork.

"I remember how you cried when the letters came. You tried to hide it, but I knew how much you missed her."

"I was afraid something would happen. And now I feel the same for you, Dai Ling. Like when you were little and those kids captured you and . . . "

"They didn't capture me, Ma. I agreed to be buried. And that's when I started to play cello. Remember, I told you I heard music under the earth?"

"No, you were playing two years already. You started when you were almost five years old."

"But that's when I *really* started to play, after I escaped. I don't *remember* playing before that."

"You coming in? Have some tea?"

"No, Ma. I just wanted to thank you. I know you would have gone back if you hadn't had to pay for my lessons."

A sudden shower fell through the sun's rays, transforming the garden into a crystal of rainbow patterns glancing off each surface. Xian Ming turned her face to the sky to hide her tears. The rain stopped as suddenly as it had begun.

"Good for the garden," she said, wiping her face with the back of her hand, leaving muddy streaks across her cheeks and forehead, "Good for the earth." She remembered how Dai Ling's music, floating from her open window each spring, had warmed the earth as she turned it, how she had expected their ritual to continue, in rhythm with the seasons, how precious was each moment of her daughter's life that escaped her own greed for repetition.

~

Talya was waiting in the reception room when he opened the door.

"I brought your books back," she said, rising with the pile in her arms.

Jia Song immediately hid his shock behind a polite mask as Talya fumbled to get one hand underneath the books, balancing them on her wounded arm so that she could offer her other hand to Jia Song. But he remained rigid, hands clenched at his sides. After a moment of awkward silence Talya dove in, filling the small room with a rush of words—her appreciation of the books, her favourite parts, her opinions on the comparison between allopathic and traditional Chinese medical systems . . .

"Your father?"

"He's . . . better. He won't come to see you. He doesn't believe in TCM," she said. "But I do."

Jia Song stepped forward and relieved her of the books.

"Can I talk to you?" she asked.

"I'm busy."

"Please. It's important."

Jia Song took a deep breath, then stepped back and gestured with his long arm. Talya walked past him through the open door into his consulting room. He wouldn't sit until she was seated, five feet away from him, her back straight, hands neatly folded in her lap. She remembered her boarding school days, the PhysEd teacher who used to come up behind the girls and whack them in the kidneys to straighten their spines.

"So this is not a medical visit," he said, only the tinge of a question in his intonation.

"You know what it's about."

"Nothing must be assumed."

"Dai Ling."

His face flushed.

"I know it must be a shock to you and your wife, but . . . "

"You know nothing. For us this is more than a shock, it is an outrage."

"That's why I want to explain . . . "

"There is nothing to explain. Dai Ling is our daughter. Without her we have nothing."

"But she's devoted to you."

"She is lost to us."

"No, no, you don't understand . . . "

"It is *you* who do not understand!" He rose from his chair as though lifted by an invisible force, his face dark with emotion. "We are Chinese. We come to this country and we do our best to fit in. We learn another language, we work hard, we make a home for our daughter and learn from her about the Canadian way of life. But still we are Chinese people. Our history is in China, our ancestors are buried in China. It is our daughter who holds us here in this new life, and all this is for her, the bearer of our future."

"That's an awful lot to put on one person."

"You give no importance to family responsibility because you are part of this dead culture which cuts the body, measures it, weighs it like a piece of meat. The western body has lost its dignity . . . "

"I don't disagree, Dr. Xiang, but surely this is another topic. And incidentally it's not true that . . . "

"We Chinese see ourselves as part of one unbroken wholeness called Tao, a singular relational continuum. In the seventeenth century Western culture suffered a dissection of mind from body, which removed man from nature and set him up in conflict with himself, trying to control nature. That is what your Western medical system is based on. "

"I know! The Renaissance Europeans began to see themselves as independent of the life around them and thought they could dominate and exploit their environment without being affected by it. So we've created a toxic, carcinogenic world, but this is a long way from Dai Ling and her sexual orientation."

"Dai Ling is a young girl. She will grow out of this."

"And if she doesn't you'll continue to disown her?" They stared at each other, neither willing to back down. "And what about the irony of *your* conflict, Dr. Xiang?" Talya blurted. "As an immigrant you're part of this sterile culture now, and you're trying to control Dai Ling."

She thought he might strike her, the force of his energy was so great, but he held still, his body and face rigid, almost trembling as he spoke.

"I trusted you, Talya. I made you welcome in my house, but you have no respect. You do not understand how we live. I did not know . . . "

"Dr. Xiang, please . . . Our relationship, me and Dai Ling — truly, it doesn't warrant so much pain." She leaned forward and he pulled back, his hands coming up to ward her off as she continued. "She misses you terribly. She hasn't talked about it, but I can see." Talya noticed a muscle twitching in Jia Song's jaw. She wished she could touch him, but she didn't dare. She didn't know how to reach him. "Please don't hurt yourself like this, don't hurt Dai Ling! There's too much pain. I see it everywhere — at the hospital, in my father's house, Dai Ling awake in the night crying. If you don't act soon you'll lose her. I may lose her too. This could destroy our relationship."

She was surprised by her sudden tears, which she stifled, but not before Jia Song had seen. He dropped his hands into his lap, his shoulders slumped as though something in him had been realized.

"I will tell you something."

His voice was low and husky, different from his usual tone, as though there was something caught in his throat trying to silence him. *Like a barb,* Talya thought, *Like a fish caught with a barb in its mouth.*

"I had a young brother in China. We grew up together in the house of my aunt, because my parents were working in the countryside and could not look after us. We were raised as Communist Youth to give our loyalty to the Revolution, this must always come first. When he was fourteen years old my brother denounced our father."

"For what?"

"The matter is unimportant. It was unjust. But my father was sent to a labour camp. He died there, and my mother killed herself."

Talya caught her breath.

"I no longer have a brother."

"You disowned him?"

Jason nodded.

"But didn't you talk to him? Couldn't you have . . . "

"In China political difference is final."

"But it wasn't political, it was family."

"In China we did not separate the two. My brother is dead."

Talya exhaled a long breath shaking her head. "Why are you telling me this? I know you'd like me to disappear from Dai Ling's life if she doesn't 'grow out' of me first."

"You will be a doctor, but you are not a suitable companion for my daughter."

"I get it. You've lost almost everyone — your father, your mother, your brother, so why not your daughter as well, is that it?"

"You misunderstand me. It is because I have lost so much that I am not willing to risk losing my daughter."

"Then talk to her. Here's the phone number." She pushed a card into his hand, but he refused it.

"The decision is for Dai Ling," he said.

Something in his eyes reminded Talya of Dai Ling, and she softened and said, "You're right, I don't really understand you, but I recognize that you're a very powerful man behind that mask of civility. You have a vast country inside you, don't you? Centuries of history, layers of culture, memories that even you don't know, so how could we poor Canadians expect to have a clue? My ancestors are from Russia and we have our story too, but I don't quite believe it yet. I admire your sureness, your confidence in your own identity. It's all about imagination, isn't it, how we see ourselves? There's no truth, but so many ways to imagine. And the creations of the imagination can't be controlled. They're a mystery. They are simply there, ghosts who insist on speaking."

"Ghosts . . . yes, ghosts of the ancestors, watching over us. In this way we are determined, Talya, by our own ghosts."

1564: Adriatic Sea

VESALIUS' SHIP SAILED OUT OF THE Laguna Veneta into the Gulf and down the Dalmatian coast of the Adriatic. He stood on deck watching the City of Venice shrink. The last landmarks he saw distinctly were the tower of San Marco and the tower of Chiesa di San Giorgio on the tiny Isola di San Giorgio Maggiore. Venice became a haze of pastel forms floating in the water, all her islands merging finally into one jewel, imprinted on his retina.

He turned then and walked the length of the ship to the prow where he stretched out his arms to the future. He laughed as salt spray flew into his face, flecking his beard with foam and crystals until he sparkled. He felt there was not a happier man in the world at that moment.

Once again Vesalius had presented his letter of recommendation from the king, to the captain of the Venetian fleet this time, for safe passage to Palestine. Accompanying him on the vessel as far as Cyprus was Giacomo Malatesta di Rimini, general of the Venetian army.

"Ah, a pilgrimage," said di Rimini, stroking his beard thoughtfully, "It is your time of life, I suppose. Taking stock."

"In a manner of speaking," Vesalius replied.

The voyage passed pleasantly for Vesalius despite his preference for dry land. He loved nothing better than to travel and was oblivious to the cramped conditions and enforced idleness. He felt himself rocked in the cradle of the sturdy Venetian vessel as they passed out of the Adriatic into the Ionian Sea, past the beautiful island of Zante, known by the Venetians as Fior di Levante, and along the north coast of the Mediterranean island of Kriti, where they docked briefly at the eastern port of Candia.

As they sailed on through a blue expanse of tranquillity to Cyprus, he read Pero Tafur's *Travels* and Wey's *Itineraries*, with advice for pilgrims on how to proceed in the Holy Land. *On arriving at Jaffa, the port of Jerusalem, make haste to secure one of the best asses,* counselled Wey, *You shall pay no more for the best than for the worst.* Pero Tafur advised seeking the help of the Franciscan monks at Mount Sion, near Jerusalem. A letter of safe conduct from the local Saracen governor, he said, was essential for Christian pilgrims who did not want to be robbed or murdered by the Muslim Saracens.

Signor di Rimini disembarked at Cyprus and Vesalius, filled with anticipation, continued on to Jaffa. There he joined a group of fellow pilgrims and, escorted by the prior of Mount Sion and the local Saracen officials, travelled thirty-nine miles overland to Jerusalem, his body still swaying to the rhythm of the ocean. Vesalius was consumed by the desert. He lost himself in the infinite expanse, his eyes unable to anchor on the shifting horizon, empty of all landmarks.

Palestine is the Holy Land because it is a place of nothingness, he thought. *I am nothing here and nothing exists save my knowledge of other places. I am drowning in this emptiness. I am without reference.* He retreated into his mind for safety, but his mind sank and he was obliterated, despite his efforts to hold onto the mirage.

Vesalius gave thanks for the sanctuary of the Holy Sepulcher, Church of the Resurrection. He worshipped the Virgin and her son on his knees in the coolness of her enclosure. He began to understand the refuge of the body, the generous body which stretches to accommodate the growth of life. His fingers worried the rosary beads, counting them off, recording his prayers.

He lost count of the days as he travelled to and fro, to the Mount of Olives, to the Pillar of Pilate where Christ was bound and scourged, to the mound of Calvary where the true cross had stood, and which reminded him of the Galgenberg gallows on Montagne de la Potence. He walked in the desert and discovered a wealth of plants from which he collected samples to be used for medicines. One morning he woke to a glory of desert flowers, bloomed overnight in the warming spring air. These he collected for their colour and for their perfume.

Vesalius lost all sense of time. In the recesses of his mind he knew that he must take ship from Jaffa in the month of July to return in time to take up his post. Meanwhile, the sands stretching before him rendered time meaningless. He laughed when he thought of his life in Madrid, of his wife's frenzy to reach Cette in time to keep an appointment with her lover. The wound had healed sufficient that he could think of Anne now and remember with pleasure their love for each other. The harsh land of Palestine reduced everything to the eternal. *My life is beginning again. I am cleansed and I return full circle to Padua.*

That night he dreamed of Helle Straetken, and in his dream the mud and dirt of the lane had become a paradise of sweetly scented flowers blooming on a bed of twisted vines. He rose from the ground, flying higher and higher above the wooded copses of Galgenberg, above the fields and the lake where boys were swimming, splashed with laughter, above the Bovendael. *I am free!* he shouted in his dream, *I am flying!* He swooped over the crest of the Galgenberg peak and stared into the jewelled eyes of an angel hanging there. No more a twisted, tortured criminal disintegrating on the gibbet; here was a jewel-studded creature with shining wings, opening and closing its eyes heavenward. It had no arms, only wings, huge and muscled, which it lifted with great exertion and spread slowly in the sun, like a newborn creature drying its dark flesh, drinking the dew of Heaven into its body.

When he woke Vesalius knew it was time. He bundled his belongings, joined a caravan and returned through the now familiar desert to the port of Jaffa.

Xian Ming and Jia Song sat at the kitchen table. They picked at their food until finally Jia Song pushed his plate away.

"Zhuzi, you sick?"

"No appetite."

Xian Ming laid her chopsticks down. "Dai Ling came today."

"In my house? I forbid it!"

"She was in my garden. We talked. She's sad."

Jia Song turned, as though he might get up and leave the room, as he so often did now, sitting alone in the front parlour all evening while Xian Ming cleaned and cleaned her kitchen until there was nothing left to scour. But he simply shifted position and crossed his long legs.

"She asked about you. Wants you to forgive her."

He looked up sharply. "Will she come home and stop her foolishness?"

Xian Ming shook her head. "Zhuzi, you disowned your brother, and now you . . . "

"I had no brother!"

"Of course you have a brother. Isn't it time to forgive him, and then perhaps you can forgive our daughter?"

"It is time for the truth." Jia Song leaned forward intently, grasping Xian Ming's hands. "I had no brother. I lied. I had no brother."

"Zhuzi, what is this? All these years you told me . . . "

"Ma was forced to abort little brother."

"What? I don't believe it. Why did you lie to me?"

"To hide my betrayal . . . my father's death . . . Ma's suicide . . . "

Xian Ming cupped his face in her hands as he wept. "My husband, my husband, tell me what it is." She patted his face with the corner of her apron, drying his tears. "Tell me, Zhuzi, I will help you."

He pushed his tea cup away, the chopsticks, his rice bowl, everything, to make space for his arms, spread wide as he leaned forward. "When I was five my Ma got pregnant. It was the time of the one-child policy. Our county was a Family Planning Model County. If we'd stayed the birth control officers would have forced her to abort, so we went to Beijing to stay with Auntie until after the birth, but without a permit the police could have arrested Ma, so she tied a cloth tight around her belly to hide little brother. The astrologer told us it was a boy and we were so happy, waiting for him. Then one night I heard them in the corridor. I went out. They were leaving. A neighbor had denounced Ma. My parents fled, but Auntie told me they were caught and they cut the baby out of her."

Xian Ming's hands flew to her face, covering mouth and nose as though she were praying.

"They were sent to the country to work in agriculture", Jia Song continued. "I didn't see them for two years. Auntie told me that Babá was a writer. I was proud of him, I bragged at school — 'My Babá is writing a story.' Then my teacher took me to the countryside — two days on the train — I was so happy to see my father, so proud, but Ma was crying, I didn't understand. Then they made me bear witness against my father. I watched him swallow the pages of his story, torn into little pieces and forced into his mouth until he choked."

Tears spilled and splashed onto Xian Ming's plate as she reached for Jia Song's hands, covering them with her own.

"Ma told me the story was about little brother and the destruction of our family. She scolded me for speaking. at school. 'Never tell the secrets of the family,' she said. 'Never tell, it is dangerous, see what you've done now, my son.' They sent me back to my aunt in Beijing and I pretended that it was little brother's fault, for trying to come into our family. I began to believe it, that it was *he* who had betrayed our family with his existence. I had to tell myself this lie, or I couldn't go on living."

Xian Ming stroked his face. "It wasn't your fault. You were only a child. How could you have known?"

"When news came of Babá's death and Ma's suicide, I shouted at my brother and disowned him forever. I was seventeen, just starting university. I met Wu-Li and Jiang-Gang. They were leading the student movement for democracy. I went to a meeting, then I threw myself into political action, to fight the injustice I carried in my heart."

"I remember how you were when we met, angry about everything, but when Dai Ling was born you changed. And I thought in this new country everything would be different."

Jia Song shook his head. "We were the end of a lost generation, the ones who missed our proper education because we were recruited by the Red Guard. We believed we could change the world and we were betrayed. We all became traitors. That is what happens, over and over. I am a traitor and I cannot forgive this."

"My Ma was right. She was afraid of your political extremes, that I'd lose you and end up a widow like her. But you're still fighting, Jia Song, now you're fighting our daughter, and she's fighting back. It's her I've lost."

"Did I tell you I'm going to specialize in surgery?"

"Uh-huh. What field?" Elliott asked.

"Don't know yet."

Their heels clicked, echoing down the long corridor

"Ob/gyn would be easier."

"It's not about ease, Elliott. You know that. I *love* it."

"How about forensic?"

"The *living* body. I want to heal, not analyze," Talya said. When I pass my LMCC I'm going to apply for a surgical residency."

They sidestepped a gurney trundling down the centre of the corridor, and slipped through the swinging doors into the lobby, by a bank of elevators.

"Going up?" Elliott asked.

"Down . . . to my locker, and home to Dai Ling. I'm going to Europe, Elliott. I've decided."

"You're crazy."

"I know. I'm going on a pilgrimage, taking a few weeks leave. I'll join her in Padua, after."

Elliott gave her a hug. "I'll miss you, Tal. You're my inspiration, you know."

"Gimme five!" she said, and they clapped left hands, her med coat sleeve slipping down to reveal her scar. Talya saw Elliott looking at it and she laughed. "What you going up for?"

"Check on a patient. I don't have a private life . . . yet."

"What happened to your haemotologist?" Talya asked as the up elevator came and Elliott stepped in.

"I'm trying something new . . . celibacy," he mouthed silently as the elevator door closed.

~

"Ray? Ray, are you up there?"

Dai Ling was about to leave when Ray stuck his head out the window.

"Dai Ling! Haven't seen you in ages."

"Can I come up?"

"I'll come down."

Seconds later Ray flung the door open and hugged Dai Ling. "What's up? Where've you been?"

"Not on this street, that's for sure, not after what happened."

"So what are you doing here now?"

"Ray, my dad called me. He wants to talk."

"That's good news, Dai Ling. He's ready to talk."

"I don't know. Maybe he just wants to yell at me. I'm so scared. I feel like a little girl again. How's it going with Dee-Dee?"

Ray's big smile said it all. "Don't even ask. It's just too great to talk about. And guess what? I got an A+ on my Japanese film seminar paper."

"What exactly were you being graded on, Ray?"

"Don't bug me. It was probably marked by the TA."

"Did you have an affair with her too?"

"Him!"

"Oh, well I know you're not gay. Just kidding. I'm so scared, Ray. Look, I'm shivering," she said, jumping up and down. "I'd better go. He's waiting. Wish me luck."

"I'll do better than that," he said, taking a thin gold chain from around his neck, a small jade piece dangling from it, "I'll give you some of mine." He clasped it around Dai Ling's neck and kissed her lips.

"Oh Ray, I love you," she said, her eyes filling with tears.

"Friends forever!" he said. "Go on, Dai Ling, be brave."

She went down the laneway, opened the side gate and stood at the back door. She didn't know whether to knock or just walk in, but Ma was at the window waiting for her and she flung the door open and hugged Dai Ling.

"Come on, come on, your Babá is waiting."

Jia Song stood in the doorway, the long hallway stretching behind him, a smile hovering on his lips. When Dai Ling looked back on that day later in life she always saw them like this, waiting for her, their prodigal daughter, to come home and drag them into this new world.

When he arrived at the port of Jaffa he learned that the Venetian fleet was not expected for another month.

"There's a pilgrims' ship in port, sailing for Venice tomorrow. I'll be on it myself." The man had a pock-marked face. "Georg Boucher," he extended a meaty hand, "from Nuremberg. I'll take you to the captain if you wish."

"Most obliged," Vesalius said, pumping Boucher's hand. "If there's passage, I'll take it. I'm in haste to be home."

With his chin jutting and his beard spading the way, Vesalius strode along the dock and up the gangplank of the pilgrims' passenger ship, carrying his meagre pilgrim's bundle. The captain, eager to cram the decks, took him on and promised, for a sum, to provision him for the voyage. Vesalius shared a cabin with Boucher. He was a devout fellow who'd been to Jerusalem to give thanks for the birth of a son after ten fallow years of marriage.

They set sail into a choppy sea and sped along with the wind behind them. There were passengers to disembark at Candia, but the weather changed and soon they were tossing in twenty foot waves, which swept across the deck, driving passengers and crew below. The ship was blown south along the African coast and for full forty days was unable to reach land. It was all the captain could do to keep the old vessel from crashing to smithereens in the storm as hope of reaching Kriti receded. Vesalius was assailed by sea-sickness, fear and, finally, hunger. The provisions proved insufficient as the storm continued unabated. Only the passengers who had provided for themselves fed, secretly in corners. The rest went hungry on a dwindling ration of ship's biscuit. Their water was discovered to be contaminated when a drowned rat was found, sunk to the bottom.

"Mother of God, we'll all be doomed with the plague!" Boucher exclaimed, sweat breaking out on his pitted forehead.

When the first man died his body was thrown overboard for fear of contamination and Vesalius realized with horror that he might not survive this voyage. He busied himself with the dried leaves of his desert plants, crumbling them to a fine dust, reconstituting them with soft wax rolled into pellets for ease of swallowing. He dispensed his remedies to the crew and to the praying passengers. Ambition was forgotten. Everyone prayed for mere survival. Two more died in the night, their skin darkened with fever, and were tossed overboard at dawn.

Vesalius lurched into the wheelhouse. "I beg of you," he said to the captain, "do not let your men throw me to the sea if I succumb."

"Ship's rules," the man replied, surly with fear.

"I have a horror, you see, a horror of drowning . . . "

"Ain't no dead man drowns."

He wrenched the wheel as the ship keeled and the mast creaked ominously in the relentless gale. Vesalius, pale and shamed, retreated to his cabin, where he lay shivering. He listened to the snores of Georg Boucher, faint beneath the screaming of the wind, the ripping of the sails, the cracking and creaking of the exhausted vessel. So he lay as the fever took hold of him, melting the waxen herbs in his belly, cooking his body to a rich darkness. He heard his mother, Isabel Crabbe, shouting down Hell's Lane, *Nicolas, Andreas, Franciscus! Come for your dinner! Come, you naughty boys!* His winged feet carried him up over the walls of the city, over the fields of Galgenberg. He plunged deep into the lake where it was cool, so cool, and swam with open eyes. *Where are you, my brothers, where are you?* he wept. He swam to the surface of the lake and gasped as his head emerged from the water, but his throat was on fire, the world was burning and there was nowhere to go but down.

Vesalius woke gasping for water, but Boucher was not there. When he tried to stand his legs would not hold him and he collapsed on the floor of the cabin. "I am dying," he said, in the moment before darkness engulfed his mind. So, when he heard the splashing of the waves, the splashing and crashing, over and over, he took it for the impact of his body upon the water as he was thrown, over and over, from the doomed ship. He drowned a thousand deaths until all his fear was gone and he surrendered. Then the world was still and silent, as it is in the deep. His blood stood still and Vesalius listened, rapt, to the silence of his heart which had ceased its beating. *Ah, it is the heart, the activity of the heart which circulates the blood!* A smile broke upon his face as Anne's words echoed down the years . . . "Look to your heart . . . your unwilling heart . . . it is your heart, Andreas, that I require."

He began swimming to the surface where he saw a great light, and when he turned to look back he saw his body floating free. He didn't understand at first, the perfection of the creature he recognized as himself. Then he remembered everything, knowledge ricocheting through him; all the bodies he had explored, searching, searching for the elusive Soul, the vacant perfection of the flesh filled with blood and organs, still warm but stagnant without the enlivening spirit. Vesalius knew himself then as answer to his own quest; he was the eternal Soul, the intelligence of memory leaving the flesh. He was flooded with ecstasy as he knew his freedom once again. He thumbed his nose at the bearded man floating underwater and his spirit filled with the music of the spheres as he turned, pointing himself Heavenward.

"Land ahoy!" the first mate yelled, "Land ahoy! Land ahoy!" He ran screaming along the deck, running in circles, until he fell to his knees, weeping hoarsely. As the ship neared the island of Zante, sailing into shallow waters, the captain gave orders to drop anchor and, this done, the small boats were lowered to transport the men to shore. It was a sparkling day after the storm, a day such as the one upon which Andreas had set sail from Venice.

As his shrouded body was lowered with the first boat, the captain gave strict instructions for it to be laid on the beach, high above the tide line, so that it would not be swept out to sea. But Georg Boucher took charge of his friend's remains, bobbing with them the short distance to shore, his hand trailing in the warm azure waters of the Mediterranean. He arranged for the body to be transported high up on a cliff overlooking the ocean and there he prayed as Andreas Vesalius, two months short of his fiftieth year, was laid in a shallow grave.

As coincidence would have it, at this time in October of 1564, a Venetian ship had put into the port of Zante. Aboard was a goldsmith of Venice who, hearing of the recent burial of Andreas Vesalius, and out of regard for his great anatomical endeavours, arranged for a humble headstone to be laid.

They rented a car and Dai Ling drove, climbing into the mountains surrounding Padua while Talya looked dreamily out the window at passing vineyards and olive groves. Christie had wanted to come along, but Dai Ling had said no; she wanted Talya all to herself. She had just joined her after a short trip to Greece. Their final concert of the tour was the next night in Padua. This was a free day.

Up and up they climbed, the car whining as it geared down, each curve of the road revealing a new and more breathtaking vista. They stopped in the village of Petrarca and looked through a wrought iron gate at Francisco Petrarca's house.

The red-tiled roof was barely visible through an overgrown garden which sprawled onto the path. It somehow reminded Dai Ling of the Kulikovsky house, even though it was quite different. Pomegranates hung from a gnarled tree by the gate, seeds bursting from the over-ripe fists, split like aged leather.

They drank muscadet in a cool wine cellar lined with jars of cherries and peaches bottled in grappa. Tall jugs of olive oil threw their green reflection onto slim bottles of wine vinegar and jars stuffed with fat olives. Dai Ling sipped the cold sweet wine, watching Talya's mouth, remembering the paleness of her lips as her blood had soaked through red silk bandages and dripped into the earth. Everything had changed.

"And how was Milano?" Talya asked, holding her in a steady gaze.

"Full house. Another standing ovation. But I'll be glad when it's over. It's been a long trip. And I've missed you."

The tour had started in Amsterdam and moved on to Brussels, Paris, Strasbourg, Basel, and Milan. Talya had flown to Athens, connecting with a flight to Zakynthos, and had arranged to meet up with Dai Ling in Padua.

"Did you find it?"

"Yes. He's buried by the ocean, high on a cliff where there's always a breeze carrying spray from the water crashing on the rocks below. It's barren up there but further inland there are green slopes and olive groves.

"What did you do?"

"Without you?" Talya shook her head, her eyes eloquent.

"Truly."

Talya shrugged. "Walked around. Sat in the sun. It was hot and dry and I felt parched." She raised her glass and clinked Dai Ling's glass, slippery in her fingers from the frosted wine.

Driving back in the early darkness, they passed through several small villages before Dai Ling pulled over by the ruins of a Roman villa.

"What is it?" Talya asked.

"Something shining by the roadside in the curve ahead. Look."

They walked under a full moon. The night air was humid, filled with the aroma of box hedge and the sound of crickets. When they reached the curve they found a whitewashed statue of the Virgin surrounded with fleshy cyclamen.

"A sanctuary!" Dai Ling exclaimed.

They stood in the reflected light and she turned to Talya and kissed her illuminated face. Over Talya's shoulder she saw the outline of the villa, heard a dog barking. She thought of Ruby and imagined her sleeping, with Nick in the new condo, her paws twitching as she dreamed, her soft black nose quivering.

As they walked back to the car there seemed to be an aura of light around it. *It's the full moon,* Dai Ling thought, *and the light from the sanctuary. There's light everywhere tonight.*

On the seat of the car was a package which Talya had taken from her backpack when she'd arrived the day before. She lifted the package now with both hands and sat with it in her lap. "Tomorrow we'll go to Del Bo," she said.

"What's that?"

"The faculty of Medicine at the university, where Vesalius held the chair of Anatomy."

"No, I mean . . . "

Talya silenced her with a kiss.

A bank of screens flooded the wall of the café, each one occupied by a young traveller or a student from the University of Padua.

"Any messages?"

"Uncle Vassily. There's a heat wave in Montréal. They're sleeping in the basement. Aunt Riva says 'Don't drink the water.'"

"Look, there's a message coming in."

"It's from Dad!"

Natáshenka, moya dochka, *How are you, my darling? I'm back in the saddle, enjoying the new condo. Going out for lunch with Cam today. Holding on the house warming until your return. Regards to Dai Ling. All my love, Dad.*

Everything has changed, Talya thought. The green oval of the Prato del Valle was surrounded by canals with little bridges crossing them, the park studded with glistening white statues. The statues crumbled into the white dust of memory and flew on a sudden gust of wind.

"What's wrong?" Dai Ling asked, holding onto Talya's hand, pulling her down beside her on a stone bench. "You're miles away."

"I'm right here," she replied. She felt the warm stone of the bench on her bare legs, the pressure of Dai Ling's fingers, playing, playing her, filling her with sound as she returned.

"What *is* that?"

Talya carried the package under her arm, a box wrapped in brown paper, tied with string. She'd been up before dawn, sitting at their open window as Dai Ling slept, watching Venus the morning star, bearer of light. She remembered her Greek now, her mind refreshed by the trip to Zakynthos. *Phosphorus* . . . the Greek name for Venus . . . Φοσ — light . . . Φοροσ — bearer . Phosphorus, spontaneously flammable in its pure organic form, bound in chemical form within the bones and teeth, essential element of all living organisms. Phosphorus which may remain a thousand years in deep soil and at the bottom of lakes and rivers. She had watched, fascinated, in chemistry class as Mr. Bernstein had removed a small white circle, like an eyeball, from a jar and set it glowing in a petrie dish. Venus, up from the ocean before sunrise, igniting the day.

"What *is* it?" Dai Ling insisted, bringing her back.

"You're so curious. I love that."

The courtyard was hushed as they entered. Stones rang under their feet, echoing in the silence, and their whispered words travelled along the colonnade, snaking up and down pillars. On the walls surrounding the courtyard were plaques with the family crests and emblems of generations of faculty members. From the far corner Talya heard a familiar voice . . . *We must separate the construction of the universe from considerations of* . . . . She grasped Dai Ling's hand and pulled her across the courtyard to a heavy wooden door that stood slightly ajar. She edged her body inside and, yes, there was the platform that Galileo had built for his lectures, with four wooden steps ascending, cordoned off like an artefact.

Rows of smartly dressed men and women were attending a lecture. She could see through an archway into the next room and heard a woman speaking rapidly in Italian. Some people turned and stared at them. *I have a right to be here*, Talya thought, but Dai Ling tugged her hand and they left the hall and walked down the colonnade to the other end of the quadrangle. There they entered a long room with walls of panelled wood. Along one wall, displayed in glass cases, were the skulls of men who had served on the medical faculty.

Talya paced up and down, staring into the eye-sockets of each skull, then she placed her package in the centre of a long refectory table, untied the string, folded back the crinkly brown paper and removed the lid. A faint haze escaped and ignited immediately in greenish tongues of flame flickering so fast that Dai Ling couldn't be sure she'd actually seen them. She leaned in closer as Talya lifted a fragile object from the box and set it down on the darkly polished wood. It had a reddish-brown hue, and yes — Dai Ling gasped as she realized what it was — unmistakable now, darkened teeth still clinging loosely to the jawbone. Talya laid an envelope on the table next to it, addressed to the Dean of Medicine, inside a note.

This is the skull of Andreas Vesalius, to be displayed with his colleagues in his rightful place, here in Padua where he discovered and mapped the interior of the human body.

"I've brought him home. It's what he would have wanted. He was trying to get here."

"That's *his* skull? But how do you know? How did you get it?"

"There was a stone with his name engraved. It's almost illegible now, but it was enough."

Dai Ling stared at her, incredulous, but Talya felt quite calm now, just as she had felt when she had finally found the place and started digging with an improvised shovel made from a sharp rock. No one had known where he was and she had almost abandoned her quest, anxious to get to Padua and see Dai Ling, when a bristly-chinned woman in a black head scarf and shapeless dress had pointed her to the edge of the cliff. She had hesitated before following the widow's direction; it was late in the day, the evening star already signalling the darkness, but something had pushed her forward.

The earth had been dry and crumbly, surprisingly easy to dig once she was through the top layer. It seemed to her then that the earth emitted a faint light and she began to work with her hands, but in reality the moon was up and it shone brightly enough. There was no coffin. She supposed there had been a shroud, from the shreds which disintegrated in her hands. She bundled the poor skull in her shawl, and held it close to her as she replaced the earth without disturbing the rest of his bones. She knew that Andreas Vesalius, although a man of the body, had lived in his head, and that his head belonged in Padua.

As she had left the grave Talya had smiled up into the star-speckled sky, the brittle roundness of the skull resting on her breast. She had carried the skull to her room at the taverna and transferred it there to the box she'd brought with her from Canada, a small collapsible hatbox. She'd had no doubt that she would find him and transport him until she had arrived on the island of Zakynthos, then everything had seemed different from how she had imagined it. Her Greek was rusty and when it came back to her no one had heard of Vesalius, let alone his burial place. She had followed her nose, exploring the island, but felt no sense of recognition, no guidance, until the last day, when in truth she had lost heart. Then the old woman appeared and Talya had almost ignored her. She'd been impatient at that point, already thinking of her reunion with Dai Ling in Padua. It was in this divided state that she had approached the cliff's edge. She had felt the grave before she'd seen it, surprised and yet not at all surprised, the paradox of her existence, always pulled in two directions before she arrived at a completely new place. Once she had recognized the place, squinting at the broken inscription of his name, she wondered how she could ever have missed it, how she had managed to wander all over the island instead of walking straight to the grave. But then she realized that her imagination was a free agency that surrounded and guided her, always dramatically tensed against the determination of her body, her form, the rules of the world in which she existed. Whenever she thought thus she was once again pedalling away from Dai Ling, east on Bloor, across the Don Valley Bridge, a creature of perpetual motion escaping and catching up with herself.

Talya looked up now and smiled at her sweetheart. "There's more," she said, and took her hand. The next room was smaller. Talya began to feel a tingling at the back of her neck. She turned and found herself staring through an archway into the operating theatre. Dai Ling followed her into the womb-like, windowless theatre, remembering Xian Ming's fears.

Talya walked slowly to the centre where the cadavers had been placed, brought from the nearby hospital. She felt her hand reach for something, then her arms rose in a triumphant gesture as though she were going to conduct an orchestra. A sharp smell stung her nose and entered her lungs, shocking them. There was a rushing sound in her ears and she closed her eyes as the theatre pulsed around her. Something clattered to the floor. She felt a pulling in her belly, blood on her tongue, her body lifted into the air. In the moment before everything went black she flew across a great body of water and stared into the ancient eyes of the horned creature that had lived inside her mother. As she entered the creature, merging with it, the floor rose up to hit her.

When Talya came to Dai Ling was kneeling over her, holding her head. She felt a trickling down the back of her skull and when she reached to touch it her hand came away sticky with blood.

"You're hurt."

"I'm all right."

"You're not. Oh, Talya, what happened?" Dai Ling was almost weeping.

"Head wounds bleed a lot."

"You lifted up your arms and then . . . I heard something . . . a screaming. Was it you?" She dabbed at Talya's head with a kleenex.

"No, it wasn't me. It's okay, I'm all right."

Dai Ling helped her up and they walked slowly out of the theatre, through the small ante-room and into the courtyard.

People from the seminar were bursting through the heavy door, milling about, talking excitedly.

Talya breathed deeply, filling her lungs, and exhaled into a clear sky, the jade pendant trembling at her throat as she spoke. "I'll return the anatomy book when we get back."

"Oh, Mrs. Fox will be so relieved. It's a rare book, you know. You weren't even supposed to have it out. Someone slipped up. What will you tell her?"

"That I lost it, then I found it while I was clearing out my father's house."

They walked across the quadrangle and under the ancient stone archway onto the street. "How's your head?"

Talya, still staunching the blood, removed the kleenex and looked at it. "It's stopped bleeding. I'll get rid of this." She stepped towards a waste disposal bin on the kerb.

"No!" Dai Ling held onto her arm. "We must burn it. Your blood is a prayer and the paper is your wish, remember?"

"Of course. I forgot." Talya tilted her face to the sky and closed her eyes, smiling. "I'll be ready to leave Padua after your concert tonight."

The concert hall was full. Talya watched as the musicians entered with their instruments. She saw Dai Ling sit with her legs astride, the cello resting on her body. She listened to the familiar cacophony of sound as the musicians tuned their instruments. Then a hush, a breathless moment in which the orchestra became one body and the audience waited for the music to begin. The conductor lifted her baton and Talya watched as Dai Ling's arm rose and hovered like a bird preparing to dive. Then she closed her eyes and her bow swept firmly across the strings of her cello, striking the first echoing chords of the *Elgar Concerto*. She was home and Talya was with her as the wind instruments entered, as the cello climbed an ascending scale and introduced the haunted melody.

Acknowledgements

Many thanks to all the people who have helped me as readers, critics, and advisors on a multitude of topics. Thanks to my sisters, Sally Goodwin and Bridget Goudie, for listening to the first pages; to Fan Chen and Gloria Lee for invaluable advice about Chinese family culture; to Alix Allen for sharing her Romanov heritage; to Kati Marshall, Ellen Coburn, Laura Chalfin and Bob Henderson for essential information on the medical world; to Sarah de Rose, Kye Marshall, Jean Woodley, Cath Gray and Janey Bennett for musical inspiration and advice; to Ariane Crawford for unstinting help with Russian names and customs; to Marc Was for help with Flemish names; to Brock MacLeod for a wonderful lecture on the Renaissance; to my brave friend, Mary Wright, now deceased, for sharing the details of her alternative cancer treatment; to Aija Mara, Tom Knott and Louise Jarvis for their comments on very early drafts; and, to Judith Irvine of the University of Toronto Medical Faculty for information about student schedules.

Thank you most especially to Seán Virgo, an editor of extraordinary skill and sensitivity, who pushed me hard and inspired me anew in the final stages.

My gratitude to everyone at Thistledown Press — particularly Al Forrie and Jackie Forrie — for their belief and support.

Thanks as ever to Joy Gugeler for her generosity with editorial advice and encouragement during the long journey.

Bibliography

Books

Excerpts cited are page numbers from *My Sweet Curiosity*

Beinfield, Harriet, and Efrem Korngold. *Between Heaven and Earth: a guide to Chinese medicine*. New York: Ballantine Books, 1991. (Excerpts pp. 216-218)

Hogarth, Burne. *Dynamic Anatomy*. New York: Watson-Guptill Publications, 2003. (A paragraph on p. 25 is paraphrased from this book)

McNamara, Sheila. *Traditional Chinese Medicine*. New York: BasicBooks, 1996. (Story of Shen Nung, the Red Emperor and Divine Husbandman, p. 187)

O'Malley, C.D. *Andreas Vesalius of Brussels 1514-1564*. Berkeley and Los Angeles: University of California Press, 1965.

Saunders, C.M. and Charles D. O'Malley. *Vesalius: The Illustrations from His Works:* with biographical study. Cleveland: The World Publishing Company, 1950. (Excerpts pp. 34, 50-51, 101)

Also of inspiration in my research were the following books and movies, together with numerous books and internet postings on the Romanov Family, Reproductive Technology, and the Renaissance.

Ma Jian , *Beijing Coma.* Toronto: A.A. Knopf Canada, 2008.

Lam, Vincent. *Bloodletting and Miraculous Cures.* Toronto: Anchor Canada, 2005.

Sobel, Dava. *Galileo's Daughter.* London, UK: Fourth Estate, 2000, 1999)

The Tianenmen Papers, edited by Andrew J. Nathan and Perry Link. New York: Public Affairs, 2001. From materials compiled by Zhang Liang .

Brothers of the Head, a movie co-directed by Keith Fulton and Louis Pepe, adapted by Toni Grisoni, from a novel by Brian Aldiss (Potboiler Productions)

Twin Falls Idaho, 1999, a movie directed by Michael Polish, co-written by Michael and Mark Polish, identical twins

Websites

Gene Expression (www.gnxp.com), Aug 13, 2003, article on ectogenesis, "The Real Threat to Roe V. Wade – Fake Uterus" by Sacha Zimmerman,

Slate online magazine (www.slate.com), July 29, 2005 article, "The Organ Factory" by William Saletan

"Genealogy of the Romanov Imperial House", www.timohaapanen.net

Songs

"The Second Time Around", written by Cahn/Van Heusen (Lyrics copyright EMI Music Publishing) (p. 60)

"Cheek to Cheek", written by Irving Berlin (Lyrics by Bobby Harris, Eric Fearman, Steve Cox, Sennie R. Martin, © EMI Music Publishing, Irving Berlin Music Company) (p. 235)

"Blue Skies", written by Irving Berlin (Publisher Hal Leonard Corporation) (p. 235)

Author photo by Enrique Molinas

Amanda Hale's first book, *Sounding the Blood*, was a Fiction finalist for the BC Relit Awards, and was one of *Now Magazine*'s top ten novels of 2001. Her second book, *The Reddening Path*, has been translated into Spanish, and is available in English as an audiobook. Her poetry and short fiction have appeared in numerous publications, and she won the 2008 *Prism International* literary non-fiction award.

Hale lives on Hornby Island in British Columbia.